Soul's Survivor

Soul's Survivor

Navi' Robins

www.urbanbooks.net

Urban Books, LLC
300 Farmingdale Road, NY-Route 109
Farmingdale, NY 11735

Soul's Survivor
Copyright © 2020 Navi' Robins

ISBN 13: 978-1-64556-191-0
ISBN 10: 1-64556-191-7

First Mass Market Printing March 2021
First Trade Paperback Printing March 2020
Printed in the United States of America

10 9 8 7 6 5 4 3 2 1

This is a work of fiction. Any references or similarities to actual events, real people, living or dead, or to real locales are intended to give the novel a sense of reality. Any similarity in other names, characters, places, and incidents is entirely coincidental.

Distributed by Kensington Publishing Corp.
Submit Orders to:
Customer Service
400 Hahn Road
Westminster, MD 21157-4627
Phone: 1-800-733-3000
Fax: 1-800-659-2436

Chapter 1

Inner Demons Never Sleep

The heat from the afternoon sun seemed to intensify as gunfire and terrified screams surrounded him from every corner of the small village. Dozens of midnight-skinned bodies lay mutilated in pools of blood that seemed to boil under the scorching hot African sun. In his arms lay an African girl no older than 5 . . . eyes wide open and lifeless. Her body was riddled with the bullets that violently snatched the life of a promising future full of potential. Regardless of her age, she was raped and gunned down like a rabid dog by monsters disguised as men, who didn't care how young and innocent she was, nor did they heed her screaming pleas for mercy. They violated her small, innocent body repeatedly with vicious malice that seemed more demonic than human, stripping her of the happiness she stored within her soul—right before they murdered her. They laughed, howling like wolves as her body shook violently from the force of the countless bullets that pierced her tiny and broken body.

She was the most beautiful soul Dr. Daniel Bennett had ever known, and now that soul was gone, leaving behind the violated and mutilated shell it once occupied. Tears streamed down his face like rivers of pain and anger as he felt her blood pour over his arms and hands into the reddish dirt beneath him. He was so engulfed in his grief that he didn't notice the multiple assault rifles now pointed at him, the men that held them yelling in a language he didn't understand . . . nor did he care to. Everything that he cared for was taken right before his eyes to the sounds of automatic gunfire and at the edge of a machete. Eventually, he looked up at the men that threatened him with their weapons of genocide. The revelation of staring into their evil faces made the blade of his tragedy cut even deeper. They all resembled the child in his arms, possessing the same ethnic features and ultra dark skin complexion that was common among most of the people that lived in the southern region of Sudan.

How could people be driven to hate themselves this way?

One of the men bent down, pushing the barrel of his smoking-hot rifle on the doctor's cheek. Pain shot through his face as his flesh burned against the barrel of the rifle.

"What are you doing here, and where are you from?" the man asked with a thick Sudanese accent. He possessed deep and dense scars all over his face, and in his eyes burned an evil inferno that appeared insatiable. He was clearly their leader, indicated by the way the sound of his voice silenced the other men.

"Are you American?"

The sound of his voice angered the doctor, as his accent was all too familiar to him, being the same accent the girl spoke when she was alive. Looking the man in the eyes and without thinking of the consequences, he hawked up phlegm from his throat and forcefully spat it in the man's face.

The leader's eyes turned red with rage, right before he struck the doctor in the face with the back end of his rifle. The force of the blow slammed the doctor to the ground shattering his jawbone and throwing the little girl's body out of his arms and onto the dirt like a rag doll. Before the pain could set in, he was being stomped and pounded with boots and rifle butts all over his body. Their strikes were inhumanly violent, and it seemed each blow meant to kill him. Every time he appeared alive, they would hit him again, even more violently. The beating seemed to last for an eternity until suddenly, everything stopped. The doctor was in so much pain he could barely breathe. He kept his eyes shut, lying in a fetal position, afraid to see what was coming next. He could feel the bright sun shining on his face, and when he decided to open his eyes, he was looking at the group of men pointing their guns at him, awaiting the order from their commander.

"You spit in my face? I was going to let you go free, but now you will die for your insolence . . . ready, aim, fire . . ."

Daniel's sweaty body jumped up as he screamed at the top of his lungs. He was disoriented, and the darkness made it difficult for him to figure out he was safely in his own bedroom. Once he accepted his surroundings, he flopped back down on his pillow, exhaling forcefully. Looking over at the clock on his nightstand, the time 3:45 a.m. glared back at him. Trying to forget his nightmare would be an impossible task, so he slowly climbed out of his bed and headed for the bathroom.

Looking in the mirror, he shook his head at his drenched reflection. Sweat poured from every pore on his caramel-colored body, and looking down at his boxers, he noticed they were soaked as if he'd peed himself. Twisting his muscular body to the left and right, he frowned at the multiple bullet entry and exit scars he had all over his torso. Leaning on the sink, he turned on the cold water and threw a handful on his face.

I might as well get ready for work and head in early. My ass ain't going back to sleep anytime soon.

Still in front of the mirror, he pulled down his boxers, revealing his entire naked form. Staring at himself, he began to examine his body with pride. The longer he stared, the ugliness of his scars seemed to overtake the image . . . until all he could see was a scared and damaged 35-year-old man. His head once held high began to slowly hang downward until all he could see was his well-endowed manhood and size thirteens. He began to feel a frigid chill of regret run up his spine as he tried to fight back the tears of heartache and loss. He was the example of what a once strikingly handsome and successful doctor could become if he comes face-to-face with death and regret. Having seen enough, he slowly walked into the shower and turned on the cold water to wake up an already frightened body . . .

Chapter 2

Empty Routine

9:00 a.m., University of Illinois Hospital

Chicago, Illinois

"Doctor Bennett? Can you hear me? We have two gunshot victims in ICU, and Dr. Kohlman called in sick again."

Daniel sat behind his desk, staring off into nothing as his mind drowned in the memory of his past until an uninvited voice snapped him out of his daydream. He looked at the nurse and nodded his head, acknowledging he heard her. Satisfied that she'd gotten the message across, she turned to leave, but something she said grabbed his attention, so he called out to her before she could walk out of his office.

"Did you say Dr. Kohlman called in sick again?"

Turning and smacking her lips with an attitude, the nurse responded, "Yep, that's three times in the last two weeks too. Something needs to be done, Dr. Bennett. This neighborhood needs two doctors on duty in ICU at all times. It's like a war zone out there, and we are losing more patients than we are saving because we are short-staffed."

"I know, but we have to make do with what we have, and complaining about Dr. Kohlman won't save another life. It definitely won't give you job security. I'm okay with you voicing your concerns because I agree with you. But be careful with other people here, because Dr. Kohlman has ears everywhere. You remember what happened to the last nurse that complained about him?"

The nurse nodded her head and grinned at the doctor before responding, "Yeah, you're right. Sorry, Doctor."

"No need to apologize, I get it. I really do, but I also want you to keep working here because you are one of the few nurses that actually care. It's not just a paycheck for you. Losing you would be devastating, so I'm just giving you some sound advice. Watch your back, okay?"

"Sure thing, Doc, and thanks again."

"You're welcome. Let ICU know I'm on my way now."

The chaos in the ICU would be overwhelming for most, but for Daniel, it was just a routine. After experiencing horrors most only watched on television, nothing surprised him. He still gave his best and tried to save as many patients as he could, but regardless of the outcome, he remained numb to it all. It mattered, but not enough to garner a real emotional response from him. To Daniel, death was just a needle's tip away from everyone, and the sooner we realized it, the better off we would be. Watching so many young men and women from the West Side of Chicago come through the ICU due to gang violence was concerning, but what could he do? People are irresponsibly violent, and no matter how many bullet holes he patched up, organs he replaced, or lives he saved, people would always be the same: violent and hateful.

Sometimes he would be so zoned out in his routine that he wouldn't notice he'd worked a fourteen-hour shift without stopping to eat until one of the nurses would force him to eat something. Dr. Kohlman was the head doctor of the hospital, but was so engulfed in his hatred of minorities that he was either taking the day off or complaining about *having* to save another "leech." Daniel could only imagine the names he called people of color around his dinner table when he was alone or with like-minded people. The fact that Daniel was African American made their professional relationship a difficult one to maintain, but Dr. Kohlman seemed to tolerate it as long as Daniel kept coming into work so that he didn't have to.

Eleven gunshot victims and countless other emergencies later, Daniel found himself in the bathroom, washing the day's drama from his hands and looking at a reflection that he loathed to his core. Suddenly, the bathroom door flung open and in walked his college buddy and cancer research specialist, Dr. Timothy Avers. Timothy graduated at the top of his class and was considered one of the few people on the brink of finding a viable cure for cancer. With all the breakthroughs he made in treating cancer, he just couldn't seem to find a cure for himself. He was the worst disease to women, and he left a graveyard of broken hearts in his wake. He was an expert surgeon at using his intellect and success to his advantage in getting what he wanted from women, and all he ever wanted was sex.

He was an attractive, dark, mocha-skinned genius and a doctor, a potent combination that seemed to cause any pair of panties to fall around a pair of ankles, with Tim sliding in between them. On the surface, it would seem Tim wouldn't be the type of guy Daniel would hang with, but Tim was a riot to be around, and he provided a much-needed escape from Daniel's timid and frigid life. Usually, he would be smiling brightly because it was Friday and they would go out to a local bar or club to hang out . . . Well, Daniel hung out. Timothy would be on the prowl. However, he seemed angry as he stomped into the bathroom, and his demeanor momentarily alarmed Daniel to the point of almost caring . . . almost.

Timothy kept pacing back and forth in the bathroom, clearly trying to get a reaction out of Daniel. Daniel was content with just letting him pace around, as long as he didn't bother him with whatever was making him upset. After another minute, Daniel became annoyed and decided to give Tim the attention he craved.

"What's up, Tim?"

"Nothing. I'm cool."

Nodding, Daniel continued to wash his hands. He knew that Tim wouldn't end it there, but he wished he would.

I'm really not in the mood for his whining.

"Huh, what you say?" Timothy asked.

"Nothing," Daniel responded, quickly reaching for a paper towel to dry his hands and hoping to escape the bathroom before Tim talked him to death.

Moving quickly toward the door, Daniel tried to make his escape, but Timothy wasn't having it and stopped him before he could open the door.

"Wait, Danny . . . Something's up."

"But you just said nothing was up," Daniel protested.

"I know. I didn't want to talk about it, but now . . ."

"Now, you do," Daniel responded, exhaling deeply.

"Yeah, but if you're busy, it's cool."

Daniel knew his last statement was pure bullshit. It wasn't cool if he didn't listen to his story, which more than likely would include every minute detail of another disappointing night, with another strange woman. Rolling his eyes and shrugging his shoulders, he moved away from the door and walked back toward the sink. Leaning against it and folding his arms, he nodded toward Tim so that he could begin talking.

"Okay, so I met this WG—"

Interrupting him, Daniel asked, "WG?"

"Yeah . . . WG . . . a white girl . . ." Tim responded, confused at Daniel's unfamiliarity with the acronym. "Anyway, I met this *white girl* last week that I've been dying to fuck, and do you know what this bitch had the nerve to tell me this afternoon?"

Daniel remained silent, staring blankly at Timothy. He was clearly not amused with the story thus far. His nonchalant attitude made Timothy feel stupid, but he really needed to get this off his chest, so he continued.

"This bitch told me that she couldn't sleep with me until I meet her parents. I'm like 'Bitch, I'm not trying to meet your folks. I'm just trying to make you call *me* daddy.' Just once, maybe twice, if she's any good. Other than that, I'm not trying to be her man."

Most would question Tim's story, finding it hard to believe the conversation went as he's describing, but Daniel knew all too well that more than likely, it went *exactly* as he described. Tim had very little respect for women, and he didn't hide it. He constantly called them bitches to their faces when they wouldn't give him what he wanted.

"I'm sure she didn't like that now, did she?" Daniel asked sarcastically while looking up at the ceiling, appearing bored and unconcerned.

"Hell naw! The bitch got beside herself and started calling me all kinds of niggers *and* bitch-ass niggers."

Daniel's eyes widened as a very rare smile started to grow on his face.

"Oh, *now* you're amused? So, you like it when a white chick calls me a nigger, huh?"

"Hey, dude, you called her a bitch first. Seems like you were asking for it. I'm not saying you shouldn't be mad, but what did you expect?"

"Not the 'N' word," Timothy yelled back at Daniel.

"I bet she wasn't expecting to be called a bitch either when she invited you to meet her parents. But again, she did give you her number, so she was also asking for it too," Daniel chuckled.

"Oh, so, now you're a comedian? To hell with you, Danny. She had no right using the N word. No right at all."

"Hey, I'm not saying she did but . . . anyway . . . So *that's* why you're upset?"

"No, that's just the beginning of it. So I hung up on her, and this bitch goes on my Facebook page and posts a bunch of crazy shit on there."

"How crazy?" Daniel asked, becoming more intrigued by the woman's need to make Tim pay for disrespecting her.

"Photos of lynchings and slaves being sold. Then, to top it off, she posted a comment saying she owned me through her inheritance from her father."

After hearing about the woman's final assault on Timothy's Facebook page, Daniel leaned backward, laughing hysterically. He could barely stand as his stomach muscles heaved and shook from the laughter that bellowed from his mouth. He hadn't laughed this hard in over three years, and he reveled in it as long as his sad body would allow.

Now, pissed and embarrassed by Daniel's reaction, Timothy decided to leave, and Daniel reached out, stopping him from exiting the bathroom.

"Wait, I'm sorry for laughing so hard," he chuckled, trying to hold in another round of laughter.

"So hard? You shouldn't be laughing at all. That's racist as fuck! She's a racist, dude, plain and simple, and she exposed herself all over my page."

"She's a racist, yet she gave you her number and wanted you to meet her parents? Come on, Tim, that doesn't make any sense. If she were a racist, you wouldn't have gotten past hello, let alone an invitation to meet the folks."

"Maybe she was setting me up to get lynched or something!"

"I doubt it. She more than likely has some serious issues with being called a bitch and decided to respond with something she knew would bother you just as much as being called a bitch bothered her. Both of you are insane. I think you should marry her."

"Fuck you very much, Doctor. No thanks. I'm never calling her again."

"I would hope not . . . She might take away your freedom next time around."

Starting to laugh again, Daniel turned toward the mirror to wipe away the tears from his eyes. "So, does this mean we aren't going out tonight?"

"Hell no, we are hitting up that new martini bar on LaSalle tonight!"

"You sure you don't need some time to lick your wounds or double-check your freedom papers, just in case she really *does* have a claim on you?" Daniel teased, laughing so hard again, he had to lean on the sink.

Timothy stared at Daniel with eyes filled with anger. Shaking his head while walking out of the bathroom, a sudden thought made him pause before he stepped out the door.

"It was good seeing you laugh, Danny, even if it's at the expense of my civil rights being violated. See you later tonight . . . and don't you dare stand me up like you did the last time."

"Oh, I'll be there, hoping the 'WG' is there as well. You may have to dance for your freedom tonight, Toby."

"Man, fuck you, dude," Tim responded while laughing.

Chapter 3

Opening Old Wounds

For several months, Daniel had been getting calls from an unrecognized number. They always called around the same time each day: 8:00 a.m., 1:00 p.m., and 5:00 p.m. Daniel wasn't in the mood for anything out of the ordinary, so he decided not to answer the calls and deleted the voice messages without listening to them. He felt his life already had an overabundance of drama, and he didn't need any more added to his plate—especially from someone he didn't know.

It was a beautiful Wednesday morning, and Daniel was on autopilot in the ICU and trying to save lives in the process. Summer was in full swing, and so was the gang violence in the city. The innocent were always the ones delivered to the hospital dead on arrival and the combatants alive and kicking—at times literally kicking, trying to keep the cops off of them. Daniel would shake his head as he looked on at the state of the youth today.

Someone should drop them all in the middle of a warring third world country and see how tough they really are, he thought to himself.

He'd just pulled five bullets out of a twelve-year-old girl who miraculously survived a gun attack intended for her gangbanging father. Dr. Kohlman seemed disappointed that she survived and made a comment about "another future welfare queen allowed to live another day in my great country." Daniel's unwillingness to allow himself to care made him ignore the doctor's racist comment and continued to fill out the little girl's report. Daniel had no illusions about Dr. Kohlman, and he knew that the doctor more than likely believed Daniel was too afraid to speak up. Daniel was far from afraid. He just didn't see any reason to reprimand a racist that decided to become a doctor. No other profession outside of law enforcement brings different races of people in direct contact with one another than medicine. Anyone in their right mind that wanted to be separated from another race would've chosen another profession suited for their separatist beliefs.

Seeing that Dr. Kohlman chose medicine shed light on his lack of proper brain function, and Daniel considered arguing with him about his racist views a waste of time. After giving the little girl's family the news of her progress, he decided to retire to his office to take a quick nap before he jumped back into the chaos again. Daniel routinely closed his office door before heading out into the madness of the ER. In his mind, his office was his fortress of solitude, and keeping the door closed kept the madness of the outside from infecting his sanctuary. So, when he arrived outside his office, and he noticed his door was slightly ajar, he swallowed deeply, cringing at the thought of someone invading his quiet place.

He slowly opened the door, and standing at the front of his desk was a man in military uniform, accompanied by two women occupying his office. One of the women wore a navy-blue business suit and had a long, blond ponytail that flowed midway down her back. She wore a pair of glasses that covered her ultramarine-blue eyes that were the color of a tropical sea. She was a very attractive middle-aged white woman, and the lack of makeup other than some red lipstick made her beauty more apparent. Her elevated chin and rigid posture let Daniel know that she was a determined woman, and she wore her pride like the suit that covered her thin, athletic frame.

The other woman possessed a beauty that surpassed anything Daniel had ever seen. Her skin was like the color of expensive dark chocolate, so dark it seemed to absorb the sunlight that poured through the window behind his desk. Her hair, just as long as the other woman's, was also in a ponytail, allowing her beautifully maintained locked hair to flow down her back. She possessed a pair of captivating light brown eyes that seemed to pierce through him, exposing the shattered man that stood before her. She was tall, at least a foot taller than the average woman, with a curvaceous yet physically fit frame that was so inviting, Daniel unconsciously begin to lick his lips, imagining the amazing secrets her naked body could contain.

She destroyed every stereotype concerning the unattractiveness of darker-skinned women. Looking at her, Daniel assumed either she had to be married or well on her way because he couldn't find a reason any man would be unwilling to marry such a beautiful woman. They were all looking at the doctor as he walked into the office, each of them with an expression that detailed what they expected from him. The uniformed gentleman watched him closely, making sure he didn't pose a threat to either woman in his office. The businesswoman looked at him like a woman on a mission, and she couldn't continue her journey until she got what she needed from him.

The other woman just smiled at him with compassion in her eyes. Her attitude toward him caught the doctor at a disadvantage, and he began to look away from her piercing gaze.

Trying to keep his eyes off the beauty standing next to his desk, he cleared his throat before speaking.

"How can I help you?"

The businesswoman reached out to him, shaking his hand firmly. Her hand was soft, and she had the most frigid look on her face that he's ever encountered. He knew that whatever she wanted, she was not here to play games.

"Hello, Dr. Bennett, you're a hard man to get on the phone. My name is Meagan Quinn. I am from the United Nations War Crimes investigation team. It's a real honor to meet you. I would also like to introduce Ayana Burundi, who is also from the United Nations. She is our top counselor for survivors of war and genocide."

Ayana smiled brightly as she held out her hand. When Daniel took her hand in his, warmth immediately began to flow up his arm, and then traveled throughout his entire body. His hand immediately began to sweat as the softness and intricacies of her hand seemed to fit perfectly in his own. Her handshake wasn't as firm as Ms. Quinn's, but it was embracing, and he felt his nerves come alive with excitement. Startled by his reaction to merely shaking her hand, he pulled back and began to move toward the other side of his office, trying to avoid eye contact with the smiling goddess near his desk.

Noticing his reaction, Ayana shook her head, smiling brightly, exposing a mouthful of pearly white teeth that seemed to sparkle in the sunlight. The contrast of her white teeth and dark skin made her even more amazing.

He could tell she was used to this kind of reaction from other men, and it amused her.

"It is also an honor to meet you, Doctor," Ayana said, still smiling. Hearing her voice startled him, and he began to sweat all over his body. Her accent was heavy, her words spoken like poetry as she pronounced each letter and said each word with meaning. He'd heard someone speak like this before, years ago when he was a volunteer doctor in southern Sudan, and he never dreamed he would hear that melody again. Actually, he prayed he would never have to relive the nightmare of that melody because it reminded him of the young dead girl in his arms and a village slaughtered right before his eyes.

Ayana was Sudanese, and Daniel feared they were here to ask of him the unthinkable. Feeling a deeper kind of fear grip his body, Daniel tried his best to calm his nerves in order to deal with the possibilities of this visit. After going over every possible scenario, he discovered none of them were favorable for him keeping the little sanity he had left. His nerves were in a frenzy now, and he decided to have a seat at his desk to stop his legs from shaking like twigs in the wind.

"Doctor, Ayana and I are here because we need your help in bringing a monster to justice. United Nations Security Forces captured Kronte a few months ago, the man responsible for the murder of your daughter, and we are building a case against him. If we are successful, he will spend the rest of his life in prison, and his followers will disband."

"And when you say 'help,' you mean testify in court, correct?"

"Exactly. The hearings will be held in Juba, and your testimony could help secure his conviction."

Realizing his worst nightmare has come knocking on his office door, Daniel immediately decided he wanted no part of reliving an ordeal that nearly claimed his life.

"Listen, you said that this guy attacked other villages, so I know there are other witnesses that will have a more damaging effect than me."

"That's not entirely true," interjected Ayana. "Many people that survived his massacres are too afraid to testify for fear of retaliation. The United Nations has him in custody, but his murdering gang is still at large in South Sudan, intimidating my people from testifying."

"Listen, Doctor, you were there during one of their raids. You witnessed everything, and they even attempted to murder you," Meagan continued. "Your testimony could inspire others to come forward, once they see that this man won't get away with the atrocities he's charged with. I know you went through a lot over there, and we are asking a lot of you, but what's the point of surviving such an ordeal if the man responsible is allowed to get away with it?"

"Evil people get away with a lot nowadays. As a doctor in one of the worst areas in this city, I see it every day. So many murders with very few convictions, but I don't see the United Nations coming into my office asking for testimony for all the little dead black or Hispanic boys and girls that are murdered right up the street from this hospital. I have yet to see a tribunal being held for the drug dealers and gang leaders of this city. Where is the outrage for them, huh?"

Ayana's bright and welcoming smile began to dissipate with each word that came out of the doctor's mouth, and by the time he paused from his geopolitical tirade, her face was twisted with disgust at the man in front of her.

"I heard a lot of things about you, Doctor, but being a coward wasn't one of them. I am ashamed that I held you in such high regard and disgusted that you and I breathe the same air. It's men like you that allow men like Kronte 'The Terror' Kroma to flourish and their evil infect this entire planet."

The melody of her voice was now more aggressive, and she sucked her teeth before storming out of his office. Daniel leaned slightly to the side to try to sneak a quick peek at her swishing backside to confirm what he secretly thought to himself when he first saw her.

Damn, I knew it! She has an amazing ass. One down, one to go, he thought to himself while watching her leave his office.

Meagan, forcing a smile, attempted to ease the damage that Ayana's rant may have caused.

"Listen, Dr. Bennett, I completely understand your apprehension, but I can assure you that you will be safe from any retaliation by his followers if you would just—"

Cutting her off, Daniel responded, "You are right. I will be safe because I'm *not* going within 10,000 miles of that trial. I would say I'm sorry, but I'd be lying. I paid my dues to the motherland, and I don't intend to give another ounce of blood to that godforsaken continent. Let Africans handle their own business, and let Americans do the same."

Now looking at the doctor with the same look of disgust, Meagan sat there staring at him for a few seconds longer before preparing to leave his office. Then without warning, the door flung open and in ran Timothy, anxious with something to say. Daniel could tell from his expression that Timothy had either something vulgar or disrespectful to say about women on the tip of his tongue, and he threw both of his hands in the air, attempting to warn him before he let it slip out. Timothy's excitement prevented him from seeing Daniel's gesture, and he yelled out, "Dude, white bitches are fucking crazy!"

His words seemed to explode like a grenade in the office, and Daniel cringed at the thought of what could be going on inside Meagan's head after hearing his proclamation. Now guilty by association, Meagan looked at Daniel, shaking her head and immediately left his office with the silent uniformed escort quickly following her. Burying his head in his hands, Daniel grunted and then chuckled at the events that just unfolded in his office.

Looking completely lost and confused, Timothy whispered, "Oh shit! Was that a white woman?"

Chapter 4

Unforgettable

The time, 4:05 a.m., glared back at Daniel from the digital clock on the nightstand. The red light from the clock barely seemed to penetrate the darkness of his bedroom. The horrible nightmare of the massacre in Sudan continued to haunt him, and with Ayana and Meagan's arrival, it seemed the nightmares took on a life of their own. The nightmares now seemed to concentrate more on the pain of his beating and the multiple gunshot wounds he received from his attackers. Even after waking up screaming, drenched in sweat, he could still feel the pain of his legs being broken and the searing burn of the bullets piercing his flesh repeatedly. He stumbled, falling to the floor when he tried to walk to the bathroom, his legs refusing to follow the orders of his brain to move.

He sat up on the floor and began rubbing his legs while gritting his teeth. He knew his body was healthy, and the bones in his legs were completely healed, but his mind refused to let go. His body felt like it was losing blood at an alarming rate from the healed bullet wounds on his torso. He tried to fight back the tears of anger and pain, but an emotional tidal wave came over him, and he broke down, sobbing on the floor. Unable to move, he decided to lie there and let his emotions take over until his body had enough, and his brain would come back from the past and into the present . . .

Later that day, Daniel was sitting in his office, staring at the wall when he heard a light knock on his door.

"Come in."

It was Timothy, looking worried and concerned. "Hey, dude, did I fuck up something big yesterday? Because you left in a hurry and didn't say anything."

"Naw, not really. You actually may have helped."

"Huh? How so?"

Daniel decided to fill Timothy in on the reason why the three visitors were in his office yesterday afternoon and how his outburst helped him.

Timothy sat there listening attentively, and once Daniel was done, he stood up and began walking around.

"Listen, I won't pretend to know or understand what you went through over there, but don't you think you were unreasonable . . . just a little bit, bruh?"

Daniel remained silent and just shook his head.

"Hmmm, so that chocolate dreamboat was here for you? Dude, with all that body that woman has and that face? Oh my God! Bruh, I would've followed that ass to Jupiter and testified against God himself if she would let a brother hit . . . mmm-mmm . . . I'm usually not into dark-skinned girls, but that one right there . . . woooweee! She was bad!"

Daniel laughed at Timothy's rantings about Ayana's beauty.

"All that beauty will get you killed too, Tim. What they are asking me to do could put my life in danger all over again."

"Or it could give you some closure."

Shocked by Timothy's comment, Daniel decided to leave the office and get away from him, before he started trying to have a heart-to-heart. Timothy, seeing Daniel's reaction, quickly ran to the door, shutting it, and standing in Daniel's escape route.

"Nope, I'm not letting you get off that easy. You need to hear this. You haven't been the same since you came back from Africa. It's like even though your body is here, you're breathing and you talk . . . well . . . something like talking . . . It's like the Danny I grew up with died in that village, and the man standing in front of me is someone else. You're my boy, and I got your back regardless, but you can't keep going on like this. It's not healthy."

Daniel stood there, giving Timothy a blank stare showing no emotion whatsoever. Looking in his eyes, Timothy couldn't tell if his friend was even listening to him or if his soul left the room, leaving behind this empty shell of a body. Feeling uncomfortable with the way Daniel was looking at him, he looked down at the floor before stepping aside. Daniel quickly opened the door and walked out of the office, leaving Timothy standing alone in the room, confused.

Daniel's mind was racing a hundred miles a second as he hurried toward the ICU, attempting to escape Timothy's assessment of his state of mind.

The nerve of him! Who the fuck does he think he is? He doesn't know anything about what I went through. I'm perfectly fine. I don't need anyone telling me what I need to do. I know what's best for me.

Aggressively walking into ICU, Daniel began yelling out orders to the nurses on duty, startling them in the process. It had been years since anyone has seen him this aggressive. It was clear to everyone that he was furious about something, and they all decided to tread lightly while he vigorously moved from one patient to the next, blaring out orders and demanding their undivided attention. By the end of another twelve-hour shift, he was physically and mentally exhausted, and more than likely had burned a few bridges with the nurses on duty.

Driving home, he began to reflect on his behavior and was instantly overwhelmed with deep feelings of shame and remorse. He was extremely mean today, and as his behavior replayed repeatedly in his mind, he could barely sit still in the driver's seat. Attempting to calm his nerves, he turned on the radio and quickly turned it off again once a song began blasting through his BMW's speakers, demanding all women in the club to shake their asses and grab their tits.

What the fuck was that shit? They actually play that on the radio now?

Daniel didn't consider himself old enough to be converted to listening to anything other than "old-school" music, but with the direction music was headed in nowadays, it may start him much earlier than anticipated. With nothing to take his mind off his shameful behavior earlier, Daniel was forced to drive home in silence, tortured by the memory of his actions in the ICU. After showering, he collapsed on his bed, praying for one night of restful sleep so that he could have the strength to face his coworkers and muster up the courage to apologize to everyone . . . including Tim.

At 2:58 a.m., Daniel could feel the heat of the sun, but his body remained frigid. He could feel the life slowly ooze out of him from the countless wounds his attackers inflicted on him. His body, screaming out from the indescribable pain of dying slowly, lay in a pool of his blood while a few of his would-be murderers watched. They were smoking and laughing, seemingly amused by the spectacle of a man dying at their feet. Their disregard and lack of remorse for their actions tortured him as his body's organs began to shut down, preparing his body for the coming darkness of death. How could men like this be allowed to get away with these acts of evil? How could they be allowed to live another second, let alone another day? He would soon be gone from this earth, and these men would remain, allowed to continue their wicked campaign to eradicate an entire nation of people.

All he wanted to do was help, to give back to a people that needed and deserved more than the oncoming genocide. Good things are supposed to happen to good people and bad things to bad people. Daniel gave up so much to be here, working countless hours without pay in a hostile environment to help a people he didn't know but grew to love like his own family. He taught, he healed, counseled, prayed, and allowed himself to learn. He thought a higher power ordained his mission, but in the end, the only payment he received for his sacrifice was pain, loss, and death. There were no words that could be spoken that could describe the pain his soul endured. Soon, he found it hard to keep his eyes open as his lungs stopped working. Blood began to fill up in his throat, and he felt himself suffocate on the metallic and salty taste of his blood. How ironic that the thing that gave him life would also deliver the final blow of his demise . . .

The burning in his chest became unbearable, and his eyes widened as he began to lose himself, struggling to breathe . . .

The loud thump of his body falling from the bed and hitting the floor shook his bedroom, jolting him from his nightmare when his head struck the nightstand. Gripping the side of his head, he rolled on his side while gritting his teeth. He wanted to curse, but he was still trying to catch his breath. He began to wonder if he would've killed himself had his body not fallen to the floor from his struggle to breathe. The nightmares were getting worse. The fact that he was on the verge of suffocating in his sleep made it evident. Suddenly, the sound of his cell phone's ring tone filled the air. Reaching for it, he looked at the display to see the same strange number that's been calling him for months.

Without thinking, he accepted the call, placing the phone to his ear. Breathing heavily, he spoke into the phone. "Hello, who is this?"

At first, the only answer he got was silence, and after waiting for a response for a few more seconds, he decided to hang up; then Ayana's familiar voice filled his ear.

"Hello, Dr. Bennett, this is Ayana. I know it's not a respectable hour to call you, but I couldn't sleep until I apologized for what I said to you the other day."

Still disoriented, Daniel remained silent, trying to process the reality that Ayana was the person that's been calling him for months.

"Hello? Dr. Bennett, are you there? Did I interrupt something?"

Shaken out of his daze by her question, he immediately answered, "Interrupt something? Why . . . no . . . what . . . Why would you ask that?" he stuttered.

"Well, you sound like you are involved in something physically challenging," she responded, giggling. "You are breathing pretty hard, Doctor, and you seem distracted."

Looking at the clock and noticing the time, he responded sarcastically, "I'm distracted by the loss of sleep this phone call at three in the morning is causing."

"I'm sorry, Doctor. I just wanted to apologize for my behavior the other day. I let my emotions get the best of me."

"Apology accepted, but this could have waited till morning."

"Yes, but the morning isn't promised, so we should take the opportunity when it presents itself. I'm happy that you've accepted my apology, and again, I'm sorry for disturbing your workout session."

"It's fine. I wasn't working out anyway."

Ayana became increasingly concerned for the doctor because his breathing never improved throughout their call. Had he admitted to being in the middle of a workout or even a sexual encounter, although awkward, it would've explained his condition. As much as she didn't want to offend the doctor further, she was concerned, and her nature wouldn't allow her to hang up. Something troubled her. Knowing what she did about survivor's guilt, she felt she knew exactly what troubled the doctor. She was afraid to push further, knowing if he became angry, she might lose any chance of him changing his mind about testifying. She couldn't quite understand why, but she felt his well-being was more important than his testimony. Bracing herself for his anger, she decided to probe deeper.

"How long?" she asked softly.

"How long what?" he answered, confused by the question.

Without hesitation, she responded, "How long have you been having the nightmares?"

Daniel's finger immediately pressed the *end* call button on his phone, and he tossed it across the room. He didn't even think about it. It was an automatic response after hearing the question.

How did she know? Who is this woman?

Again, the phone began to ring a few seconds after it hit the floor. Daniel just sat on the floor, listening to the ringtone. He felt frozen and lost in his dark bedroom, sitting on the floor like a frightened child awaiting punishment for misbehaving. Ayana terrified and intrigued him. She reminded him of a time when he cared about more than his job, but now, the only thing that mattered was the distraction of the chaos of the ICU and how that chaos helped him to forget. He just wanted to be left alone . . . no emotions, no memories, and no reasons to give of himself, besides being a doctor. Let the suckers care . . . He was fine with not giving a shit. However, since Ayana showed up in his office, things were taking a turn he didn't like, and he felt like he was losing his mind.

The phone continued to ring repeatedly.

Damn it, that woman is persistent!

Knowing she wouldn't stop calling, he decided to walk over to the phone intending to answer it and yell, demanding that she stop calling him before he files a harassment lawsuit.

Slowly picking up the phone, he looked at the number again.

Ayana.

Inhaling deeply, he accepted the call, and just before he went into his threatening rant, he heard her say, "Meet me at the coffee shop downstairs in your building in half an hour."

Without thinking, he responded, "Okay."

After hearing his response, she disconnected the call immediately, not giving him a chance to change his mind. Ayana knew that he wasn't going to stand her up, especially because he would be curious about her knowing where he lived.

He can't help anyone if he doesn't help himself, she thought as she reached for her coat and headed out the door to meet him.

After ending the call, Daniel stood in the middle of his bedroom, covered in sweat and confusion.

How does she know where I live and that there is a twenty-four-hour coffee shop in my building?

Chapter 5

Defibrillator

The thought of not showing up did cross Daniel's mind, but sitting here across from Ayana and taking in all of the intoxicating effects of her, he was glad he did show up. She had a concerned look in her eyes, and her face was void of the beautiful smile she'd greeted him with the first time they met. Even without her smile, though, she was still amazing, and the few people that were sitting in the coffee shop kept staring at her as if in a trance.

"I'm happy you decided to meet me. I know it's very early, so I won't waste any more time and get straight to the point. How long have you been having nightmares?"

"What nightmares?"

"Doctor, let's not play childish games, okay? You are a man that many people depend on to save their lives. Being in this state is dangerous for them and yourself. So, please, don't insult me by pretending you have no idea what I'm referring to."

Daniel remained silent while forcing himself to look at her. She reached across the table, holding his hand, and without saying a word, he instantly felt her compassion, assuring him that it was okay to trust her.

"Four years."

The words spilled out of his mouth with ease, and his mind tried to grasp the realization that no one has been able to pull that out of him since his near-death experience in Sudan. Not even all the sessions on a psychiatrist's couch could pull those two words out. He barely knew this woman, and she was already getting him to tell a secret he vowed to take to the grave. He wanted to bolt and run back to his condo upstairs, locking his door and changing his phone number. But somehow, no matter how afraid he felt, no matter how vulnerable she made him feel, he remained seated with his hand in hers. She kept gently running her incredibly soft hands on his, the gesture easing his anxiety.

How can this man function with so much pain inside of him?

Knowing the pain that he kept inside of him, yet he continued to save lives in one of the most violent neighborhoods in this city, spoke volumes of his courage, and Ayana felt ashamed for calling him a coward. His bravery was incredibly rare, and she'd met some amazing people in her life. Most would've chosen another profession, something with very little responsibility, a job where no one depended on them. Not this man, though. He stood against the evil that had invaded his soul and continued to ease others' pain while disregarding his own.

"So, are you going to tell me I need therapy or closure? Somehow, tying my cure with testifying against the warlord?" he snapped at her, suddenly becoming angry with himself for easily opening up to this beautiful stranger. Unmoved by his anger, she smiled and responded, "No, Doctor, in your current state, you would hurt the case more than help it. I would not recommend you testify."

Shocked by her response, he leaned back in frustration while shaking his head.

"So what was the point of this meet and greet, Ayana?"

"I want to help you."

Laughing loudly and startling the other patrons in the coffee shop, Daniel slapped the top of the table, clearly amused by her desire to *help* him.

"Help me. How can *you* possibly help *me?*"

"You are not the only one that has suffered and experienced loss in the Sudan, Doctor. Millions have suffered worst fates than your own. Don't assume or believe your experiences are the worst that those evil men can conjure up because I can assure you that your assumptions are false. That is the problem with people from so-called first world countries. The suffering of the third world isn't a concern until you get a taste of it. What you experienced, albeit horrible, is just a small sample of what my family and I have had to endure."

Becoming increasingly offended by her words, Daniel decided to get up and leave. He'd heard enough, and there was no way he would allow anyone to downplay what he went through—no matter how beautiful and caring they appeared to be. Seeing he intended to leave, Ayana reached out and took hold of his hand. Her soft hands firmly holding his prevented him from getting up from the table. His attempt to leave her alone at the table was upsetting her, and she wasn't going to let him get off that easily.

"You are not leaving. I didn't come over here for you to leave me alone at this table. Now, sit down and stop acting like a baby."

Her refusal to back down angered him further.

Oh, man, I'm so out of here, he thought.

Snatching away from her grip, he stood straight up and began to push his chair under the table.

"Thank you for your visit, and I appreciate you are trying to *help me,* but I don't *need* your help. I don't need anyone's help. Have a nice day, Ayana . . . oh, and by the way . . . lose my number. I would hate to testify in another court concerning a restraining order."

He then quickly turned and left the coffee shop, leaving her sitting at the table alone and in shock. Watching him leave, she felt like she just had a conversation with Dr. Jekyll and Mr. Hyde. His passive-aggressive behavior was a clear indication that if he didn't get help soon, he would implode and lose the little piece of the man he used to be forever. She tried to be understanding of his outburst, but she couldn't get past the embarrassment she felt while everyone watched him leave her at the table as if she were a desperate woman begging for a date. Not wanting to remain here while people whispered and stared at her, she quickly got up and left, leaving behind a tip for the waiter even though they never got a chance to order.

He doesn't need therapy. He needs a pacifier and a diaper change, she thought while she walked out the door . . .

It was the weekend again, and Daniel and Timothy decided to spend their Saturday night at one of Chicago's hottest reggae clubs. The loud club music could barely drown out Timothy's half-drunken laughter after listening to Daniel tell him that he demanded Ayana to lose his number. Daniel wasn't amused at Timothy's response and started taking shot after shot in frustration. Noticing that his friend was drinking himself into a coma, Tim reached over and stopped him from downing another shot glass full of Patrón.

"Dude, you need to grow the fuck up, seriously. You've held back your emotions so long that you don't know how to act. Now that Ayana is bringing them out of you, you get angry when you should be happy, you get happy when you should be angry, and you run when you should be horny. Any other man that had Ayana anywhere near their building . . . Hell, even if she were ten miles away, would've tried to get her in their house. Man, at least they would've been nicer to her."

"Yeah, even though she got their number without them giving it to her?"

"Fuck, yeah! What do you think? She works for the UN, not mall security. The Chicago PD can get your number, so I would expect a UN official would be able to get it too. I'm not sure why she was at your building that early in the morning, but for me, those are prime booty call hours."

Timothy began to laugh, and then he continued, "I know a lot more is going on than what you're telling me, and if you don't want to tell me, that's cool. But don't think I'm stupid. I know there's more to this story besides a phone call, and then she just pops up at your building. She wanted something besides coffee at four in the morning."

Ignoring Timothy's last comment, Daniel took another shot and turned around on the bar stool. He was half-drunk and looking at the dance floor for some much-needed sexual stimulation. Thinking about Ayana seemed to send his sexual appetite into overdrive. He knew he didn't have the patience to share a bed with a woman, but at least he could grind and gyrate on a strange woman that was willing to do the same to him.

Near the DJ booth, he noticed a very attractive woman dancing alone. She wore a very revealing dress that seemed painted on her incredible body. She was built for action, and she didn't hesitate to shake and twerk, showing off what she had to offer. Licking his lips, he took another shot and got up from the bar with intentions of taking her body for a test drive.

Timothy, noticing what Daniel was about to do, stopped him momentarily to give him what he believed would be some valuable advice.

"Dude, be careful with that one. If you ain't willing to hit that, I wouldn't even get her started."

Looking at him in disbelief, Daniel gave him a drunk smirk and backed away. "How do you know that? Have *you* fucked her?"

"Hell no! I don't know that bitch, but I know her type. She wants dick and money, not necessarily in that order. That body is made for making babies, bruh. She's looking for that one good payday, and you being a doctor . . . well . . . Let's just say she would fuck you right in this club if you let her."

"Whatever, dude. You don't know everything about women. You think you do, but you don't."

"I never said I did, but I do know about women like *that*. Okay, let's make a gentlemen's bet . . ."

"Hell naw, I'm not betting on any ass, dude."

"No, not that. I wager that if you walk over to her and try to dance with her without saying you are a doctor, she will act like you ain't there. But . . . but . . . Tell her you are a doctor and see how she responds. Just try it."

Thinking about it while watching the woman bounce and gyrate next to the massive speakers, Daniel nodded in agreement.

"Okay, so what's the prize?" Daniel asked.

"If I lose, I refrain from sex for ninety days."

"Bullshit! Tim, you know you can't go ninety hours without sex."

"True, but you know I'm a man of my word."

Nodding in agreement, Daniel accepted his end of the wager.

"But if *you* lose, you have to call that fine-ass Ayana and do whatever she wanted you to do."

"Fuck no," Daniel snapped.

"So, you're a bitch now? You were all gung ho about my end of the bet, but you can't do yours?"

"What is it about Ayana? Why do you want me around her?"

"Because in the short time she's been around, you've actually started to show some signs of life, even if they are annoying as fuck at times. Before, I couldn't get any meaningful emotional responses from you. Now, you're talking more, and none of this started until Ayana showed up. So, maybe with a little more time with her, things will work themselves out. I know it's a long shot, but I'm a doctor trying to cure cancer, so I'm used to long shots."

Daniel didn't want to play this game with Timothy, but he really needed to prove that Timothy wasn't as skilled with the ladies as he thought he was. Yeah, sure, a lot of women were as he described, but not all of them. He wanted to prove him wrong for once. Despite his fear of losing the bet and having to be around Ayana and her attempts at *fixing* him, he accepted the bet and started making his way toward the dancing woman.

Timothy watched his friend maneuver across the dance floor. He was excited to see how it would turn out, and he was confident that he was accurate concerning his assessment of the dancing woman.

He's gonna feel so stupid when she rejects him.

Daniel moved slowly, staring at the woman until he caught her eye. She looked back at him and gave him a mischievous smirk. She caught him watching her, and she liked it. Still moving toward her, Daniel never took his eyes off her. The longer he stared at her, the more sensual her movements became. She turned to the side while dancing, exposing the perfect crescent moon that was her ass. Daniel was only a few feet from her as he continued to push forward in her direction. He was now so close that he could smell the sweetness of her perfume, feel her body heat, and the sweet smell of the fruity chewing gum she had in her mouth. Timothy stepped away from the bar, so he could get a better view of the coming rejection, but what happened next made his mouth drop. Instead of Daniel walking up to her, he proceeded to walk past her as if she weren't there, sending a strong feeling of rejection in the woman's direction.

The woman, now shocked and intrigued by Daniel's reaction, quickly and forcefully grabbed his arm and pulled him close to her. Wrapping her arms around him like a mother's embrace and without uttering one word, she began to dance with him. Pressing every curve against his body, she seemed desperate to get as close to him as humanly possible. Daniel accepted her embrace, and the two embarked on a rhythmic journey so sexual, Timothy was sure Daniel was going to pop before it was over.

Seven songs later, a sweaty Daniel returned to the bar with the biggest smile on his face. Timothy's face made it clear he wasn't happy with his loss and the consequences he would have to face. Daniel could tell Timothy was confused at how things played out, and he was all too eager to give him the lesson he should've learned ages ago.

"Dude, you forgot about me, didn't you? All the game you have, you got from yours truly. Just because I've been focused on other shit doesn't mean I don't know how to get a woman's attention. It also helps that a brother is considered quite attractive by the ladies. I don't need a profession. I got all I need with me at all times to pull any woman I want. You just forgot, young Padawan learner, who your master is . . . May the force be with you, and the pussy be away from you for the next ninety days."

The thought of being sex free for three months started to sink in, and Timothy immediately felt faint. Watching his reaction caused Daniel to laugh loudly as he ordered a drink and handed it to his friend.

"Tim, you look like you need a drink."

"Gloat all you want, Yoda. I will honor our bet, but I still believe you should give Ayana a chance."

"How about you take this drink and give celibacy a chance . . . Father Avers."

Timothy immediately gave him the finger, while gulping down the drink his friend just handed him.

Laughing loudly, Daniel headed back out on the dance floor, looking for another dance partner.

Chapter 6

Breaking Point

The next afternoon, Daniel sat in his office, rocking back and forth in his chair, twirling a writing pen in his hand. His mind wandered beyond the confines of his office, replaying the conversation between himself and Ayana the other night.

"Dr. Bennett?" The nurse's voice called out to him from the doorway of his office.

"Yes, Ms. Davis."

"There's someone here to see you."

Instantly feeling annoyed, Daniel assumed it was either Meagan or Ayana.

"Who is it?"

"He wouldn't give his name, but he's definitely not from around here."

"Not from around here?"

"Yeah, from this country . . . from the US . . . I believe he may be African or Jamaican . . . I'm not completely sure."

Now confused, Daniel told the nurse to show in his guest. She returned with a dark-skinned man of such a massive stature that Daniel was afraid he wouldn't fit through the office door. He wasn't an obese man, but a man built like a tank. His muscles bulged through the three-piece grey suit he wore, and while watching him step through his office door, Daniel was surprised a suit existed to fit a man with such a large frame. The man smiled and began to speak with his hand extended to greet the doctor.

"Hello, my name is Satu, and I am here as a representative of Kronte and the freedom fighters of Southern Sudan."

His introduction caused Daniel to freeze in his chair as a cold sweat started to build all over his body. Seeing his reaction, Satu smiled brightly and sat in the seat on the other side of the doctor's desk. As he slowly took a seat, Daniel secretly reached down and quickly entered the security code of his gun safe located in an opening on the right side of his desk. The quiet yet sharp clicking sound of the safe's door lock disengaging made the doctor cringe, hoping the gigantic man that was making himself comfortable didn't hear it.

"I assure you, Doctor, I am not here in an aggressive capacity. I am here to deliver a message from our wrongfully imprisoned leader. He sends his condolences for your loss in Sudan, but he assures you that neither he nor his followers had anything to do with that raid. Because of this fact, he hopes that you would refrain from testifying in the courts, falsely accusing him."

Daniel's hands were now cold as ice, and he began to rub them together, attempting to warm them. His nerves were in a frenzy, and sending this hulk of a man to his office to relay this message was the definition of intimidation. Daniel assumed Kronte thought this large man would instill a fear in him that would keep him silent. Daniel was nervous, not because of the man, but what his presence caused him to relive. It was as if the universe was hell-bent not only on torturing him in his sleep but also while he was awake.

Satu, noticing the confusion on the doctor's face, grinned while reaching into his inside jacket pocket, which made the doctor jump back in his chair. His reaction sent a look of satisfaction on Satu's face, and then he slowly pulled out a large, yellow envelope.

"Kronte also wanted to give you this gift, a token of his appreciation and sorrow for your loss in his country."

Looking confused, Daniel stared at the envelope now lying on his desk. "What is that?"

"A gift of $100,000 US. He knows that he can't replace a life, but he believes this can be the beginning of many gifts that can help you forget . . . with your cooperation, of course."

Daniel's emotions were now in freefall, and fury began to boil inside of him. He wanted to attack Satu with the butterfly pocketknife in his coat pocket, but he wasn't sure how the hospital staff would take him slicing and dicing a man in his office. He tried his best to calm his nerves and decided to lean back in his chair and give Satu a very concise piece of his mind. He'd had enough, and it was time for him to let his guest, *and* the one who sent him, know.

"Your leader must really be a generous man to pay $100,000 in restitution for someone else's crime. I mean, you did say he didn't have anything to do with the raid, correct?"

"You are correct, Doctor Bennett."

"One hundred thousand, huh? I take it your leader, being so generous *and* innocent, didn't want to appear desperate by offering more. I get it. Thing is, I'm confused concerning a few details, especially the claim that your boss wasn't present and responsible for the massacre in the village and the attempt on my life. They didn't fail from a lack of trying. I can tell you that."

"What are your concerns? Like I've said, my leader wasn't responsible for that raid."

"Hmmm, that's strange, because I remember clearly while I was getting my ass beat and shot up, your leader was one of the men pulling the trigger. Actually, I clearly remember spitting in your boss's face. Now, I know the sun was bright that day, and usually, it can play tricks with your eyesight, but your leader . . . well . . . You know, you hang with him all the time . . . He's a pretty dark-skinned man. I mean, standing next to him in the sun is like hiding under a very luscious tree. So, I'm sure the bright sunlight wasn't a factor in me seeing clearly. Also, the emblem on your suit that represents your (*cough*) freedom fighters . . . The men that raided that village also wore the exact emblem.

"Now, unless your organization has some imposters, and your boss has a twin brother, it's hard for me to accept his claim of innocence. You see, where I'm from, if it walks like a duck and quacks like a duck . . . well . . . It's a fuck of a duck. And now you come in here with a gift of $100,000 . . . well . . . for recompense for a crime he didn't commit. Satu, keep it real with me . . . It's not a gift, is it? It's hush money, right?" he asked sarcastically.

"Listen, I too have a message for your boss. Tell your boss he can take his gift and shove it up his degenerate ass. You don't scare me, and neither does he. Now, take that envelope and get the fuck out of my office!"

Appearing offended, Satu sat quietly. His smile was gone, and he had a look in his eyes that revealed violent intentions. He decided not to leave the office and possibly try to intimidate the doctor further.

"Or what, Doctor? You'll call security?"

"Security? Nigga, if you don't get the fuck up out of that chair and out of this office, I will fill your ass up with some hot shit!"

From his gun's safe, Daniel pulled out the biggest handgun Satu had ever seen. He jumped to his feet in terror, grabbing the envelope, and quickly started backing out of the office.

"Satu, it would be in your best interest if I never see you in this hospital again. I also implore you to leave quietly. If you threaten me in any way or utter one word on your way out, I will attempt to shoot the black off your ass. That's a lot of shooting, but I got refills here so . . ."

Shaking his head, Satu quickly backed out of Daniel's office and ran down the hall toward the elevator.

Americans and their guns, Satu thought, stepping inside the elevator alone.

Looking out his office door, Daniel watched Satu until the elevator doors closed. Still holding the chrome-plated hand cannon, he began to pace back and forth in his office in a daze. His thoughts were spinning like a hurricane in his head as he tried to grasp the magnitude of what just occurred in his office. Kronte and his henchmen would not give up so easily, and Daniel feared that once the warlord found out he couldn't buy him out, he would resort to other means to silence him. Running wasn't an option. Men like Kronte didn't gamble, and he wouldn't stop looking for him and would use those closest to him to draw him out. Taking the money would've only allowed Kronte to bend him over anytime he wanted, taking all kinds of shit that wouldn't be worth the money exchanged.

All he wanted to do was to be left alone and allowed to live his life the way he wanted to live it. Now, he was being forced to make decisions against his will, and Daniel hated that. Just thinking about it caused his jaws to tighten like a vice grip as the pressure caused his teeth to grind in his mouth. With the gun still in his hand, his fists tightened as his anger grew. He unconsciously placed his finger firmly on the gun's trigger while slowly closing his fist. He was lost inside himself, his rage and feelings of entrapment caused his emotions to become unstable, like a house of cards. In his confusion, he didn't notice the loud clicking sound that kept echoing inside his office until Timothy's voice snapped him out of his nightmare.

Timothy was looking at his friend as if he were a madman. His eyes kept moving from his hand to his face, searching for any clue about why Daniel was standing in the middle of his office, repeatedly pulling the gun's trigger with the barrel pointed directly at his temple. The Glock 43's safety was still on, so the gun never discharged, but the scene was still very disturbing. Timothy was afraid to say anything that might cause Daniel to snap, causing him to do the unthinkable.

Timothy stood in the doorway in complete silence, afraid to move or make a sound. Daniel was looking at the floor with a tormented look in his eyes. Timothy saw his friend was in a lot of pain, and he didn't know how to help him. Each time he pulled the trigger, Timothy's heart seemed to stop beating. He was sweating now, and the stress from what he was watching was taking a serious toll on him. Not wanting to expose Daniel's breakdown to the rest of the hospital, Timothy slowly closed the door behind him and raised both hands in the air, before deciding to call out to Daniel.

"Danny, Danny, what are you doing, man?"

Daniel was unresponsive, appearing not to notice he wasn't alone any longer.

"Danny! Bruh, what are you doing?"

Daniel appeared to be trying to listen to something, as he slightly turned his head in Timothy's direction. Feeling that his friend was coming out of his trance, Timothy decided to speak louder, hoping that Daniel would come to his senses before his thumb accidentally hit the safety switch.

"Danny, what is that in your hand, bruh? Look at your hand."

Daniel seemed to understand and turned slowly toward the hand that held the gun. Upon seeing the shiny barrel directly in his face, he quickly jumped back, covering his face as if someone else were holding the weapon. Noticing that the gun was in his hand, Daniel examined it before letting his arm drop to his side. Exhaling deeply, he turned to face Timothy, whose frightened eyes were filled with questions that demanded answers. Watching Daniel walk over to his desk and slide the gun back in the drawer, Timothy became furious at how calmly Daniel was behaving. It was as if he just walked in on him eating lunch instead of about to eat a bullet.

"You wanna tell me what the fuck that was about?" Timothy asked, without trying to hide his anger.

"Not really, but I don't have a choice, do I?"

"Hell no, you don't! Look, man, I'm too backed up for this stressful shit. I can't even release the stress I'm feeling right now, so you need to tell me what's going on."

"Okay, fine. Have a seat."

Refusing to say a word or sit, Timothy folded his arms and remained standing. His posture of defiance amused

Daniel, and he smiled while he calmly took a seat behind
his desk. The fact that Daniel continued to smile aggra-
vated Timothy to the point of madness, and he secretly
wanted to knock that smile right off his friend's face.

"So, are you going to talk or sit there smiling at me like
some kind of car salesman ready to fuck me over on a
ten-year car loan?"

His comment wiped the smile off Daniel's face, causing him to shake his head, annoyed at Timothy's attempt
at forcing him to reveal things he didn't care to talk
about. Knowing he had no choice, however, Daniel told
Timothy about the conversation he'd just had with Satu.
Once he was done, Timothy still had a look of disbelief
on his face. He knew that Daniel was still leaving a lot
out, and he wasn't going to be shortchanged, not after
what he just walked in on.

"What else, Danny?"

"That's it. That's everything."

"Hey, asshole! I know there's more, and you need to
spill it. I'm not fucking around. I'm your boy, but I will
go to the board about this. You are a danger to yourself
and the patients with that suicidal bullshit, and I'm in
short supply of patience and an overabundance of sexual
frustration, so don't test me."

"Hey, you can't blame me for your sexual frustration.
You came up with that—not me."

"Danny, I'm not playing . . . I want it all, and I want it
now. Spill it!"

Daniel, seeing that Timothy wasn't going to let it
go, decided to explain everything, including his violent
nightmares, but kept assuring him that he had things
under control, and he shouldn't be worried.

"I shouldn't be worried after I walked in on you with a
gun to your head? Yeah, that seems real reasonable."

As Timothy continued to complain, Daniel's shattered mind tried to pull itself together. Momentarily closing his eyes, he attempted to bring himself into the present, but Timothy's constant complaining made it difficult to concentrate. Clinching his fists, Daniel inhaled deeply and said, "Listen, I understand you are concerned, and I would love to delve deeper into this, but right now, this isn't the time or the place for this discussion. I need to get back to the ICU, and the last thing I need is for someone to overhear this conversation and misunderstand the situation."

"Misunderstand the situation? Dude, screw that! If they overheard this conversation, they would get exactly what they should from it. Your ass is unstable, and you need help . . . *serious* help. It's one thing to be standoffish and cold like a robot, but it's another to point a loaded gun at your head and continuously pull the trigger."

"The safety was on . . ."

"Danny, I don't give a flying fuck," Timothy snapped back.

"Keep your voice down," Daniel warned, looking toward his office door. "This is why I said we need to talk about this later."

"Cool. Tonight . . . We will get real deep into this madness, and I swear, Danny, if you play stupid with me tonight, I *will* inform the hospital board. You may hate me now, but you'll thank me later."

"You wouldn't do that to me."

"Ha! Try me, Doctor Doom. Just try me."

"Okay, tonight. Come by my condo around nine. Now—"

Before he could finish, Timothy quickly turned and stormed out of the office without saying a word.

Appearing unconcerned about his friend's abrupt exit, Daniel stood up and began getting himself ready for another long shift in the ICU.

Tonight is going to be very interesting.

Chapter 7

Acceptance

This muthafucka better open this door, Timothy thought as he continued to knock on Daniel's door. He'd been knocking for a couple of minutes, but the minutes dragged along like the final minutes at work right before a three-day weekend.

Timothy's anger began to change to concern the longer he knocked. He could hear the sound of Daniel's television from inside the condo, and he knew Daniel wasn't the type of guy to leave anything on that wasn't being used. Either he was ignoring him, or something was wrong, and a terrifying thought popped in his head. The image was like a dark nightmare that unfolded in the most gruesome fashion as his mind created a scene of Daniel's lifeless body lying across his living room floor. A massive hole of damaged flesh appeared on the side of his head from the bullet that tore through his brain and came out the other side. Blood poured out of his head like a river, and his lifeless eyes stared up at the ceiling.

Timothy began to panic as his knocking turned to banging and kicking. Eventually, he started attempting to break the door in, and after six tries, succeeded in tearing the door off its hinges. The resulting loud crash bounced off the condo's walls, and pieces of wood and metal flew across the black granite floor. Running toward the living room, Timothy noticed an empty bottle of vodka, and a sharp pain filled his chest as the realization of his nightmare began to unfold. Daniel wasn't in the living room, and Timothy frantically began checking every inch of the 2,400-square-foot penthouse condo.

Glancing in the master bedroom, he noticed that Daniel's bed was a mess—again, out of character for Daniel, who was a neat freak. Taking a closer look, he noticed that the sheets on his bed were all pulled over to the far side of the bed, toward the large floor-to-ceiling windows that opened up to a breathtaking view of Chicago's skyline and lakefront, the lights from outside casting eerie shadows on the walls and ceiling. He ran over to the side of the bed to find Daniel on the floor, fighting to breathe. His eyes were closed. His body lay flat as he gasped violently for air. Timothy immediately kneeled to his side, trying to figure out what was preventing Daniel from breathing.

Daniel seemed to be dreaming, and whatever he was going through appeared so real that it was affecting his body. He tried everything he could to wake him, but nothing was working. Daniel's caramel skin began to turn a dark blue as his body struggled to survive without oxygen. Timothy felt himself lose control as he repeatedly slapped his friend, trying to wake him from the nightmare that was killing him. He was sweating excessively, and tears filled his eyes. The mixture of sweat and tears burned like hot peppers as he repeatedly wiped them and continued to strike Daniel's face. So caught up in his terror, he couldn't hear himself as he screamed for his friend to wake up.

Each passing second was a lifetime in hell as he helplessly watched his best friend die in front of him.

"Please, please, wake up," he moaned and begged through his tears as he pulled on his sweaty shirt, clawing at himself like a man driven mad with grief.

Suddenly, Daniel's eyes shot open, revealing a look of horror as he screamed, "Victoria!"

Seeing an opportunity, Timothy reached down and slapped his friend with all the strength his exhausted body had left, ripping his friend from his deadly nightmare. Timothy's strike caused him to bite his tongue, and the pain sent shockwaves through his mouth. The taste of blood filled Daniel's mouth as he shook his head in pain.

Looking around, he noticed he was on the floor, and his body felt cold and wet. Forcing himself to sit up, he saw Timothy sitting on the floor next to him breathing heavily, his face drenched with tears and sweat. He was clearly terrified by what he'd just seen, and he looked at Daniel like a stranger and not as a friend.

"What happened?" Daniel asked. His body felt like he'd been locked inside a washing machine filled with rocks and set to spin.

"You were having a nightmare so violent, you almost died. I think that if I weren't here, you would've."

Unable to look Timothy in his eyes, Daniel looked down at the floor and asked, "How did you get in here?"

"I broke your door down. The condo association will be calling you about that, I'm sure," he replied, trying to lighten the mood.

Daniel remained silent for a few seconds, before gathering the nerve to look Timothy in the eyes and say, "Thank you, thank you for saving my life."

"What the fuck is going on with you, Danny?" Timothy asked, unable to ignore the elephant in the room any longer.

"To be honest, I don't know. I started having these nightmares immediately after I got back from Sudan. At first, they terrified me, but after a while, I became used to them. Ever since Meagan and Ayana came to my office asking me to testify against the man responsible for the raid on the village, my nightmares have gotten much worse."

"Are they about Victoria?"

"What?"

"The nightmares . . . Are the nightmares about Victoria?"

"Not specifically, but she's in the nightmares."

"So it's about when—"

"Yeah," Daniel replied before Timothy could go into details. "Why did you ask about Victoria?"

"Because you kept yelling her name when you were under."

Daniel's body began to slouch as the exhaustion of his ordeal started to take a bigger toll on him. It'd been years since he dared say her name. He purposely tried to forget it, but no matter how much he tried to ignore or hide his pain, his subconscious mind wouldn't let it go. Feeling succumbed with grief and gratitude, Daniel decided to tell Timothy everything, including Ayana's real reason for her 4:00 a.m. visit. When he was done, Timothy, still sitting on the floor, shook his head in disbelief.

"I can't pretend to imagine what you went through over there, but you can't carry on like this. You need closure, and this trial can give that to you. You can't hide from this any longer, Danny. You have to face this, and get that part of your life behind you and under control."

"The trial will only make things worse."

"Why do you feel that way?"

Daniel exhaled forcefully and told Timothy about his uninvited visitor. After he finished, Timothy nodded his head slowly, attempting to find the silver lining in today's events.

"Yeah, but you are looking at this all wrong. God sees what you are going through and presented this opportunity for you to heal and move on."

"God? Really? Now, some mystical being is looking out for me? Where was he when I needed him? Where was he for Victoria? Oh, I get it. He works in mysterious ways, right? Let me tell you what I've learned about mysterious ways. Wherever there's mystery, there's death. The death of an entire village and a 5-year-old girl isn't mysterious. It's evil. There isn't some kind of hidden agenda that will work itself out down the road. There is no God . . . There is only us and what we do. And if there were a God, and he sat by idly while those people were slaughtered in cold blood, I don't want anything to do with him."

Looking at Daniel like a lost child, Timothy scoffed while rubbing the back of his neck. "Okay, okay . . . Well, if it's not God, it's something. Life, Karma, Buddha, whatever! I don't fucking care at this point what or who it is. What I care about is you taking advantage of this opportunity to find closure. Reality is you really don't have a choice, because Kronte and his people won't stop until either you accept their bribe or you aren't able to testify. Period. They tried to kill you the first time and failed. It's still a miracle you survived that, but I can assure you there won't be another miracle. So, put him away for good or be prepared to look over your shoulder for the rest of your life—however long that may be."

"Fuck! I'm not ready for this, man. I'm *not* ready."

Shrugging his shoulders, Timothy replied, "Doesn't matter now. You have to get ready because it's time for you to face what happened over there, and maybe I can get my old friend back."

"Ayana told me I wasn't ready to testify, and if I testified in my current state, I would ruin the case they are building against him."

"I can see her point. My advice is to let her help you get ready. If she can help where the other doctors couldn't, then I'm all for it. Let her."

"It's not that simple."

"Yeah, I know you're attracted to her, and that can get complicated . . . or it could make things more interesting. Either way, I think you should give it a shot, because next time, I may not be around to save you."

Nodding in agreement, Daniel forced his body to stand as he slowly walked into the bathroom. Before closing the door behind him, he turned, grinning at Timothy who was still on the floor, and said, "If I do die, that would mean our bet is off, and you can get you some much-needed genital-to-genital stimulation and maybe find a reason to comb your hair and shave. Damn, bruh, the lack of sex got you slipping. I almost didn't recognize you at first. I thought a homeless man broke in the condo."

Feeling embarrassed and amused, Timothy ran his hand through his unkempt hair and laughed.

"Kiss my ass, Danny. Your teasing of the afflicted isn't funny. I feel handicapped or something, like I have an abnormally large organ."

"Maybe we should call the fire marshal so that he could give you a ticket for your balls being filled over capacity and posing a public safety hazard," Daniel teased before closing the bathroom door.

"You mutha . . . You got jokes, I see," he yelled.

Chapter 8

An Uncomfortable Arrangement

It took Daniel three days to track down Ayana and Meagan, and another four days before she returned his call. Back in New York, Ayana was busy with a laundry list of things to tackle, and returning the call of the rude and immature Dr. Daniel Bennett wasn't at the top of that list. He was nothing like she'd expected and was worse than she feared. He was so closed off and self-centered that he'd rather insult her than listen to what she had to say. After leaving the coffee shop, she vowed to never contact him again, especially after his threat of suing her for harassment.

What type of man sues a woman for trying to help him?

She was content in not hearing from him again . . . until he started leaving multiple messages everyday this week. Her assistant said he sounded desperate, and no matter how many times the assistant told him that Ayana didn't want to speak with him, he kept calling. Complaining to Meagan only made things worse, because she became upset that Ayana wouldn't call back the most solid witness in their case against Kronte. Ayana wasn't concerned about the doctor being a potential star witness. She was concerned about his well-being . . . well, until he left her high and dry at the coffee shop. After that, she allowed her anger to take her out of character, and she couldn't have cared less if he leaped to his death from his much-needed perch in the sky.

His constant calling began to weigh on her conscience, and she finally decided to call him back. Staring at her desk phone, she took a deep breath, trying to relax. She wanted to make sure she remained professional and that she would allow his previous behavior to be water under the bridge if he behaved himself. However, if he got out of line one time, she wouldn't hesitate to curse him out and hang up in his face. She'd come too far in life to be disrespected by a crazy doctor that refused to admit he had a problem. The phone only rang twice before the doctor's deep voice answered, sending pleasant vibrations through her ear.

"Hello, Ayana? Thank you so much for calling me back. I want to apologize for my behavior. I was dealing with a lot, and I wasn't sure who I could trust."

Rolling her eyes while listening to him, she kept twirling her hands in a gesture for him to move the conversation along and skip the pleasantries.

"How can I help you, sir?"

Her no-nonsense and professional demeanor threw Daniel off, and he was at a loss for words. He thought after offering his sincere apology, she would be more receptive to him, but his assumptions were wrong. Ayana also assumed that she could forgive his behavior at the coffee shop, but after hearing his voice again, the scene began to replay in her mind of being left hanging at four in the morning, and she couldn't bring herself to overlook his immaturity. She decided to keep things strictly professional yet cordial.

"Dr. Bennett, are you there?"

"Yes, I am."

"So how can I help you, sir?"

Clearing his throat once he accepted the new dynamic of their relationship, he proceeded to update Ayana on the events that had transpired in his office not too long ago. A very uncomfortable silence followed as Ayana remained quiet. She tried to calm her nerves after hearing everything the doctor had to say. She'd heard about the almost legendary selfish attitude that Americans possessed, but she'd never come in direct contact with it until this moment. Meagan was from the US and a native of New York, but she was one of the most selfless people she knew. She always thought Americans were unfairly getting a bad reputation, but after meeting Dr. Bennett, she began to understand that maybe the reputation wasn't ill placed. She felt he wanted her help only because he was concerned about his safety and not because he wanted to bring Kronte to justice.

Oh my God, I can't stand this man.

"Dr. Bennett, let me recap so that you and I are on the same page, okay? So you supposedly got a visit from one of Kronte's henchmen, and he offered you a bribe that you turned down."

As selfish and self-centered as this man is, I'm shocked he didn't take the money, she thought.

"After carefully assessing your situation, you've discovered that you have no choice but to testify in order to protect yourself from retaliation for not taking the bribe. Am I on course so far?"

"Yes, Ayana."

"Call me Ms. Burundi, please," she responded coldly.

"Really? So that's where we are now?" Daniel asked, clearly becoming frustrated with her attitude.

"And where might that be, Doctor? I am clearly trying to maintain a professional tone with you. When I tried to be more of a friend to you, you punished me. So, for me to remain objective and do my job, we must maintain a professional relationship. Or will that also be a problem for you, Dr. Bennett?"

Momentarily taking the phone from his ear and pointing at it angrily, Daniel balled up his fist while swinging in the air without uttering a sound. After completing his three-second tantrum, he placed his cell phone to his ear and began to speak. Attempting to match her cold demeanor, he responded, "No, professionalism is never a problem for me, so as long as we maintain that and stay out of coffee shops at 4:00 a.m., we should be just fine."

His response sent vibrations of anger through Ayana's body, like the tremors of an earthquake. Her arm swung down hard in an attempt to hang up in the doctor's face, but she stopped herself.

He wanted to get a rise out of me, and if I hang up on him, he will get the satisfaction he wants.

Refusing to be outdone by a man she believed wasn't worth her time and effort, she put the phone back to her ear, smiling, and began to speak in the most pleasant voice. What she planned to say next, however, wasn't pleasant at all.

"Dr. Bennett, as much as I would like to continue to stroke your ego and babysit you, I can't. I have a full schedule that is dedicated to people with real problems, people who really want to solve them. The fact that Kronte has taken notice of you is the only reason you want my help. Not because of the millions of lives that've been lost and more that will be lost if Kronte's allowed to go free. My services are not for people who only think of themselves. I work for the United Nations, not the United States or the United States of Daniel.

"So, in response to your request for my assistance, I will have to decline with great satisfaction . . . oops, I mean great *dis*satisfaction. Now that we got that out of the way, is there anything else you would like to say before I disconnect this call?"

"Yes, it's called the United States of *Dr. Bennett,*" he responded and immediately hung up the phone.

Hearing the click from the doctor hanging up in her face sent her emotions raging as she slammed her handset back on its receiver. The sound caused her secretary to leap into action, rushing to her door to find out what was wrong.

"Is everything okay, Ms. Burundi?"

Not wanting to take her frustrations out on the innocent secretary, she withheld her need to yell at someone and calmly replied, "Everything is fine, Mrs. Brown. Just a slight misunderstanding on the last call."

"Can I get you something?"

"Sure, you got some tequila?"

Mrs. Brown, in shock, immediately started laughing, which caused Ayana to follow suit.

"No, but I know a place not too far from here."

"That sounds great. How about you, Meagan, and I all head down there after work?"

Surprised that Ayana invited her, she quickly accepted the invitation and walked out of the office to make reservations for later that evening. Once Mrs. Brown was out of her office, Ayana took a deep breath and continued to work on the case files that were covering her desk.

***

A few hours later, Timothy walked into Daniel's office anxious to hear the good news that Ayana would help his friend, but after seeing the aggravation on Daniel's face, he knew things didn't go as planned.

"Don't tell me she said no!"

"Yep, she surely did."

"Why? What did you do, Danny?"

"Me? It was her! I apologized, I was cordial and nice, and she still couldn't let what happened go. She wanted to remain 'professional.' Then she started insulting me, saying the only reason I came to her was that I was afraid of what Kronte and his boys would do to me."

Timothy laughed at Ayana's misconception that Daniel was afraid of Kronte and his men.

"She doesn't know your place of origin, does she?" Timothy teased.

"I guess not, but fuck it. I don't need her. If she doesn't help me, I'll find someone else, or go it alone."

Hearing Daniel's comment alarmed Timothy, but he decided to remain silent. He didn't want to reprimand Daniel and cause him to shut him out as well. Daniel had seen many professionals when he got back from Africa, and it was apparent none of them did a damned thing to help him. Ayana's specialty was situations like what Daniel was dealing with, and Timothy secretly decided he was going to make her work with his friend, even if he had to pay her an exorbitant fee. He had to admit that he didn't expect Ayana to allow herself to be just as immature as Daniel. She had to have feelings for him, and his rejection of her trying to help him must've hurt her feelings. Therefore, he was going to play on those feelings, no matter how deeply she tried to bury them.

Later on that evening, Timothy stood in the middle of his living room while he waited for Ayana to answer her phone. She eventually picked up, and he could hear loud music in the background.

Damn, she's at a club on a Monday. I like this girl.

"Hello, this is Ms. Burundi. Who's calling?"

"Hi, Ms. Burundi, this is Dr. Timothy Avers."

"Who?"

"Dr. Timothy Avers, Dr. Bennett's colleague."

As soon as she heard the name Bennett, Ayana's anger immediately grew, and she was prepared to curse Timothy out and hang up. However, she was curious about how he got her number and why *he* was calling her, besides the obvious.

"Oh, the 'white bitches are crazy guy,'" she replied sarcastically.

Refusing to be deterred by her sarcasm, Timothy decided to play along. "Yep, the same, and ain't nothing changed. They still crazy!"

His reply caught Ayana off guard, and she found herself laughing at his comment, which eased her anger, and she calmed down, willing to hear what he had to say.

"If you are calling on your friend's behalf concerning me assisting him, I want to be up front with you. I'm not interested. I'm sorry if that disappoints you, but that's my final decision."

"I understand completely. My boy can be a real dick sometimes, but I want you to reconsider once you've heard everything I have to tell you."

"Listen, I'm out of the office, so if this is going to take long, you can call me in the morning, Doctor."

"Yeah, right. After you get drunk in the club, you won't be in the mood to hear a damn thing I have to say in the morning. I assure you I will be quick, and you can get back to your twerk session."

Laughing at his comment, she replied, "I'm much too old to twerk, Timothy."

Damn . . . With all that ass, she would be a winner.

"Understood. Again, I will be brief," he replied while imagining Ayana twerking and shaking her amazing body to the head-banging beats that were blaring in the background. Snapping out of his brief Ayana-inspired "twerk fantasy," Timothy began to detail his experiences with Daniel and his near-death episode on his bedroom floor.

The more Timothy explained things that Daniel conveniently left out, the more her heart began to ache for the doctor. She had no idea he was so tormented and haunted by his experiences in her country. Things began to make sense and explained his hostility toward her and the idea of going back to Sudan. To hear him better, she moved into the ladies' room, and Timothy could hear the echo in the background. Noticing the club music was now muffled, he felt optimistic that he was making headway with her.

"Does he know you called me?" she asked.

"No, he doesn't, and I'm sure he won't talk to me for a while after he finds out I told you everything. But he's like a brother to me, and if something isn't done, I fear I will lose him. So, will you help him?"

"Yes," she replied without hesitation. "But his condition is extremely severe, and to help him, he's going to have to endure a few things he's going to find uncomfortable."

"Whatever, whatever he needs to do, I will make him do it," he responded excitedly.

"Okay, Dr. Avers . . . I need to finish up some cases here in New York, but I can be there within a week."

"Call me Timothy."

"Okay, Timothy . . . I'll be there shortly. Oh, and by the way, my friend Meagan is white, and she's *not* crazy. Just so you know," she teased.

"If that's the case, have her call me," he played along. Then after thinking about his current situation, he continued. "Wait, have her call me in about two months."

"Why two months? Even though I don't think you are her type, I'm just curious."

"I'm going through a kind of cleansing period, and I can't enjoy the company of the opposite sex."

"Ha! You assume she would even go there with you. You *are* funny, Timothy."

"Not assuming, but at the same time, if she did, I don't think I could resist, and I have to keep my word. Rather, stay away from the fire than play with it and get burned."

Shaking her head and laughing loudly, she said goodbye to Timothy and ended the call. Then she turned and looked at herself in the bathroom mirror and smiled while praying that she wasn't making a mistake. Dr. Bennett's condition was more severe than anything she'd ever come in contact with, and she needed to devise a plan that would help him. She felt sorry for him and still hated his guts for his behavior, but she couldn't bring herself to refuse to help someone that tormented.

Meagan is going to think I'm freaking insane.

Chapter 9

In-Home Care

Eight days later. Chicago, Illinois

"No! Hell no! She is not . . . Oh, hell no! Timothy, you are way out of line if you think I agree to this! Over my dead body, bruh!"

Daniel was standing in his doorway, yelling at Timothy and Ayana. Timothy was standing there with his arms and hands filled with Ayana's luggage. Daniel was led to believe they were coming to talk, but when he opened the door, he knew exactly what was going on, and he wasn't having it. Ayana stood there, rolling her eyes, trying to remain patient with the crybaby in front of her. She wanted to force a smile but decided she wasn't going to pretend with the doctor. She wasn't excited about moving in here with him either, but for her to watch him closely, there was no other way. He needed to be in the comfort of his own home so that she could help him more effectively.

Timothy, annoyed and tired of standing in the hallway holding Ayana's heavy bags, forced his way past Daniel and walked into the living room, dropping the bags in the process.

"Dude, shut your whining and let that woman in here. Ayana, come in please," Timothy said while waving her in.

Now, furious beyond comprehension, Daniel slammed the door behind her and began screaming at Timothy.

"This *isn't* your house! You don't pay any bills in this muthafucka! You can't tell someone to just come in here without my permission."

"Well, look at that? I just did, and she's in your condo because I told her to come in." Looking at Ayana, Timothy gestured for her to have a seat on the couch. She smiled brightly and sat down while looking over the condo.

This place is beautiful. How could such a toad live in a place like this? she thought.

Daniel's skin was heating up with anger and beginning to turn a different color. Seeing his deep anger, Timothy walked over to face him.

"Whether or not you like it, this *is* happening. In-home therapy. She's great at what she does, and I'm sure she can help you. I can't stay here anymore, dude. I just can't. You need someone that can help you while you take a vacation."

Eyes wide with surprise, Daniel couldn't believe what Timothy was saying to him.

"What vacation?"

"Oh yeah . . . The vacation you will be taking, starting today. Call the hospital and let them know I will be taking over your duties for the next month or so . . . Yeah, I checked your vacation time, and you got over five months accumulated. So you are good on that front. You two can have all the time you need to get your mind back on track."

Hearing that Timothy decided to halt his research to help him, Daniel immediately calmed down. Timothy was on the verge of making a big discovery on the road to curing cancer, and for him to drop everything to cover for him demanded that he shut down his rampage.

"I didn't know you did that, Tim. I'm grateful, but you shouldn't have to pay for my crazy shit."

"Dude, you are like a brother to me. It's the least I could do. Plus, I felt kinda bad going behind your back and setting this up without your permission."

Looking at Timothy as if he wanted to punch him in the face, Daniel nodded his head, then looked at Ayana. She was still as beautiful as she was the first day he met her, and as much as he despised having her invade his personal space, he couldn't deny he'd rather it be her than anyone else.

Looking at both Daniel and Ayana, Timothy smiled and decided it was time for him to leave. He didn't want to be around when the bombs over Baghdad started.

These two need to bone and get it over with . . . stat.

"Well, would you look at the time? A playa gots to roll. So much to do, and tomorrow, I start working in the ICU. You two have a wonderful evening. I'll check on you both tomorrow evening. Hopefully, you haven't killed each other by then."

Without hesitation, Timothy closed the door behind him, leaving Daniel and Ayana sitting in the living room together. The air in the room seemed to leave as soon as the sound of the door closing echoed through the condo. Neither of them would look at the other, and both remained silent for about ten minutes before Daniel decided he needed to make the best of this arrangement.

"Are you hungry? I could order something to eat if you'd like."

"No, I'm fine. Timothy took me to a restaurant. I just need to shower and get some sleep."

"That's fine. The guest bathroom is right down that hall, and there are clean towels in the hall closet."

"Thank you. You have a great place here."

"Thank you, and thank you for agreeing to help me," he replied, looking at his watch. "It's getting late, and I'm going to turn in. If you need anything, I'll be in the bedroom."

Nodding, Ayana stood up to take a shower.

He better not try to sneak a peek. I need to make sure there aren't any hidden cameras or secret holes in that bathroom.

Standing up, Daniel took in a deep breath of her perfume. An intoxicating fragrance he'd never smelled before, it quickened his heart rate each second it invaded his nose. Trying to prevent himself from getting aroused from her scent, he quickly left the living room and went into his bedroom, closing the door to prevent the smell from following him . . .

3:02 a.m.

Daniel was awakened by the sound of Ayana screaming his name. She was hysterical, her face filled with a fear he'd only seen once, and that was on Timothy's face the first time he saw him have another episode. Relieved after seeing him come out of his attack, Ayana fell back on the carpeted floor, exhausted and shaking.

"Oh my God, Dr. Bennett, are you okay?"

Lying on his side, Daniel felt exposed and vulnerable. He was covered in sweat and only in his boxers. He was afraid to sit up and face the woman who'd seen his weakness in its most terrifying form. His body felt limp and overworked, and his muscles ached while his lungs burned as if he'd just inhaled a large amount of smoke. Suddenly, he felt Ayana's soft hands reach for his arm, trying to help him to his feet. She saw he was fighting against her, so she stopped pulling his arm and knelt by his side. Placing her hand on his shoulder, she called to him.

"Daniel, look at me. Look at me."

Seeing him refusing to look at her, she slid down and got on her belly so that she could be level with him on the floor. Reaching for his chin, she gently turned his head toward her and looked into his eyes. In her eyes, he saw compassion he hadn't seen in a very long time. He'd been so closed off. No one seemed to care about him. No one really gave a damn about what he's been dealing with until tonight.

"It's okay. All you have to do is stand up," she pleaded. "Just stand up. We will get through this, but you have to stand up first. Can you do that for me?"

Nodding, Daniel began to lift his body off the floor. The cold air from the air-conditioning hit his sweat-covered body, and he shook momentarily before reaching over on the bed to get his robe. Ayana stared at him, and no matter how much she tried to keep herself from looking at Daniel with longing eyes, she couldn't help it.

Jesus, this man is fine.

The sweat seemed to enhance every muscle and chiseled feature on his body. He was in excellent shape, and his body screamed power and stamina—something she'd been missing for a very long time. Nevertheless, he is a client, a very disturbed yet incredible-looking client. Successful, intelligent, oh yes . . .

Girl, pull yourself together. Remember, I have to keep this strictly professional. I am here to help him, and complicating things with sex will only make matters worse because it would never work out between us. But I can't keep my eyes off him. I think he's noticing me looking at him like a great big chocolate bar . . . I need to find something else to do. I think I'll go back to my room . . . This is getting weird now.

Daniel stood there, smiling at the look on Ayana's face. She appeared in a daze as she looked over his body while he slid into his bathrobe.

Wow, she's staring at me like she wants to pounce on me right now! I guess all those nights at the gym is finally paying off.

"Ayana, is there something you need?" he asked, with a mischievous grin on his face.

Noticing his facial expression, she quickly snapped out of her daze. "No, Doctor, I'm fine."

"Thank you for helping me. I guess you being here with me isn't a total loss after all."

What the hell? I actually needed that from him, because I thought maybe I was wrong about this asshole. Hmmm, men just don't know when to keep their mouths shut.

"I guess not," she replied, smiling as she walked out of his bedroom and rolling her eyes.

Knowing he'd just put his foot in his mouth, Daniel looked up at the ceiling in frustration and walked into the bathroom to take a cold shower . . .

Later that morning, Daniel decided to relax on his couch and read the newspaper. Suddenly, the morning breeze from the open balcony doors blew the alluring aroma of Ayana's perfume up his nostrils. His nose flared as he peered around the side of his newspaper to watch her walk toward him, wearing a colorful summer dress that gently caressed her amazing body. The dress was a midthigh length that exposed her long, dark chocolate, well-oiled legs. The summer shoes she wore possessed a slight elevation toward the back that caused her already amazing backside to poke out even further, and her leg muscles to play peek-a-boo every time she moved. Swallowing deeply and trying to contain his excitement for what his eyes were blessed to behold, Daniel attempted to act as if he didn't see her, but Ayana caught him staring, and she smiled at his reaction.

"Going somewhere?" he asked while refusing to look up from his newspaper. He didn't want to do something he couldn't control, like drooling or howling like a dog in heat.

"Yep, we are going somewhere."

Daniel knew she was referring to both of them, but he decided to play dumb. Maybe if he annoyed her, she would just leave by herself. He didn't want to be around a bunch of strangers and would rather enjoy the comforts of his condo.

"Oh, you have a date? Lucky guy."

"I don't have a date, and, yes, he is very lucky to even be in my company, but he's too bullheaded to realize it."

"Bullheaded? Really? Is *that* how you see me?"

"Well, you *are* smarter than you pretend to be because you just tried to act like you didn't know I was referring to both of us getting out of this house. Summer will be over soon, and you won't have beautiful days like the one we have today. Also, my therapy begins with a day out of your comfort zone, and since you only travel from here to work and back, I think a change of scenery would do you good. Get you out of your normal routine."

"What's wrong with my normal routine?"

"Well, after what I saw last night, I would figure a whole lot. Looking over your medical records, you've had different types of therapy, and none of them have worked for you. So, doing the process of elimination, I concluded that the problem isn't that the therapy failed. Instead, the patient purposely rejected the treatment."

"You don't know what you're talking about. I didn't reject anything."

"So, why are your nightmares getting worse and your mental state becoming more unstable?"

"Maybe because no one understands what I went through. Ever thought about that?"

"Or you don't want people to understand and decided you would rather live a nightmare than trust someone to let this weight go."

Becoming frustrated with her probing, Daniel decided it would be better for them to leave the house and go somewhere loud so that she couldn't ask him anymore questions and make assumptions.

"Fine, let's go out."

Smiling brightly with her first victory, she stood there while watching him put on his shoes, so that they could walk out the door. Looking over his attire of khaki shorts, white T-shirt, and brown sandals, she shook her head, letting him know that he could've done better with his appearance, but she didn't want to delay any longer. She didn't have the patience to argue with him anymore. She just wanted to get the day started.

Instead of allowing the doctor to drive, they took the train to Wrigley Field. She'd bought two tickets to the game that morning, hoping a day out would help re-lax the Grinch sitting next to her on the train. This was her first time on the "L" train in Chicago, and after a few minutes en route, she found herself amused—and terrified—by the different characters that rode the train. Looking over at Daniel, he seemed relaxed and just gazed out the window, refusing to look at her or anyone else on the train, no matter how disruptive they were.

Once they reached their stop, they both stood up to leave, and as they walked out of the train, they passed by a group of young teenagers that looked at Ayana and immediately began belting out obscenities concerning her body. Like a light switch being turned on, Daniel came alive, turned around, and gave the teenagers a look that silenced them immediately. As the train doors closed, she noticed the look of fear in the teenagers' eyes as they all stared at Daniel while the train pulled away.

Wow, what was that? she thought.

The train's platform was overcrowded, and it was dif-ficult to navigate through the maze of excited Cub fans, so without thinking, Daniel reached for Ayana's hand. With her hand firmly in his, he began to lead her through the massive crowd, down the stairs, and onto the busy streets of Wrigleyville. Ayana's eyes lit up as she took in the entire scene that unfolded before her. There were bars and restaurants everywhere, all of them surrounding the vintage-looking baseball stadium known as Wrigley Field. The energy and excitement were palpable, and the music that blared out of the numerous bars made her want to get drunk and dance in the middle of the street.

She'd heard of the atmosphere of this national land-mark and the undying fans' love for the Chicago Cubs, but no words could describe the feeling she got while strolling hand in hand with Daniel. She felt like a child at Disney World for the first time. Yankee Stadium was a sight to behold, but it couldn't touch the ambiance here in Wrigleyville. Daniel looked over at Ayana and smiled at her bright-eyed expression. She was peeking into every bar they walked by, admiring the interiors and the crowds that filled each one. Daniel didn't want to take her to just any bar. He wanted to take her to the best bar, and nothing compared to the Cubby Bear here in Wrigleyville.

It was a beautiful day, and he decided to take her to the sun deck, so they could enjoy a few drinks and wait for the game to start. Two hours and several drinks later, Daniel and Ayana were laughing and having a great time together. Ayana, aware of the emotional barricades Daniel had built around himself, decided to keep their conversation light. She allowed him to speak freely about safe things, his work, his friend Timothy, and his love for the Chicago Cubs. There weren't any distractions from anyone around them, and they both behaved as if they were on their own private island where no one could touch them. Everything that troubled Daniel seemed to fade away. The only thing that mattered was the present, and the great time he was having with this beautiful African princess.

Looking at his watch, he noticed that game time was quickly approaching, so they gathered themselves and slowly walked across the street to the ballpark. Daniel caught Ayana eyeing a stuffed bear dressed in a Chicago Cubs jersey and hat and stopped to get it for her.

It's the least I can do for what she did for me last night.

"Here, just a show of my appreciation for what you did for me last night. Thank you!"

"Oh no, Dr. Bennett! Please don't buy that for me. It's cute, but I think it would be inappropriate for you to get that for me. If I want it, I can get it myself."

Her statement immediately brought the doctor back to reality, and the blissful fantasy of the day was shattered. As he slowly put the bear back, he realized he'd allowed himself to relax. The disappointment of not being allowed to show his appreciation brought his attitude down, and suddenly, he didn't want to be here anymore. For the rest of the afternoon, he was on autopilot while watching Ayana be unaffected by his mood. She was enjoying her first Cubs game while laughing and joking with the strangers that sat around them. He felt like a ghost in this social and feeling world, long removed from an emotional expression and meaningful human contact.

On the way home, Ayana kept staring at the doctor, trying to figure out what his problem was. To her, it was an amazing day, full of great food and a Chicago Cubs win. He should be feeling on top of the world, but he seemed down and angry.

"Are you okay, Dr. Bennett?"

Forcing a smile, he turned to her and nodded. He didn't want to say a word. He just wanted to go home. He had been hoping that he was making a breakthrough with Ayana. The entire day leading up to the stuffed animal fiasco, he was finding himself drawn to her. He felt comfortable with her and caught himself imagining what life would be like with her. Daniel understood keeping things professional, but he thought that maybe she felt what he felt. Her reaction to his gesture made it clear that things weren't as he wanted or seemed. He vowed never to allow his emotions to get ahead of him again. It was just safer for him that way.

Ayana wanted to talk, but he wasn't in the mood, so he retreated to his bedroom. He'd been lying in his room watching TV for about three hours when he heard a light tapping on his door. Confused, he got up from his bed and opened his door to see Ayana standing there in her pajamas, with a pillow and her cell phone in her hand. From the way it looked, she intended to join him in his bedroom. Without saying a word, she smiled and walked past him and started fixing one side of his king-size bed to sleep on.

What the fuck?

The look on his face, like a deer caught in headlights, caused Ayana to giggle as she bent over to plug in her cell phone in the wall socket behind his nightstand. Her pajamas were plain and modest, but Ayana's incredible body could turn a flag wrapped around her into sexy lingerie. Watching her bend over by his bed caused his manhood to respond immediately, and he quickly tried to twist his legs to hide his growing excitement. While still fishing for the socket behind his nightstand, she turned her head around, watching him watching her. She was struggling to find the socket, and the strained look on her face while bending over, looking back at him, sent Daniel over the edge, and his ecstasy could no longer be contained. His pajama pants a few seconds ago were covering his feet, but now, due to his excitement, they were ankle length, trying to make room for the growing and rising muscle between his legs.

Ayana, noticing his erection, nearly fell forward on top of his nightstand as she tried to stand upright. She'd temporarily forgotten the reaction her ass got from men when she bent over in front of them. Now, standing up facing him, she gave him a disapproving look while she glanced at his obvious arousal.

"Uh, Dr. Bennett, I want to make it perfectly clear that my reasons for sleeping in the same bed with you have nothing to do with you using that impressive, yet unwanted monster you have there. After last night, I think it's in both of our best interests if I slept as close to you as possible to stop your attacks before they go too far. That's all. No sex, no cuddling, grinding, or touching. You stay on one side of the bed, and I'll stay on mine."

With all that ass? Yeah, right, I'd like to see that mountain range stay on just one-half of my bed, he thought.

"I understand sharing a bed with me is going to be awkward, especially after seeing your reaction, but I'm sure we can work this out until you can have a good night's sleep without an attack. We are both adults, right?"

That's what I'm afraid of, he thought while nodding in agreement.

"I'm going to go to the bathroom . . . to . . . h-h-h . . . hand . . . take care of . . . get myself together," he stuttered.

"Good idea. I'll be here when you're done."

Closing the door of the bathroom, Daniel walked over to the mirror and stared angrily at his manhood, still standing erect like a bridge between his pelvis and the granite top of the bathroom sink. He leaned forward and started banging his head on the mirror, trying to get the image of Ayana's fully expanded ass and those light brown eyes out of his mind.

I'm so screwed.

Chapter 10

Change Can Be Traumatic and Orgasmic

The next day, Ayana decided to have lunch at a small and intimate café a few blocks from Daniel's condo. The afternoon sun seemed to make everything sparkle and shine outside the café's veranda, where Daniel and Ayana were seated. If it weren't for the huge green table umbrella providing ample protection from the glaring sunlight, it would be difficult for either of them to see each other clearly. However, the protection it provided gave Ayana the eye contact she needed to read the doctor's every emotion and reaction. She chose this public place for many reasons, but her main focus was taking full advantage of the lunch-hour crowd. The noise of the crowded veranda and traffic made it easier for their conversation to remain private as Daniel went into detail about his two-year experience in Sudan. The crowd also provided the illusion of distraction, which eased the doctor's discomfort toward her. Ayana knew that he was physically attracted to her, and he was embarrassed and frightened by his desires. Feeling like they were on a date or alone would cause him to retreat within himself in an attempt to contain his sexual yearnings for her. The crowded veranda eased that fear and allowed the doctor the comfort he needed to speak freely.

Ayana remained silent as she attentively listened to his accounts of life in her native country.

"When I first arrived in Sudan, I didn't know what to expect because my idea of Africa was so screwed up because of what we're told in the US. I really didn't know what I was going to have to get used to when I arrived. But as soon as my feet touched the African soil, a feeling of belonging came over me, and I don't know how or why, but it felt like home." She watched his reactions to everything he said to weed out the unimportant things.

"I was there for about three months when they brought Victoria to the village." Daniel suddenly paused, and his face seemed to glow in the sun's light as he smiled brightly, looking off into the distance. Suddenly, the smile vanished, and the clouds of pain returned. He momentarily closed his eyes and inhaled deeply.

"She was so frail and sick," he continued. "Many nights, I would stay up with her, giving her ice baths and checking her fever. She was in really bad shape. No one expected her to live past a week. But Victoria was a fighter, and much to our surprise, she pulled through."

What Ayana noticed was every time he would talk about the little girl Victoria, he would look down at his plate and clench his hands tightly. Victoria seemed to bring out deep anguish that caused the doctor an extreme amount of internal guilt and pain. After listening to Daniel for almost two hours, Ayana concluded that this young girl was a very important, damaging topic, and her death could be the anchor that was holding the doctor back from reentering the real world. The connection between the doctor and the young girl must have been strong for her death to have such a lasting and violent response to his subconscious.

This was strange because, from her experience with other survivors, this level of guilt and pain was only associated with close family members or the biological children of the survivors.

Daniel continued to speak about Victoria, leading up to the day of the massacre, and the guilt he expressed was more like a father instead of the expected doctor-patient relationship.

I need to learn more about this little girl and her relationship with the doctor, she thought, while she continued to listen to him.

Once the lunch crowd began to dwindle, Daniel paid the waitress, and the two of them walked out of the café. He seemed emotionally exhausted, and as much as she wanted to delve deeper, she knew it would do more harm than good at this point. As they walked back to his condo, Daniel made sure to keep a safe physical distance from Ayana. He didn't want to accidentally brush against her, sending waves of sexual desires through his body while aggravating her to anger. The other night, she made it clear she had no intention of ever pursuing anything beyond a professional relationship with him, and her bland demeanor toward him solidified her stance.

It had been almost a week since they've shared the same bed, and Daniel hasn't slept much. Ayana believed she was making progress, but Daniel's lack of violent dreams was due to his insomnia. It was impossible for him to rest while she lay next to him in a bed once cold, now invaded by the warmth of her beautiful body and intoxicated by the sweet smell of her body lotion. Every time she moved in her sleep, he would fantasize her moving closer to him, placing her warm, soft hands on his shoulders, inviting him to turn over and look into her longing eyes. Then she would lean closer to him as they would kiss, wrapping their arms and legs around each other in an explosive embrace of lust and passion.

He remained excited all night as he lay awake, trying to calm himself down. As the sunlight peered over the Chicago skyline, he would eventually start to fall asleep, only to be awakened by her movements again. Her vibrations caused his mental fantasy to replay in his head again, preventing him from falling back to sleep. Every night, he danced alone in this mental sexual Flamenco, and as much as he hated to accept it, he knew eventually he would have to start "taking care of himself" before lying next to her to get any ounce of rest. The thought of having to masturbate while sharing the same bed with this beautiful woman did some serious damage to his ego, but he understood and accepted his previous behavior was to blame for his current predicament.

Aside from his sexual torture, Daniel did feel a change come over him. He was starting to relax more, and he felt comfortable talking to Ayana about his time overseas. Unlike the other doctors and psychiatrists, she never said a word while he told his story. Even after he was done spilling his guts, she would just smile and remain silent, and then they would take a walk or do something else that would take his mind off his most recent verbal revelation. Hearing the words come out of his mouth, without anyone else assuming what he was going through, was a huge difference from what he was used to, and that difference seemed to be working.

Once they got into the condo, Ayana's cell phone began to ring immediately. The first few times, she just smiled and ignored it, but after a while, she seemed worried and walked into the guest room to take the call. Daniel decided while she was in her room that he should try to "take care of himself" during her distraction. He felt it shouldn't take him long at all because Ayana would definitely be his point of reference, and by the way she lit his fuse, he knew he might break a world record on speed of delivery. Smiling to himself, he quickly started for his room, and then behind him, he heard a loud whimper, and then her bedroom door swung open. Ayana was hysterical as she frantically ran in the living room, snatching the remote control and turning on the TV. Daniel turned around, concerned by her actions, and once he was close enough, noticed she was trembling as if she were locked away in a freezer.

Her attention was completely on the television, and she didn't notice Daniel standing next to her. The TV screen was covered in devastation as black smoke and fire bellowed in the distance. The female voice narrating the disturbing scene was clearly British as she explained in gruesome detail about another village on the border of Southern Sudan attacked by Kronte's forces. Daniel's heart immediately sank as he looked at Ayana's face filled with pain, sorrow, and tears reflecting the light from the TV. She was breathing heavily, and he could tell she was fighting with all her strength not to break down and lose herself in her sorrow and anger. The more the narrator revealed, the worse Ayana got, until the pain was so heavy on her that it forced her down to her knees.

She was now wailing uncontrollably and gripping at her dreads in an attempt to yank them out of her scalp. Daniel felt useless, as all he could do was watch her soul bombarded by the terror on the screen. He wanted to hold her, but he was afraid of rejection. How could he stand there, watching her break down and offer no form of compassion? His fear of leaving her alone in her pain began to outweigh his fear of rejection, and he slowly kneeled in front of her, blocking her view on the television. Ayana's red and misty eyes, now blocked from seeing her family's village burning, stared at Daniel.

She was angry and confused at his decision to block her view from the television. However, looking in his compassionate eyes, she noticed his eyes were glossy and wet from fighting back tears that were determined to stream down his face.

Why is he about to cry?

Before she could try to rationalize his emotional state, Daniel wrapped his arms around her. His embrace was secure and warm as he placed her head on his shoulder. His emotional energy immediately began to transfer into her body as she felt the warmth of his soul. She could feel his compassion, strength, and concern for her, but most of all, she felt his love. His embrace was more than a physical gesture of compassion. He wanted her to feel and experience the emotional transference and connection. She slowly closed her eyes and exhaled. The longer he held her, the more relaxed she began to feel. Her tears were still flowing, but the weight of her sorrow and anger seemed to lighten as she shared her emotional turmoil with the doctor, and he received it without hesitation.

Feeling her embrace him back and relax in his arms warmed Daniel's entire body, and tears began to roll down his face as he began to breathe slowly and listen to her silent weeping. For what seemed like a sweet eternity, both of these scarred souls remained in this deep embrace until the sun relinquished itself to the oncoming darkness of night. Eventually, Ayana pulled away and sat back on the floor, looking at Daniel smiling brightly. Her face, still moist from tears, seemed to radiate the same excitement she had when they first met in his office. She seemed pleasantly surprised at Daniel's reaction to her. The doctor was unaware he was blushing, and even in the failing light, Ayana could see the warming of the blood in his cheeks. Her giggle made the doctor aware of his bashful expression, and he turned away. She quickly reached out, held his face in her hands, and turned it toward her. She slowly shook her head, and without saying a word, Daniel knew exactly what she was saying to him.

While wiping the remaining tears from her eyes, Ayana stood up without saying a word, walked into the guest bathroom, and closed the door. Ten minutes later, Daniel heard the shower spring to life, waking him out of his daydream. He rose to his feet, stood in the middle of his living room, and smiled. Deep inside, he felt that his decision to take a chance and allow himself to feel, sharing those feelings with Ayana, was the beginning of something new for him. As scary as his feelings were, he was excited to discover just how much he could bring himself to care about this incredible woman. After relishing the moment awhile longer, he decided to take a shower as well. Somehow, he felt tonight was going to be a lot more interesting than any of the nights they'd shared since she's been here.

When Ayana walked into Daniel's bedroom, he was already in bed, lying on his side while viewing emails on his tablet. He didn't notice her walking in. When she slowly climbed in bed with him, she made sure she allowed her body to go beyond the invisible barrier they both created before this night. Feeling her body that close to him sent Daniel's hormones in a frenzy as he closed his eyes, attempting to think of something nonsexual to keep his excitement from revealing itself in the form of a "teepee" under the covers. Feeling things were very different, Daniel shut down his tablet and turned around to face Ayana. He was pleasantly surprised to see her lying on her side, facing him and smiling brightly.

Smiling back, he moved closer to her, staring into her eyes as she began to speak softly to him. Refusing to break eye contact, they both lay there while Ayana told Daniel about her close family ties to the recently massacred village.

"After my village was destroyed during the war, my surviving relatives relocated to Dwendele. They made a good life there, staying out of the fighting and refusing to harbor any of combatants. They thought . . . if they stayed out of it, remained neutral, that they would be left alone. But they were wrong, so wrong."

The more she spoke of the village, the more emotional she became. Her hysteria soon returned, and to ease her pain, Daniel reached for her and pulled her close to him. He positioned himself on his back and let her lay her head on his chest. The scent of her recently showered body covered in the most seductively smelling body lotion flooded his nose and filled his head with its intoxicating aroma. He began to feel light-headed the more of her essence he inhaled. Soon, he found it hard to concentrate on what she was saying, so he momentarily turned his head away to breathe in some fresh air to dilute her alluring scent.

My God, I want her sooooooo bad!

After taking in the fresh air, he felt more focused and continued to concentrate on words that sounded like poetry as they softly flowed from her beautiful lips. By the time she was done talking and started weeping again, Daniel discovered that every remaining member of her family had been massacred by Kronte's forces, a clear message of retaliation for her continued efforts to bring him to justice for his crimes of genocide against a nonwarring populace. Even though she knew what she was doing had to be done, she still blamed herself for their deaths, and the guilt covered her like a dark cloud. Hearing her admission and feeling her pain made him feel more connected to her as they both now shared a guilt that derived from their actions. They both intended to do good things, but the repercussions were more than they could bear alone. Maybe together . . . Maybe side by side, they both could conquer their guilt, anger, and the man that shared in their pain . . . Kronte.

Moved by her pain, Daniel leaned down and placed a kiss on Ayana's forehead right above her eye. Feeling his soft lips on her forehead sent a chill down her spine, and she looked up at him and smiled. Looking in her eyes, Daniel saw the same look of longing that he'd dreamed about all these nights she'd been lying in his bed, and he didn't hesitate to put his lips against hers . . . softly. He pulled back slightly to allow her to close her eyes and exhale. The nerves on the back of her neck sprang alive as they sent pulses of desire down her back to the tips of her toes, and she wanted more . . . so much more. Seeing her accept his kiss, Daniel moved in again, this time kissing her more passionately and then slightly biting her bottom lip before pulling back again, watching her fall into a trance of passion from his kisses.

Keeping her eyes closed, she reached up to him and pulled him forcefully to her, exploring his mouth with her tongue, and he met her passion full force by wrapping his arms around her waist and pulling her even closer. Feeling his excitement so close to her caused a moan of pleasure to escape her mouth that sent Daniel over the edge, and before he knew it, he was on top of her, grinding and kissing her as she wrapped her dark chocolate legs around his waist. Being this close to her, Daniel noticed she was completely naked under her gown, and his excitement soared at the anticipation of finally being able to make love to the only woman that's been able to make him feel again. He wanted to try every position in the book with her, maybe even show off a bit, but this wasn't the right time for self-indulging antics. This was about Ayana, and he wanted to make sure he gave her everything she needed tonight.

As gently as he could, he moved her gown up her body and over her head slowly, making sure to massage and caress every inch of skin his hands touched. Feeling his warm hands caressing her made Ayana bite her lips and moan louder as she anticipated a night of passion she desperately needed and wanted from Daniel. He allowed the gown to cover her entire head while only allowing her lips to be exposed. Then he began licking and biting her lips and pulling back, teasing her desire to feel his lips and his tongue dancing with hers. Once he finally pulled the gown completely over her head, he gasped at the amazing body that lay before him.

Her ultradark skin reflecting the lights from the Chicago skyline revealed every awe-inspiring curve her body possessed. Her amazing backside seemed to spill out from under her as she moved like a snake, yearning to feel his naked body close to hers. He wanted to taste every inch of her, but when he looked down at her well-groomed lotus flower, his mouth began to water at the prospect of tasting her, so he decided to skip the appetizer and go straight for the main course. Feeling his tongue and lips tasting and exploring her secret garden so suddenly caused Ayana to yell and throw the pillow under her head across the room. He couldn't believe how amazing she tasted, and feeling her thighs press against his head excited him beyond belief. He closed his eyes and devoured her peach like a man driven mad by hunger and thirst. His prowess and enthusiasm was something Ayana had never experienced, and as much as she tried to control her explosions, she couldn't and repeatedly climaxed as he continued to taste and drink of her essence. She began twisting and screaming as she tried to push his head away, finally accepting the pleasure was too much for her, but Daniel maintained a strong hold on her as he wrapped his arms around her thighs while gripping her ass.

He could feel she was going to explode with this next orgasm, and he wasn't going to be cheated, so he intensified the movement of his tongue and lips. Screaming his name, she twisted her body and covered her head in the sheets, biting them, attempting to brace herself as she felt every muscle in her body give in to the unbelievable pleasure between her legs. Breathing heavily and shaking uncontrollably, her body went limp as she began to feel lighter than air, while still trying to regain her composure. However, Daniel wasn't finished, and he quickly spread her legs apart and slid his massive, throbbing, and rock-hard manhood deep inside of her already excited and drenched passage. Her muscles inside her tunnel contracted and began pulling him deeper inside of her. She lost her breath as she arched her back off the bed when she felt him reach deeper than she'd ever thought possible.

He was a monster and receiving him hurt . . . It hurt so damn good. She reached up to him and pulled him close to her while moving her hips in rhythm with every release and thrust. Their timing with each other was flawless as they danced to a silent song of love and passion neither had ever experienced before. Ayana's tunnel was so wet and tight, and Daniel tried to concentrate, but he couldn't, and soon, Ayana was in full control of

him. The longer he was inside of her, the wetter she became, and the tighter she contracted her muscles around
him. Her passionate and firm handshake was so intense
that he rolled his eyes inside his head and moaned deeply
every time her flower tightened around his muscle, saying, "Hello." She knew he wasn't going to last long like
this, but she'd already climaxed five times, and now she
felt that she was going to make it six very soon, and she
didn't want to do it alone. She'd been alone for so long.
She wanted to feel connected to Daniel, and the best way
to enhance that connection was for both of them to climax together.

Daniel began to thrust harder and faster as he started
to drill deeper inside of her. She felt his body and manhood get warmer in preparation for his own volcanic
eruption. She moved her hips and ass in tune with him
until she felt herself reaching her own destination of pleasure. She could feel the energy move down her chest
through her stomach, her back, in-between her thighs,
and when her climax reached its forceful conclusion, she
felt the hot explosion inside of her as he released, and his
arms began to shake like toothpicks holding up a car. No
longer able to hold his body up, he collapsed on top of
her. They were both panting heavily, covered in sweat as
they held each other and continued to kiss. Daniel, feeling self-conscious, tried to pull from inside of her, but
she locked her legs around his waist, preventing him
from disconnecting from her.

She wanted him to remain inside of her, maybe even
fall asleep in her. She didn't want this connection to
end, and seeing her reaction caused him to relax as they
continued to kiss and caress each other, refusing to allow
this moment to end . . .

Chapter 11

The Morning After

Daniel opened his eyes as the bedroom was slightly illuminated by the rising sun over Lake Michigan. His muscles felt relaxed and rested, a feeling very different from the many mornings he's awakened to a sore and overworked body due to the violent struggles in his sleep the night before. Then the events of last night dawned on him. He looked over and saw her . . . beautiful and sleeping. Her breathing was so peaceful, and her long dreadlocks seemed to cover her head like a crown. She deserved nothing less. She was a queen, and he hoped one day, she would be *his* queen. Daniel never dreamed of viewing a woman so highly after just one night of lovemaking. Before his time in Sudan, he was a bona fide player, bedding a different woman every other night, and the thought of marriage was as far-fetched as living on the planet Pluto. Now, after just one night of amazing sex . . . He wanted this woman in his life forever. He just hoped she felt the same about him because he was still a basket case.

He decided to lie next to her and just stare at the ceiling. He wanted to lie there and watch her sleep, but he didn't want to creep her out, because when *he* experienced a woman watching him sleep, it didn't feel romantic at all.

Eventually, Ayana began to move around and open her eyes. Daniel became nervous, hoping for the best, but still expecting the worst. With his luck, she may wake up blaming their romp last night on grief, vowing that it won't ever happen again. He admitted to himself that it would hurt . . . Who was he kidding? That shit would burn like fire, but he was a man, and he couldn't let her see him torn down. He inhaled, kept looking at the ceiling, and braced himself for the first words she would speak after such an amazing night.

Stretching and moaning, she sat up and looked at Daniel, smiling, before saying, "Good morning." Then she leaned over, kissing him softly on the lips and quietly climbed out of bed completely naked, heading into the bathroom. He watched in amazement as she moved into the bathroom, hypnotized by the thunderous movement of her ass and the regal pace at which she moved. Those two words and kiss revealed more to him about her feelings than he could've imagined. He sat up while listening to the sound of Ayana taking a shower and smiled as the excitement of having something to finally look forward to fill him with more optimism than he'd ever felt in his life.

I may have a girlfriend, he thought to himself, while smiling like an excited kid on Christmas morning.

When Daniel got out of the shower, he smelled an amazing aroma of Ayana's cooking in the air. Before today, she refused to boil water for him, and now, she was cooking something that smelled amazing. He quickly moved around the bedroom, trying to find something to wear so that he could see exactly what she was cooking.

Ayana moved about Daniel's kitchen like an expert in one of Daniel's white tees and a pair of white lace panties.

There were ingredients and chopped fruit on the granite countertop, and a pot or skillet sat on every eye on the stove. She knew that it was a lot of food for just two people, but she didn't care. She wanted to show this man that last night wasn't a fluke or a fling. The way he made her feel, the way he touched her, caressed her, and made love to her . . . She'd never before experienced that level of sexual connection, and she wasn't afraid to admit she was already addicted to him. As with any addiction, one must do whatever they can to keep their addiction of choice in constant supply.

She wanted to hurry and have everything ready before he came out of the shower, but looking around, she noticed that wouldn't be possible. Her shoulders slumped in disappointment when she heard his bedroom door open and the sound of his footsteps heading toward the kitchen. Accepting that her plans wouldn't go as she wanted, she stood in front of the island smiling, with a tall glass of her special tropical morning shake in hand. She was extremely nervous and hoped what she was doing wasn't too much and wouldn't scare him off. Her fears eased when she saw his face light up when he saw her. He was gleaming while looking over her with longing eyes and licking his lips. His lustful stare weakened her knees as she looked at his facial expression and imagined all the wonderful things he could do to her.

I could love this man forever.

Finally noticing the drink in her hand, he took it, placed it on the edge of the counter, and pulled her toward him, kissing her like she had been lost to him, and he finally found her cooking in his kitchen.

Seventy degrees . . .

His passionate embrace caught her off guard and made her legs shake momentarily as she held on to him tightly to maintain her balance. Pressing her body firmly against his, she seductively began grinding her midsection up and down against his excited love muscle. The sexual energy her movements sent through Daniel caused him to immediately reach around and hold on to her backside as if his life depended on it.

Eighty-five degrees . . .

Thrown in a whirlwind of lust, Daniel lifted Ayana up and atop the island. She quickly wrapped her legs around his waist while violently pushing the food and plates off the island. The loud sound of the plates and glass crashing and shattering on the marble tile didn't deter the two lustful lovers from straddling atop the island, grinding and panting wildly while they tried to rip each other's clothes off. Pushing her body down onto the hard and cool granite surface, Daniel moved down, gripping her lace panties between his teeth while pulling them off of her. Feeling his mouth so close to her sensitivity, Ayana reminisced about the amazing multiple climatic journey his experienced mouth took her on last night as her body shook.

One hundred three degrees . . .

Looking toward his right, Daniel noticed the glass of the sweet-smelling tropical shake still sitting on the edge of the island. A mischievous grin formed on his face as he reached for it while licking his lips. Seeing the glass above her, Ayana opened eyes widened, and before she could protest, he poured the cold, thick liquid on her neck and over her breasts. The chill made her jump up as the liquid traveled down the middle of her ample breasts, to her stomach, and down toward her heated lotus flower.

Daniel immediately began to lick and slurp the shake from her body. The exotic flavor of the shake mixed with Ayana's body exploded in his mouth as he moved over her body with his tongue, sending shockwaves of pleasure through every nerve.

Preheat at 350 degrees . . .

She looked down at him as he moved his head between her thighs, and then she felt his warm tongue explore her. She parted her legs in a split and raised one of them, giving him complete access. The slurping sounds of him tasting her overshadowed the sounds of the cooking food on the stove as she moaned his name repeatedly. Feeling her body give in to the oncoming climatic explosion, she wrapped her legs around his head, bracing herself for the tidal wave of pleasure that would wash over her body.

Place in oven at 450 degrees . . .

"Oh my God, I'm coming," she screamed as Daniel used his tongue to play the final note on her violin, while every nerve in her body applauded at the beautiful symphony of ecstasy his tongue conducted in flawless execution. Still shaking and holding herself, Daniel attempted to slide inside of her, but she suddenly placed her foot on his chest, stopping him, while looking him in his eyes as she bit her bottom lip. Pushing him off the island, she quickly got down, turned around, and bent over the island, spreading her legs, exposing herself to him. Daniel immediately felt light-headed, looking at her ass poking up and out, waiting for him to join with her. Excited out of his mind, he quickly reached for the white T-shirt that Ayana had been wearing. It now hung on the edge of the island. Taking the top side of the T-shirt in his left hand and the bottom end in his right hand, Daniel reached over her head, wrapping the shirt around her neck. With both hands still gripping the T-shirt tightly, he pulled her back toward him like an expert horse jockey, causing her to dip her back deeply. Immediately, he grunted loudly as he forcefully plunged himself deep inside of her. Ayana screamed at the top of her lungs as she felt Daniel invading her. The stranglehold of the T-shirt around her throat both frightened and excited her. The sensation of being inside of her, paired with his excitement, nearly ended one of the best breakfasts he'd ever had before it began, but he braced himself and began to stroke her deeply while she moved her hips in motion with him. The two lovers moved like a horse and rider in perfect sync.

His strokes became harder, deeper, and faster with each passing second. The sharp and loud smacking sounds of their bodies connecting and their moans of ecstasy filled the air in the smoke-filled kitchen. Something was burning, but neither of them cared as they continued to push each other beyond their physical limits. His muscles began to tighten as he felt himself losing his self-control. He wanted to slow down, but Ayana was in a zone as she continued forcefully pushing back her ass against him while leaning forward with all her body weight, causing him to lean back and thrust deeper inside of her. Her eyelids fluttered, and the veins in her neck began to bulge with the stranglehold of the T-shirt around her neck. Daniel's pounding began to bring on the most explosive orgasm she'd ever experienced in her life. Wanting this amazing orgasm sooner than later, Ayana grabbed hold of either side of the island and began to wildly buck and push back against her lover. Seeing there was no way of controlling her, Daniel decided to let her takeover. Taking both ends of the T-shirt in one hand, he smacked her on the ass, watching her flesh bounce to the force of his strike. The sudden and sharp pain caused her to yell out in pleasure, and she immediately began moving faster, reaching for an invisible brace in front of her. Daniel began to match her intensity, pushing deeper inside of her. The sudden and intense sensation caused her to climb on top of the island.

Oh no, you're not going anywhere!

In one quick and forceful motion, Daniel pulled her back by the T-shirt still wrapped around her neck, holding her steady, while he continued to pound in rhythm with her. She was coming, and it was so intense, she scratched and clawed at the countertop, trying to brace her body for the oncoming earthquake that vibrated her entire being. Seeing her reaction and feeling her drenched tunnel tighten around him broke away all of Daniel's mental controls, and he yelled out as he lost himself inside of her. Feeling his warm essence flow through her sent Ayana over the edge, and her body dropped an orgasmic bomb between her legs. The fierce pleasure of her climax caused her to lose control of her body, and she immediately went limp.

Daniel quickly grabbed hold of her, preventing her from falling to the floor. As if planned in perfect timing, the smoke alarm went off, and they both looked around at the smoke-filled kitchen, astonished. The food cooking on the stove, now a black, stinking mess, continued to fill his condo with smoke.

"Oh shit!" they both yelled while rushing toward the stove to turn off the flames and turn on the overhead fans.

"Open *all* the windows," Daniel yelled out to Ayana, who was already working on the windows in the living room.

"Even the balcony doors?" she asked, grinning mischievously while looking at her own naked body. "Your neighbors will get the greatest show on earth if I do that."

"Well, if you are in the mood to perform for them after the smoke clears, we could take this out on the balcony."

"Ha! You wish, 'Doctor Feel Good.' I'll go get my robe before I open *that* door."

Smiling, Daniel defiantly rushed over to the balcony's sliding glass doors and flung them open, while standing there stark buck naked with his hands raised in the air. He started yelling at the top of his lungs in full view of anyone at home or in their rooms in the hotel directly across from his penthouse condo. "Look, Ma, I'm on top of the world."

Laughing until she fell over on the couch, Ayana shook her head watching Daniel act out on his balcony . . .

Chapter 12

The Calm before the Storm

Timothy stared blankly back at Daniel, trying to process everything he'd just told him. A long, awkward silence followed, and the only thing that could be heard was the afternoon thunderstorm raging outside Timothy's office windows. Suddenly, Timothy seemed to snap out of his trance and started blinking rapidly before deciding to respond.

"So, you fucked her on the same night she lost the rest of her family, and now you two believe you found love?" he asked with an uncomfortable chuckle. Smacking himself on his forehead, he shook his head, appearing to attempt to shake off a painful headache.

"Listen, Danny, you're my boy, so I'm going to keep it one hundred with your crazy ass. That was a 'grief' fuck, nothing more. The problem seems to be that the sex was so good, you two idiots have decided to confuse it with love."

"And what would *you* know about love?" Daniel snapped back.

"Enough to know what it isn't, and this ain't it, bruh. On one hand, I'm happy you are coming out of your shell, but on the other hand, I am not cool with you mislabeling this thing you have with Ayana. Because when the fairy tale is over and reality sets in, your attitude could get worse. I just don't want you to get hurt because you've been through enough."

"So, you think she'll hurt me? I'm that weak to you?"

"Hell no! Ayana is cool as hell to me. It's not her per se, but the situation that will hurt you. The woman needs time to grieve, but she's denying herself that time by covering up her pain with sleeping with you. It's all good now . . . until the orgasms can't make up for the loss of her family. Right now, she feels like she's alone, and it frightens her, but soon, anger and regret will replace the fear, and you will be the receiver of all that negative energy. It's gonna happen soon enough, and I just don't want you to be caught in the cross fire when it does."

"For a player, you seem to know more than you should about a woman's emotions. I thought players didn't give a fuck about a woman's feelings."

"True players know that's bullshit! You can't play the game if you don't have all the pieces on the board, and a woman's emotions are the king. Don't try to redirect the issue, dude. I'm not trying to rain on your parade. Like I said, I just want to keep it one hundred with you. This situation ain't good for either of you."

"You think you know what's going on, but you don't," Daniel responded while getting up out of his seat and pacing around Timothy's office. The thunderstorm outside seemed to intensify the longer the two friends faced off, and Timothy's office windows were shaking violently as walls of water splashed against the window with alarming force. The lights flickered periodically, and Timothy looked up at them uncomfortably as he tried to reason with his best friend.

"I don't know? Okay, answer me this, Danny. Since you two have started fucking—"

"I wouldn't call it fucking," Daniel yelled, cutting off his question.

"Oh, my bad. Since you two have become 'intimate,'" he corrected himself in a mocking tone, before continuing with his question. "Since you two have become intimate, have your sessions continued?"

"What sessions?"

"The fact you have to ask that question proves my point. You both are completely off track now. Her reason for being there is lost, and both of you are burying yourselves in sex. Hey, if this were any other situation, I would give you a pound and tell you to keep banging. The whole reason why I put my research on hold and work in that madhouse you call an ICU is so that Ayana can help you, *not* bang you. Y'all need to get back on track as soon as possible because this shit won't end well otherwise."

Daniel's face was inflamed as he grit his teeth while staring at Timothy with fire in his eyes. Timothy seemed unmoved by his fury toward him and smiled, clearly amused at Daniel's reaction to what he considered the plain and incontestable truth. Timothy didn't understand what his friend expected from him . . . a pat on the back, a party, or maybe a cookie? From what Daniel told him, over the past couple of weeks, his friend has had an obscene amount of cookies from Ayana's jar, and it was time to pull his hand—or dick—out of it before it gets severed. Timothy may be a player, but he knew better than to play this kind of game. The only outcome was mutual imminent destruction. Any real player knew never to get involved in such a game because self-preservation is paramount to a player.

Nevertheless, he knew he needed to tread lightly because Danny was too far gone. He really believed that what he shared with Ayana was real love, and if he considered Timothy a threat to that love, their friendship would suffer. He needed to lighten the mood in the room before his friend stormed out of his office, irreparably scarred by his comments about his relationship with Ayana.

"By the way, how many more days before our bet expires, because some of the nurses in the ICU are unbelievably fuckable!"

Daniel stood there with his arms folded, still appearing angry, but hearing Timothy's comment about the nurses began to relax him immediately. He tried to fight the smile growing on his face, but the longer he thought about Timothy's comment and his knowledge that *none* of the nurses that worked in ICU was remotely "fuckable" caused the smile to break through his angry snarl. No matter how drunk or desperate, there was no way any man alive would consider them eligible for even a "paper bag over the head" quickie. The irony of the joke broke through, and he leaned forward, laughing until tears rolled down his cheeks. Seeing his friend's reaction, Timothy slammed his hand on top of his desk in triumph and joined him in laughter.

After laughing until his stomach muscles ached, Daniel returned to his seat, wiping the tears from his eyes.

"I think we should call it even and let you get back to your favorite pastime because I'm afraid if this continues, you might bang one of those nurses and lose every player point you've accumulated over the years," Daniel joked while shaking his head at Timothy.

"Naw, I'm cool. I'm going to see this through, but I must admit, there were times of weakness when they *did* look pretty fuckable."

"Oh no, my brother! You can't be serious!"

"Real talk, especially Ramona."

"Not Jigsaw—please, not her."

"Yep, but you have to admit, even though she looks just like that clown on the tricycle, from the neck down, she's a solid eight."

"Eight, my ass. She's no more than a four on a good day. Your lack of sex has blinded you, my brother."

An image of Ramona's body popped in Timothy's head, and he shook it in shame before responding, "You got a point." He started laughing until a loud hiccup escaped his mouth . . .

Daniel drove home in silence as he considered everything that Timothy said earlier. He didn't want to accept Timothy's assessment of his relationship with Ayana, but Tim made some crucial points that were impossible to ignore. Since their first intimate encounter, Ayana hadn't held one session with him, nor did she bring it up. They were both entranced in their desire to dilute the pain and regret they both felt with sex, and Daniel hated admitting that Timothy was right. Regardless of their disconnection from reality, Daniel was certain he was falling in love with Ayana, and he wanted her in his life. However, he knew that whatever they had wouldn't last unless he started making the hard decisions for both of them.

Walking into his condo, he could hear Ayana in the kitchen again, cooking up another amazing meal. She was an incredible cook, and she would prepare small feasts for just the two of them. Daniel feared that his chiseled frame might start to round out more if he didn't slow down with all that eating. He held his head down, feeling afraid and ashamed at what he knew he had to do. He hated challenging her because he knew once he opened this can of worms, things could get really nasty and strained between them. Nevertheless, he knew that if he really cared for her, he had to do this . . . There just wasn't any other way.

About an hour later, Daniel was seated at a candlelit dining room table that Ayana had decorated beautifully. The entire condo was dark, other than the romantic flickering lights of the candles that stood high like lighted towers on either end of the large metal and glass modern dining table. Daniel looked down the far end of the table, and his mouth slowly opened as he noticed Ayana's dark and sensual body fully exposed with only his burgundy and black tie around her neck, its tail end seductively running between her breasts. She sat upright in proper posture as she ate, seemingly oblivious to Daniel's amazed expression.

There is a God, he thought while he lustfully looked at her, unable to lift his fork to his mouth. Suddenly, his plans on lifting the masquerade became ten times harder than he anticipated, and Ayana quickly multiplied things when she suddenly looked at him smiling and said, "I'm really feeling uninhibited tonight. I feel like I would be willing to do any and everything you ask of me. All I want to do is please you tonight."

He felt himself slowly growing in his pants as he imagined every kinky desire he'd ever had and the possibility that the most beautiful woman he's ever been with was willing to fulfill them all. Still not done teasing the doctor, Ayana decided to scoot her chair closer to the table. The motion caused her ample breasts to bounce in the candlelight, and Daniel noticed every succulent movement they made. Feeling like he would burst through the seams of his pants, he tried to situate himself, because the swollen lightning rod in his pants made it very uncomfortable to sit still.

"So how was your day, honey?" Ayana asked, placing a spoonful of rice in her mouth and then removing it slowly while looking in Daniel's eyes seductively.

"It was cool," he responded, clearing his throat nervously.

Looking down at his plate, Ayana smiled.

"Honey, you haven't touched your food. Are you in the mood for dessert instead?"

Oh, you are so bad, he thought, looking up at the ceiling, appearing to have a silent conversation with God.

Ayana was enjoying Daniel's nervous reaction. He was giving her exactly what she wanted, and she wanted to be in control tonight, taking the role of the giver instead of the receiver. Daniel was the most selfless, incredible lover she'd ever had, and she wanted to reward him for tending to her every carnal desire. However, he was an alpha male, and the only way to allow him to relax and relinquish control was to make him nervous . . . shock him, and now that her mission was going as planned, she wanted to take full advantage.

"Come here, baby," she commanded while taking a huge bite out of a chocolate-covered strawberry.

Seeing her full and juicy lips caress the strawberry caused a trading of places in Daniel's thought pattern. He was no longer thinking with his brain, but with his vein, and he slowly stood up and began walking toward her. Ayana turned her chair out from under the table and leaned forward in the chair while spreading her legs. His heart was beating so fast he thought he was going to have a heart attack. Like a nervous teenager, he stood a few paces from her, afraid to move closer. Looking only at his crotch, Ayana reached out forcefully, pulling him closer to her by his belt buckle and began to undo his jeans. He felt the cool night air from the open balcony door run up his legs once his pants fell to his ankles. Without hesitation, Ayana took him entirely in her mouth, something Daniel once believed impossible. His knees immediately started shaking as he felt her warm mouth firmly close around him as her tongue massaged his throbbing muscle.

Oh hell, we can talk tomorrow . . .

Chapter 13

After the Love Is Gone

Daniel watched Ayana stomp around his bedroom at a frantic pace while the early-morning sun reflected on her totally exposed dark and smooth skin, seemingly enhancing her already "out of control" silhouette. The quiet humming of the central air seemed to vibrate along with every jiggle and sensual movement she made as she pranced back and forth in his room, flinging her arms in the air as she yelled and cursed at him. She'd been at it for a while now, but after about two minutes of listening to her ranting, Daniel unconsciously tuned her out. Now, her voice sounded more like Charlie Brown's mother instead of the melodic Sudanese tone he was so used to. He figured after getting her to do so many freaky and outlandish things last night, having a conversation concerning their status wouldn't go over too well today. But he didn't think he would go from being "baby," to "Dr. Bennett," to "Dr. Dumbass," and finally, to "Muthafucka." Actually, after briefly thinking about it, Daniel couldn't recall ever being called a muthafucka so many times in under ten minutes.

He should've been concerned with how she reacted to what he considered a series of important questions and observations about their relationship. Surprisingly, he wasn't bothered . . . not one bit, but his cold reaction to her outburst *did* bother him. He felt that he was reverting to the zombie he used to be, and although he'd grown accustomed to being cold and uncaring, the few weeks of emotional freedom he shared with Ayana made it difficult for him to consider going back. After lying on the bed a few minutes longer watching Ayana "spaz" out, he decided to put an end to her tirade.

Enough already. She's acting like I told her I had a wife or a baby mama.

"Hey, okay, I get it. You're upset. I ruined the moment by attempting to label things. But *why* are you so upset? I would think you would want to be more than my live-in fuck buddy."

Hearing his voice stopped Ayana in her tracks. She stood with her back toward him with her arms raised above her head, frozen in the last position she was standing in while she released all her anger. She just stood there for about ten seconds, not saying a word or moving one inch. Daniel slowly raised his head from the pillow, looking genuinely concerned at this new reaction from her.

Ayana stood there with her eyes closed, breathing deeply. She was desperately trying to contain herself and not act out of character any more than she already had, but the doctor was a master "nerves" surgeon. He'd cut deep into her self-control, allowing all her anger and pain to spill out into the world. It was typical "man foolery" for him to think what he said to her wasn't that serious.

Why am I upset? That asshole tells me he thinks we are going about the relationship the wrong way. That things are just sexual, and soon, we'll have nothing left unless we agree about what we are or what we are not. That my purpose here is lost in sex, and I need time to grieve. Time to grieve? He assumes too much, and he's made an ass of himself and a joke about my feelings for him. He absolutely downplayed everything I did for him. I slaved in that kitchen for hours for his stupid ass. I shaved and waxed my most sensitive parts and oiled myself down like a swimsuit model for him. I deep throated him until it felt like my vocal cords needed stitches. I made him come so hard that he ripped up two pillows on the bed, tossing feathers all over the room. After doing all of that and other things I dare not share with another soul on this planet, he has the fucking nerve to tell me it's all just sex?

The more Ayana thought about everything Daniel said to her and everything she did last night to prove to him that it wasn't just sex for her, the angrier she became. Gritting her teeth and clinching her fists, she slowly turned to face him. Her eyes possessed piercing anger that sent chills through the doctor's entire body. He immediately decided it was best for him to climb out of bed and stand up, just in case her anger got the best of her and she decided to try to harm him. Watching him climb out of bed, while never taking his eyes off her, she began to feel an uncomfortable draft blow through her. Yes, she knew she was naked, but now she felt beyond naked. She felt exposed and dirty. The way Daniel looked at her with that alarming glare made everything she felt for him feel stupid and unnatural, but she needed to regain some measure of dignity after she showed out a few seconds ago.

"Mutha . . . *breathe, Ayana . . . breathe . . ." Don't let this fool see you out of character any longer.* "Doctor Bennett, I want to first apologize for my outburst. I am a guest in your home, and I have no right to behave in that

manner. Second, I want to make it clear to you that I am
not a fuck buddy or in-house pussy, and I'm certainly not
the kind of woman to cook for a man that I just want to
have sex with. Apparently, my efforts to show you my
intentions weren't clear enough for you. So, I'll make it
perfectly clear what my intentions *were*—"

"Were?" Daniel asked, swallowing deeply.

"Yes, *were,* because at this juncture. I think it would
be unwise for me to continue with the same intentions
in mind. I wanted to love you, Daniel, and be loved by
you. Despite my better judgment and past experiences
with you, I wanted to build something with you. But
apparently, you saw my efforts only as a display of
desperation for sex."

"Ayana, no, that's not what I meant. I was trying—"

"Doesn't matter anymore, Doctor," Ayana interrupted.
"We've come to the point of no return for me. I made a
commitment to see your treatment through, and I will do
so, but I will no longer share a bed with you. We've gone
way beyond a professional relationship, and neither of us
can trust ourselves around the other. As much as I loathe
you as a human being, I can't deny how you make my
body feel. So, it's best I sleep in your guest room for the
remainder of my time here."

Daniel stood there, feeling like the walls in his bedroom were caving in around him. He never intended to
hurt Ayana with the things he said to her. After hearing
her, he began to understand just how fucked up he'd
made things. His intentions were good, but his delivery
was bad . . . *very* bad. How could he fix it? He'd been so
closed off and uncaring for so long that he didn't even
know where to begin. His entire being yearned for her,
and no matter how he tried to rationalize his feelings,

there was no denying his feelings were well beyond a simple infatuation. He did love her, and there wasn't a woman on the planet he could imagine being with other than her. It seems he always found a way to ruin things just when they were getting good.

After saying everything that she wanted to say, Ayana stood there looking at the doctor, biting her bottom lip as he seemed to be in some kind of daydream. She wanted him to say something—*anything* that would show her that he truly cared. She meant every word she said, but she was hoping to God that he would make sense of these past few weeks and change her mind. However, the longer he stared blankly at her, the more her hopes of him rescuing what they shared began to dwindle.

I can't believe I gave this man so much so soon, and all I can get from him is that goofy look on his face and silence.

With each passing second of silence, Ayana felt her heart breaking, and soon, it became difficult for her to breathe and contain her emotions. She was hurt . . . no, better yet, *devastated* by his unwillingness to fix things between them, so she decided to leave before she allowed herself to break down in front of this selfish man she stupidly gave her heart and body to.

Looking up at the ceiling, trying to fight back the tears that were forming in her eyes, Ayana sucked her teeth and started shifting her weight from one leg to another. Her skin felt cold and sticky, and suddenly, she yearned for a scalding hot shower to wash the scent of the doctor from her skin. Licking her lips, she inhaled deeply as the taste of the doctor's skin seemed to invade her mouth. She wanted to wash her mouth out with bleach and peroxide so that she could remove his taste from her tongue

forever. She wanted every sensation and feeling she had
for Daniel permanently removed from her so that it could
be easier to move on and forget how she felt about him
and the optimism she felt about finally finding a man she
could give herself to completely. Ayana had nothing but
failure after failure with relationships, but none of them
got inside of her like the doctor. He really did a number
on her, and although it's been only a few weeks, she had
already started to dream about a life with him in it.

Silly girl, tricks are for kids.

Having had enough of the doctor's blank stare, Ayana
decided to leave before things got worse. As she turned
to depart, she felt the doctor's warm and sweaty hands
firmly grip her arm and pulled her back toward him. Her
heart started beating faster as she angrily snatched away
from him, but somehow, he was able to grab hold of
her again and spun her around. Now facing him, Daniel
held her with both hands on either arm. Ayana was now
terrified, expecting the worst from him. His grip was
firm and tight as she tried to pull away, but he was much
too strong. Afraid to see the careless rage she expected
to glare back at her, she held her head down, looking at
the floor and bracing herself for the first strike or profan-
ity-laden rant intended to break her down physically and
emotionally. Daniel looked down at Ayana as she closed
her eyes and tightened every muscle in her body. She
appeared to be bracing herself for something, and when
Daniel figured out what that something might be, his
emotional floodgates erupted.

It was then that he understood Ayana's anger and fear.
Someone had hurt her, and it happened so many times
that now, she expected a violent response from every
man she met. The realization of her fear and pain tore

into him, and he slowly loosened his hold on her. He never intended to hurt her. He reached out to her only to stop her from leaving. He had no words he could put together. He wasn't very poetic or a muse with words. He'd certainly been out of practice of showing meaningful affection, and he knew any attempt wouldn't seem genuine. All he had was his eyes and the pain and love he had in them. He was hoping if he could just let her look into his eyes, she would see everything he couldn't say to her.

But looking at her now, the only thing his soul yearned for was to hold this broken and abused woman close to him, to wrap his strong arms around her tightly and completely so that no one, not even himself, could ever hurt her again.

Feeling his hold on her loosen, Ayana exhaled forcefully and started to back away until she felt Daniel reach out to her, wrapping his arms around her and gently pulling her close to him. Sweat covered his naked body, and she could hear his heartbeat inside his chest. Its rhythm seemed to be in tune with her now-relaxed breathing. Their bodies connected. Daniel began to hold her tighter and closer to him, allowing every muscular groove and indentation to connect with Ayana's curves. She wanted to push him away, but something about the way he was holding her made her relax. Still slightly afraid and unsure of Daniel's intentions, she refused to embrace him back and just let her arms hang down to her sides. Daniel noticed this but didn't stop holding her. He wanted her to feel him without saying one word. He needed to be patient with her, and even if it took hours, he was not going to let her go until she knew exactly what his show of affection meant.

Still refusing to look in his eyes, Ayana just stood there in his arms, limp and seemingly unmoved by the doctor's show of affection. She initially thought about trying to pull away, but something inside her compelled her to stay right where she was. It wasn't fear that kept her in his arms. It was curiosity, and she wanted to know where all this was headed. After a few more moments, she felt her muscles relax, and she slowly started to close her eyes as the vibrations of the doctor's emotional energy began to invade her. Before long, her head was comfortably resting on his chest, and slowly, her arms began to rise as her body and soul hungered to feel more of the affection Daniel was giving her.

She started to run her fingers up his back, running them over the multiple bullet wounds that covered it like spots on a leopard. Then as natural as breathing, she wrapped her arms around his back and exhaled . . .

"I love you."

"I love you too."

Chapter 14

Back to Work

Timothy watched Daniel walk into the ICU with the biggest smile on his face, and it nearly gave him a heart attack. He just stared at Daniel like a man under hypnosis, and soon, everyone in the ICU unit, including the patients, joined in on the rare spectacle.

"Doctor Bennett, is everything okay?" Timothy asked with uneasiness in his voice.

"Everything is great, Tim!"

"So why are you here? You have two more weeks before you return."

"I know, but I think it's time for you to get back to your research, and I get back to saving lives."

The entire room grew silent, and only the beeping sound of the heart monitor machines and the humming of the huge overhead fluorescent lights could be heard in the room. No one had seen the doctor smile or refer to his job as "saving lives," so everyone was in awe at the doctor's new attitude toward his job. Noticing the uneasy feeling invade the room, Timothy decided to pull the doctor aside and have a few words with him, hopefully to convince him to take the remaining two weeks' vacation he had left, just to be certain the sessions with Ayana were working, despite their ongoing romance.

"Dude, what the flying fuck is wrong with you? You can't come barging in like this with that goofy-ass smile on your face."

"Why not? What's wrong with me smiling?"

"Seriously? When was the last time *anyone* in this hospital saw you smile?"

Timothy's question was answered with an uncomfortable ten seconds of silence. Standing there looking at Daniel as if he were a fool, Timothy gave Daniel five more seconds before he continued . . .

"Exactly . . . You can't even answer that question. I didn't tell anyone about why you took a leave, but I'm sure if you walk in here with this brand-new 'love guru' attitude, they will put two and two together."

"So you're saying I should come back with the old me attitude?"

"No . . . Hell no! What I'm saying is baby steps, bruh! You got to ease this new you in to your colleagues. Especially Dr. Klansman!"

"You mean Dr. Kohlman."

"Nope, I meant Klansman. I can't even fathom how you worked with that racist pig for so long without beating the brakes off his ass. The shit he says to people in the ICU, and the comments he makes about black and Hispanic people are crazy as fuck! I had to remind myself repeatedly that if I fucked him up, you could lose your job because I'm covering for you."

Daniel started to chuckle, and the more Timothy ranted on about how much he hated Dr. Kohlman, his chuckling quickly turned into roaring laughter, imagining the torture Timothy had to endure listening to the racist doctor. Timothy gave Daniel a concerned and nasty look before leaning against the off-white wall behind him.

Daniel could tell Timothy's time in the ICU wasn't the most pleasant, and he longed to return to his research, but because he wanted his friend to get better, he sucked it up and endured.

That's my boy right there, Daniel thought to himself proudly.

Daniel couldn't let Timothy spend another week in ICU, so although he respected Timothy's concern, Daniel knew it was time for him to take over.

"Tim, listen, I am grateful for everything you have done for me covering for me while I deal with my crazy shit, but no matter what you say to me right now, it won't change my decision. It's time for me to come back to work and you to go back to your research."

"Danny, it's cool, man. I can handle it for two more weeks . . . I'm just—"

"Tim, stop . . . seriously . . . You have to stop. I got this. I can't keep you away from your research any longer. Every day you don't work on your research is another day thousands of people die from cancer. I can't be this selfish anymore."

"So, are you cured?"

"I don't know if I'm completely rid of my nightmares or issues, but I can say I'm working toward getting better, and that's more than I've been able to do since I came home from Africa."

Smiling, Timothy nodded and placed his hand on Daniel's shoulder, pulled him close, and embraced him. Timothy felt relieved that his friend was getting better, and he prayed everything worked out between him and Ayana because if things went south, he feared so would his progress. Stepping back and giving Daniel another look of encouragement, Timothy pulled the ICU identification card from his upper jacket pocket and forcefully placed it in Daniel's hand before saying . . .

"Fuck this place. I'm out!"

Then he quickly turned and stormed down the hallway toward the exit. Daniel watched him leave, shaking his head and grinning at his friend's antics. Once Timothy was out of sight, Daniel turned and looked at the double doors leading into ICU. The smile slowly disappeared from his face as he braced himself for the horrors of the inner city and the results of what the worst of human behavior can accomplish.

Eight hours later, Daniel slumped into his office chair and leaned forward, resting his weary head on his desk. The day's drama in ICU seemed to be much harder to deal with than he remembered. Either he needed to get back into the groove of things, or something else was different that made his work more trying than usual. He was starting to doze off until he heard a gentle knock on his office door. He slowly sat up and invited the nameless visitor in. The door opened and in walked Ayana, with the biggest smile on her face. Her presence immediately lifted the doctor's spirits, and he jumped out of his seat to greet her. She walked straight into his arms, and he wrapped her tightly in them. He could feel the frigid temperatures outside still clinging to her coat, and he shuddered momentarily. Ayana immediately started giggling at his response.

"Damn, baby, I haven't even touched you yet, and you're already shivering."

Rolling his eyes, Daniel leaned back, laughing at Ayana's crack on him. "What are you doing here? It's too cold for you to be out like this."

"I know, but I wanted to bring you something to eat," she responded while placing a bag on his desk. The aroma of her amazing cooking immediately filled his office as she began to remove each dish from the purple cloth bag she brought with her. The food was still hot as the steam lifted from it as she placed it on glass plates and set it up in front of the now-seated doctor. The smile on his face was massive as he watched her serve him with care. She would periodically brush her ass up against him or pretended she slipped and flopped down on his lap. While on his lap, she giggled like a silly schoolgirl and would say in the most seductive voice, "I'm so sorry, Doctor. I don't know what's come over me. Please don't tell."

Playing along, he smacked her on the ass and called her a "bad nurse." Both of them were enjoying their playful luncheon together, and a few times, they almost forgot the doctor still needed to eat food and not Ayana. Eventually, Ayana decided to sit on the left edge of his desk and watch him enjoy the meal she prepared for him. The doctor was thoroughly enjoying himself as he swallowed each tasty spoonful. Ayana noticed he was almost finished, so she seductively slid over closer to him on the desk and slowly placed her foot between his parted legs. She made sure she didn't allow her now shoeless foot to touch his privates, but she placed it close enough to excite him. Daniel looked down at her foot and looked up at Ayana staring at him, biting her bottom lip. She had an almost animalistic look in her eyes as she stared at the growing bulge in his pants like a hungry predator. She was ready to pounce on him and ride him until she exploded all over his lap.

Daniel slowly stood up to allow her to unbuckle his pants. She was violently snatching at his belt buckle while moaning in anticipation of swallowing his candy cane whole. Daniel was now reaching behind her and pulling her closer while trying to get a firm grip on her ass to squeeze and caress it. He loved everything about her, but he was obsessed with her ass, and he wasn't shy to show it. With his pants unbuckled and his zipper down, Ayana licked her palm before reaching inside his pants. Her wet and warm hand caressing him while attempting to pull him out and into her mouth made him roll his eyes in the back of his head and moan deeply. She didn't pull him out immediately, but firmly and slowly stroked it in her wet hand inside his pants. She played with him from the bottom of his shaft to the tip, playing with the most sensitive underside of his manhood. The sensation caused him to shiver and brace himself against his desk.

Damn, she's good.

Smiling at his reaction, Ayana slowly started to pull his pants down with her feet, never stopping with her playful, yet skilled massaging of his petrified muscle. Daniel feared that if she continued, he might pop before she got his pants below his knees, and he braced himself in an attempt to hold himself from exploding in her hand.

"Mmmm . . . I want you inside my mouth, Dr. Bennett. I need you to probe my throat with your surgical tool. Can you do that for me, Doc?"

Oh my God!

Her voice, her accent, and the way she moaned became too much for the doctor's self-control. He knew that when she finally placed him in her mouth, he wouldn't last an entire minute before he would be giving in to his uncontrollable desire to come.

Shit, I wanted some pussy too. I can't go out like a minute man, but this woman is breaking a brother down with the swiftness.

Now, gripping him in her hand, she slowly began to pull him closer to her mouth—and then a moment-ruining knock echoed on his door. The sound seemed to jolt the two hot lovers out of their world of lust and crash-landed them back into reality. Daniel quickly pulled himself from Ayana's hand and placed it back in his pants, trying to fix himself and appear normal. Ayana threw her legs over the side of the desk like a stuntwoman, and once on the other side of the desk, sat down in the chair. She was still without her boots, leaving them on the left side of Daniel's desk. They were in plain view of whoever was going to walk in the office, and with the winter temperatures outside, the shoeless woman in the chair would be a dead giveaway of what was happening behind the closed door in the doctor's office.

She tried to get back up and reach for them, but Daniel was already inviting the cock-blocking knocker in, so she sat back down and placed her hand over her face. She was silently praying it was Timothy because he would understand. Anyone else might make an issue of it. They both felt like children caught by their parents making out in the basement as Dr. Kohlman walked into Daniel's office.

"Wow, it's much warmer in your office than the rest of the wing. Do you have a personal heater going?" Dr. Kohlman asked while staring at Ayana, sitting in the chair.

"No, I think it's because my office door is closed, keeping out the unwanted draft," Daniel replied, while blankly staring at him.

"Oh, so, that explains your visitor taking off her boots in your office. Must be too hot for footwear, huh?"

"Must be," Daniel replied, still staring at the doctor as if he were an unwanted bug on the wall. Ayana could feel the tension building between the two men, and she wanted to divert a disaster. So, she smiled brightly and extended her hand, introducing herself warmly.

"Hi, my name is Ayana, and you must be Dr. Kohlman. Dr. Bennett speaks highly of you."

"As any person of color should of their superiors," Dr. Kohlman responded coldly, refusing to shake her hand. He turned his back to her and moved toward the left side of Daniel's desk, trying to sneak a peek to see if the doctor was in a compromising state . . . namely, with his pants undone or off completely. Seeing what he was trying to do, Daniel immediately inquired what he needed, momentarily stopping him in his tracks and giving Daniel the time he needed to zip up his pants.

"Oh, right! I almost forgot why I came here. It's just so hot and steamy in this room. It's messing up my concentration."

"Well, if it's affecting you that much, you could leave and email me what you need," Daniel responded sarcastically.

After hearing his response, Dr. Kohlman took a step back while folding his arms. Shaking his head slightly, he stared at Daniel like a stranger and not the man he's worked with for years.

"Well, someone's in an unusually defiant mood today."

Ayana, now beside herself with anger, sat there listening to Dr. Kohlman's remarks and his apparent lack of respect for her man. She wanted to say something—*anything* to shut the doctor's bigoted mouth, but she knew she had to keep quiet and let Daniel handle him. Nevertheless, it was getting harder each passing second Dr. Kohlman continued to open his mouth.

"This isn't defiance. It's an annoyance, Doctor. I was trying to have a private moment with my girlfriend while I ate. I understand you need something, but you've been here for over two minutes, and you still haven't said what it is you want. Very annoying . . . very."

"Oh! Oh! I'm sorry for doing *my* job as head doctor of this wing! I thought I was supposed to check in on the doctors that work *under* me. Excuse my professional intrusion."

"I don't work *under* you. I work *with* you."

"That's not accurate, but I'm not here to argue. I'm here to let you know that I will be taking the next couple of weeks off."

"Wait a minute. That's the holiday season right during Thanksgiving. You know ICU is overwhelmed every year during this time."

"Exactly, and I refuse to work tirelessly for leeches and welfare offspring that don't know how not to kill themselves or each other. I refuse to spend my holiday covered in their blood. The very thought of it makes me want to puke—right in these nice furry boots."

That was the last straw. Ayana was done. She couldn't take the doctor's putrid comments any longer, and to threaten to throw up in her favorite boots was the straw that broke the camel's back.

This asshole has to be gay or never knew his mama because someone should've warned him never to threaten a woman's shoes. Ever!

"Throw up in my shoes, and you'll be covered in your own blood, Doctor Dipshit!"

Her proud, African accent startled Dr. Kohlman, and he suddenly became afraid to look at Ayana directly. He turned to Daniel, the man he's grown accustomed to accepting his behavior without protest. He felt comfortable with Daniel and his lack of initiative to correct his racist comments. Therefore, instead of addressing the aggressive black woman in the chair, he decided to go after the docile black man at the desk.

"I think you need to teach your friend her place, Doctor. She's not in Africa anymore. This is America, and we have order and a way of doing things, and we don't allow that kind of behavior."

Daniel looked at Dr. Kohlman, shaking his head. He wanted to snap, but he knew it would only fuel the stereotypes that Dr. Kohlman clung so tightly to that made him feel superior. Although everything about Daniel concerning his education and results far exceeded Dr. Kohlman's, he still felt like he was a better doctor and a better man. Daniel decided it was time to wake the doctor up from his Matrix-like slumber.

"Listen, Doc, aside from you clearly violating several workplace harassment laws, you have also violated this hospital's rules and regulations concerning time off and reporting that time. Oh, don't look so surprised. Yeah, I checked, and you haven't reported any of the days you took off this year, hoping to cash in on those days next year at the end of February. Now, that could land you not only in the unemployment line but also in a police lineup. I wouldn't be so confident in your so-called superior position here. You are only employed here because *I* allow it. However, after your disrespectful manner toward my woman, those days are over. Concerning those two weeks you plan on taking off? Denied! You don't have any days left to take off, so I'd better see your racist, redneck ass in the ICU every fucking day during the holiday season, or you are done here. Are we clear?"

Dr. Kohlman's arrogant demeanor had now transformed into that of a meek field mouse. His usual upright stance was now slouched and sloppy, and he looked down at the floor in embarrassment. He had no idea that Dr. Bennett had the smarts to double-check his time off allocations during the year, and he felt that even though he only mentioned this year, he feared Dr. Bennett has been tracking him for much longer. That would mean tens of thousands of dollars of overpayments of falsely reported time sheets coming to light. He decided against challenging him further and started walking out of his office. Daniel, not satisfied, stopped Dr. Kohlman and demanded he apologize to Ayana.

It took every ounce of dignity he had, but the doctor apologized to her and quickly exited Daniel's office before he demanded more from him. As soon as he was gone, Ayana rushed to the door, locking it and turning off the lights, determined to finish what they started, this time, without interruptions . . .

Chapter 15

Hide and Peek

Ayana watched the reflection of the moving lights of the city on the ceiling of Daniel's penthouse, breathing deeply with her arms outstretched on either side of her naked body. The ambient light of the busy city illuminated the silhouette of the two lovers enjoying each other on the leather couch in Daniel's living room. The house was still and silent besides the slurping and licking sounds of Daniel on his knees, and his head buried deep between her thighs while she wrapped her legs around his neck as she sat on the edge of the couch. The events earlier in his office only fueled their fire for more, and he decided to leave the hospital early to continue what they started in his office after he put Dr. Kohlman in his place.

Listening to Daniel aggressively break the racist doctor down while defending her honor made her so hot for him that she couldn't take it anymore and had to have him right then and there, but it wasn't nearly enough. Now, back in his penthouse, she was feeling his warm tongue exploring her drenched and excited flower, consuming her as if he were starving.

Damn, boy!

Scratching and pulling on the leather, she tried to brace herself each time he took her clitoris between his full lips, sucking and licking it vigorously. The sensations made her bite her bottom lip and curl her toes, trying to receive the intense pleasure his experienced mouth was giving her. Suddenly, she heard a low and intense buzzing sound and immediately felt the doctor plunge his tongue deep inside of her while taking the vibrating and lubricated bullet and placing it firmly on her clit. The double sensation caused her to lift her back off the couch screaming, while frantically grappling for anything to brace herself for the coming orgasm of life-changing proportions. The nerves on her back and inner thighs sprang alive and began shooting supercharged sensations of pleasure throughout her entire body. Her eyes were bulging and her mouth wide open as Daniel continued to make love to her with his tongue while using the vibrator to stimulate her already aroused pearl of pleasure.

She could barely breathe as she kept clawing and pulling on the leather with her back still elevated off the couch, making it difficult for the doctor to delve his tongue deeper inside of her. In a single and aggressive motion, Daniel reached up, grabbed her hips, and forcefully pulled her back down, giving himself a better angle to push his tongue deeper inside of her. She instantly felt his tongue reaching deeper, exploring her walls. Ayana broke free of her self-control, and her arms started swinging wildly as she began making high-pitched coughing sounds. Undeterred by her wild and shocking reactions, Daniel continued his assault with his tongue and vibrator while holding her down firmly on the couch. Soon, the pleasure became too much for her, and she reached down, trying to push his head back and remove his hand holding the rapidly vibrating naughtiness that was sending her over the climatic edge. Daniel refused to stop. Instead, he tensed his neck and arm so that she couldn't overpower him.

Hell naw . . . You taking this orgasm. Ain't no escaping now.

After trying several times without success, she flung her hands up in frustration as she let out a high-pitched scream. She was coming, and it was going to be a *massive* one. She felt the orgasm start from the back of her neck, slowly creeping down her sweaty back. It then began vibrating between her breasts, circling her erect nipples, and as if it had a mind of its own, it moved down to her belly button before rushing down to her center, expanding down her legs.

"Danny! Oh my God!"

The orgasm sent a tsunami of pleasure through her and out toward Daniel's welcoming mouth. She felt as if she'd just wet herself as the orgasm continued, shaking her entire body like a grand mal seizure. Her leg muscles were trembling and twitching uncontrollably as her body jumped and jerked on the couch. Her eyes rolled inside her head. She seemed completely lost inside herself as the orgasm continued to intensify and lasted longer than any she'd ever thought possible. Slowly removing his tongue from inside of her while opening her legs, Daniel firmly, yet carefully, inserted his rock-hard muscle deep inside of her. Ayana immediately reached up, wrapping her arms around his neck, biting him on the shoulder as she was feeling the grooves and veins of his rod rubbing against her spot as he slid inside of her while she continued to come.

"Oh my God, you are going to send me to the crazy house, baby," Ayana breathlessly whispered in his ear.

Smiling and not saying a word, he started stroking her deeply and slowly. The sensation caused her to dig her nails into his back . . .

In a dark hotel room directly across the street from Dr. Bennett's building stood a large man in the window, viewing through a big pair of binoculars with a mischievous grin on his face. He'd been watching the two lovers for about an hour, licking his lips while periodically groping himself, growing more aroused as the pair continued making love. Suddenly, his cell phone rang, snatching him away from his entertainment. Grunting in disappointment, he quickly reached for it sitting on the window's ledge. Looking at the screen, he rolled his eyes and answered the call.

"Is this line secure?" the deep and commanding voice inquired on the other end.

"Yes, sir."

"Good, what have you found out about the good doctor? Anything we can use against him?"

"I couldn't find anything to blackmail the doctor until I discovered something much better than a bribe or threat. Something we can use to ruin the UN's plan to prosecute you."

"And what's that, Satu?"

"Ayana."

"Ayana? How the hell is she going to help keep him from testifying? She and Meagan are the ones running this circus, and if they can convince him to testify, I'm done. How deep is he in with her?"

Balls deep, Satu amusedly thought to himself. "Very deep, sir. She's living with him at the moment," Satu replied.

"Really? Now *that is* interesting," Kronte responded with satisfaction. "Listen, we only have one shot at this, so you know what you have to do. Don't fuck this up, Satu. If we play our cards right, the doctor will no longer be a problem for us, and without his testimony, they have to release me."

"Exactly, sir, I'll get right on it."

"Good work, Soldier, very good work."

"Thank you, sir."

Ayana awoke the following morning, greeted by an empty bed and a blizzard raging through the city. She stared blankly outside, watching as the angry winds rattled and shook the massive floor-to-ceiling bedroom windows. The buildings outside were being blanketed by frozen white powder with such force and intensity that it appeared as if the weight of the snow would soon cause the buildings to lean. The longer Ayana watched the blizzard bombard the city, the more she was thankful to be inside Daniel's warm and cozy condo. After lying there a few more minutes, she decided to get out of bed and begin her day. She had so much on her mind this morning after a life-changing night of lovemaking with "Doctor Feel Great." There was so much she needed to tell him, but she needed to be careful because Daniel's mental and emotional state was still very fragile, and she didn't want him to relapse.

Throwing her bare legs over the bed, she immediately felt her muscles protest at the sudden movements. She was still weak after Doctor Feel Great pushed her body to its limits, and she felt light-headed and dehydrated.

What did he do to me?

Bracing herself to stand up, she was interrupted by the ring tone of her cell phone. Ayana moaned as she reached over to the nightstand to look at the front screen of her cell.

Damn, she thought as the contact photo of Meagan glared back at her. Ayana had been avoiding her calls over the past few days, but she felt a call this early in the morning meant something serious. She accepted her call while clearing her throat.

"Hey, girl!"

"Don't 'hey, girl' me! Ayana, where have you been? I've been trying to get in contact with you since Tuesday."

"I'm sorry. I've been really busy with the doctor this week. It's been nonstop with him all week," Ayana responded while covering her mouth, trying to hold in a giggle. She felt like she was lying and at the same time, telling a naughty truth.

"Well, I hope with all that 'nonstopping,' you are closer to getting the doctor to agree to testify. The trial is months away, and I need confirmation soon."

"I'll step up my efforts and work him harder until he says yes. I'm sure I can bang him into submission."

This time she couldn't hold in her laughter, and she flopped facedown on the bed, laughing into the sheets.

"What the fuck? 'Bang him into submission'? What kind of therapy are you giving him, Ayana?"

Still laughing, Ayana tried to speak into the phone, but she couldn't, and she decided to let Meagan yell, "Hello!" repeatedly while she tried to pull herself together. After gaining her composure, Ayana placed the phone back to her ear.

"Ayana, what's going on down there in Chicago?" Meagan asked with deep concern in her voice.

"I'm sorry, Meagan. I dropped the phone under the bed. Like I was saying, I will double my efforts to get Dr. Bennett to commit to testifying. Is that why you called? You needed an update?"

"Actually, no. We have another emergency that I can't discuss on the phone. I need you back in New York ASAP."

Meagan's words seemed to send the outside frigid winds blowing right up Ayana's spine. The last thing on her mind was going outside in that madness and leaving Daniel. She thought about using some excuse to try to keep her in Chicago but decided against it. Meagan seemed very agitated and desperate. Also, Ayana knew that whenever they couldn't discuss a situation over the phone, it meant a security breach was suspected. So she inhaled deeply and braced herself for a long day.

"What are my travel options?"

"A flight leaves this afternoon. I need you on it."

"Meagan, have you seen the weather report here? There is a serious storm blowing through here. I don't think I'll be able to leave today."

"You're right. Okay, no problem. But I need you on the first flight once that storm blows over."

"Okay, I'll let you know once I confirm my flight plans."

After hanging up, Ayana flopped down on the bed and began screaming into the mattress . . .

Later that evening, Ayana and Daniel discussed her return to New York. Daniel was just as disappointed as Ayana that she had to leave, but he understood she still had other obligations. Ayana was concerned that Daniel

might have another attack while she was gone, but he
assured her he would be fine. Somehow, deep inside,
he believed that he would, and he decided to turn the
tables and pamper Ayana before she left for New York.
The weather was still horrible outside, but he braved the
tundra that had become the city of Chicago and went to
the local market to get the essentials he needed for what
he was planning that evening. Ayana's eyes lit up like
fireworks as she watched him walk through the door,
hands filled with bags of groceries and other items.

She immediately got up as if to begin cooking, but
Daniel stopped her and gently pushed her back on the
couch. Kissing her softly, he handed her the remote to
the television and whispered, "I got this tonight." Ayana's
eyes and mouth were wide open as she watched him con-
fidently walk into the kitchen. Before long, she heard
him removing items from the bags and rambling through
the kitchen cabinets. Two minutes later, he walked back
into the living room with a wineglass and a bottle of wine.
Standing next to her, possessing the demeanor of a waiter,
he filled her glass with red wine and handed her a folded
white cloth while she sat on the couch. The cloth felt cool
to the touch and was filled with something round and
smooth. When she opened it, four large, white chocolate-covered strawberries stared back at her.

My favorite! How did he know?

She looked up to find him already gone and headed
back into the kitchen. She lifted the wineglass to her
lips and let the exquisite taste of the fermented beverage
fill her mouth. Ayana closed her eyes as the taste and
sensation filled her head. She let the wine glide down her
throat and then opened her mouth to receive one of the
strawberries. The mixture of the wine and chocolate-cov-

ered strawberries sent a dizzying sensation through her, and she allowed her body to relax into the couch. By the time she had drunk her second glass of wine, she felt as if she were floating on air.

The aroma of Daniel's cooking began to fill the condo, and it smelled amazing. Never in a thousand years would she have guessed the doctor could cook. She still needed to wait until she tasted whatever he was cooking, but from the smell, he was already winning.

After an hour of watching television and trying to sneak a peek in the kitchen from time to time with Daniel yelling at her playfully to "sit your ass down," she was startled by the living room going dark. She turned to see Daniel smiling in front of an elegantly arranged candlelit dining table. She noticed that he placed their seats next to each other instead of on the opposite sides of the table.

"Dinner is served, my Queen," Daniel said, smiling, while perfectly mimicking her native accent. Her face lit up like a tropical sunrise as she walked over to the table. He pulled out her chair, Ayana sat down; then she reached for his hand and kissed it gently.

"I'm really gonna miss you, Danny," she whispered.

Not saying a word, Daniel began to serve her an Italian- themed meal that she soon discovered tasted better than it smelled, an amazing accomplishment in her book. The night progressed from the candlelit dinner to a hot bubble bath, and, finally, a full-body massage with warm, scented oils and heated rocks. By the time they were both lying in Daniel's bed, Ayana was expecting Daniel to make love to her, but he had something else in mind for her.

While lying naked on her back, still relishing in the amazing massage she'd just received, Daniel began to move up her well-oiled and relaxed body with his lips and tongue. Gently kissing and licking her body, he caused the nerves on her warm skin to react. She squirmed and smiled as he moved up to her neck. Licking along the large vein on her neck, Daniel reached out and began to run his hands up her outstretched arms. Once he had her hands in his, he held them firmly against the headboard while kissing her passionately on her lips.

She was so entranced by his passionate kisses that she didn't notice him slowly moving off the bed, still holding her hands against the headboard. When she felt the soft, smooth silk scarf being tied around her left wrist, her eyes sprang open, examining Daniel's eyes, searching for the reason why he was tying her to his headboard. She wanted to protest, but Daniel placed his index finger on her lips, smiling seductively, not saying a word. Seeing the look of love and sexual desire in his eyes, Ayana relaxed as she watched him move over to the other side of the bed, securing another red and black silk scarf around her right wrist.

Gently taking hold of both her ankles, Daniel spread her legs apart until they formed a perfect triangle, made of the most exquisite dark chocolate the doctor had ever tasted in his life. Ayana lifted her head as she watched Daniel tie another pair of red and black silk scarfs around her ankles, securing her to the bottom posts of his king-size bed. Her body was screaming out from the fear of the unknown and anticipation of what Doctor Feel Great had in store for her. Daniel then reached for the remote control that controlled the music system, and the song "There You Go" by the soul singer Johnny Gill began playing throughout the bedroom.

Never taking her eyes off of Daniel, Ayana watched him reach for a tall, red bottle that appeared to be some kind of erotic lotion. Walking over to the side of the bed, he placed a small amount of the lotion in his hands, rubbing them together slowly. He then began blowing into his hands for a few seconds, before massaging the sweet-smelling lotion on her breasts and nipples, then moving down to her excited center and massaging the remaining lotion on her clitoris.

Ayana's body immediately reacted to the warming sensation of the lotion, and she moaned in pleasure as she felt her nipples and clitoris swell. Reaching in the drawer on his nightstand, Daniel pulled out a large black feather, about thirteen inches long and four inches wide.

"Baby, what are you going to do with that?" Ayana asked, breathing heavily, feeling the erotic effects of the steadily warming lotion.

"Shhh," he responded while looking over the feather with a mischievous grin on his face. Daniel then placed the feather on her breast and began moving it in a circular motion around her hard and aroused nipples, allowing the fine intricacies of the feather to titillate the sensitive nerves on her breasts. Ayana lifted her back off the bed as the sensation vibrated through her chest and back.

"Danny!" she moaned while trying to pull free from her restraints.

As if in tune with the music, Daniel slowly traced the feather down to her belly button, around her hips, and then her inner thighs. Ayana knew what was coming next, but Daniel made sure he teased her, moving the feather closer to her center and then moving it away. He continued to use the soft sides of the feather to excite her, driving her out of her mind as her eyes rolled in the back of her head. The heating lotion intensified each touch of the feather. Then she felt it—the feather slowly running along her excited pearl, and she moaned loudly, pulling down with her arms, attempting to free herself.

Daniel smiled as he watched her go insane, continuing to slide the feather over her clitoris. His motions were slow and attentive, allowing her to feel each and every strand of the black feather running across her now-over-excited clitoris. The sensation caused every nerve in her body to erupt in intense pleasure. Her restraints kept her in place, preventing her from stopping Daniel from doing anything he wanted. Breathing heavily and squealing, Ayana closed her eyes, beads of sweat forming on her forehead and chest as her body gave in to every stroke of the feather.

Each time Daniel would notice Ayana reaching her point of climax, he would quickly run the feather up her clitoris and stop. Then when the eruption would subside, he would begin his gentle assault on her pearl of pleasure again. He played this game with her until she began growling and jerking violently on the bed, the intense desire to come driving her insane. Daniel smiled, deciding it was time, and he used the feather to play the ultimate symphony . . . and her body erupted in a round of applause that nearly caused her to break free from her silk restraints.

Ayana began to bounce and twist as her body pushed out every desired orgasmic note it wanted to play.

"Oh my God!" Ayana screamed as Daniel watched with great satisfaction.

After freeing Ayana and allowing her body to calm down, the two lovers held each other with only the sound of Ayana's labored breathing echoing through the room.

Feeling the urgency of her departure the next day, Daniel decided to open up about his time in Sudan and the events leading up to his near-death experience.

"Before the village massacre, I'd been to Sudan once before."

"Really? I had no idea."

"Yeah, the first time I went was with a large group of doctors and a couple of celebrities. I'd just graduated and was doing my internship in Boston. It was scary at first, but soon, I really got into what we were doing there. Then something amazing happened . . ."

Daniel paused. Ayana could feel the muscles on his chest tense up as he turned his head away. Feeling that the conversation was going into very sensitive territory, she began to rub his bare chest and gently kiss him on his neck.

"It's okay, baby. It's just you and me here. Continue."

Clearing his throat, he continued, "There was a baby that was abandoned in the bush and was bounced around from village to village. The people were very guarded about the parents of the baby, and no matter whom we talked to, no one wanted to go into details about this baby. Anyway, the baby was in horrible shape, starving, sick with malaria, and a slew of other diseases. I nursed the baby back to health. It took months, and I found myself staying longer than anticipated. Once the baby was well, I began to search for her parents, but as before, I found nothing. No one, and I mean *no one,* would take the baby in—not even the Catholic missionary school in the area.

"During that time, I found myself bonding with the baby, and so, I decided to adopt her. Usually, the process takes months or years, but it seemed like everyone was trying to get rid of the baby, and I obtained adoption rights within weeks. She was so beautiful, and I named her Victoria because she always carried herself like a queen. I got her papers taken care of and brought her back home with me. Because I was still an intern, she moved in with my parents while I was in Boston. Since my father is a pastor, I was certain she would have a great upbringing. Then things in Sudan started getting bad, and I decided to return to help the refugees and victims of the massacres there.

"I was there for so long, and I missed my baby, so I decided to send for her to be there with me during my last month. My parents and the people in Sudan warned me not to bring her . . . but . . . I wouldn't listen . . . I was too arrogant, and I thought being an American would protect us both. But, I was wrong . . . I was so wrong . . . my God . . . Victoria . . . I miss her so much! They murdered her in cold blood in that village that day. Raped and shot her down like a dog! And I couldn't do anything to stop them. They made me watch as they raped her repeatedly. Kronte . . . was the ringleader. He was the first to rape her, and the first one to shoot her. I should've listened . . . She would still be alive if I would've just listened."

Daniel began wailing as the pain of his guilt ran down his face. Ayana reached over to hold him, but he pulled away, leaped out of bed, and ran over to the window. Ayana, terrified of what he might do, jumped out of bed after him, grabbing him from behind and wrapping her arms around him. During their sessions, she knew Victoria was a crucial part of the doctor's pain, but she had no idea it was this bad. She wasn't expecting it to be this horrific and devastating. While she held him in her arms, she wept along with him, feeling completely

connected with his pain. There was something important
she needed to talk to him about concerning her past, but
after hearing his confession, she knew this wasn't the
right time. Actually, she didn't know when that time
would ever present itself. It was too bad to put in words.

"Baby, I'm sorry. I'm so very sorry."

The two lovers remained at the window, holding each
other, watching as the snowstorm continued to bombard
the city below . . .

Chapter 16

Getting It Out in the Open

The next morning after having its fun with the city, the blizzard passed on, and the two lovers headed to the airport. Daniel stood at the security checkpoint entrance watching Ayana walk down the corridor toward her terminal until she disappeared around the corner. Sighing heavily, he pulled his leather driving gloves out of his black pea coat and turned to walk out toward the visitor's parking lot. The frigid winds smacked him in the face with a burn that immediately caused him to swear aloud, startling a few people within hearing distance. He quickly lifted the collar on his coat and put on his gloves.

Daniel slowly stepped onto the icy walkway, gritting his teeth with each step, praying that his balance wouldn't betray him. As the frigid air blew across his face, he regretted not bringing a hat along, as his ears immediately began to feel the bite of the below zero wind chill.

The airport was overcrowded with stranded passengers from the day before, so the drop-off lanes for departures were jam-packed with cars and traffic attendants bellowing orders for parked cars to move along or be ticketed. Daniel quickened his pace as he neared the crosswalk leading to the parking lot, but right before he stepped onto the street, a huge blacked-out SUV pulled directly in front of him. The SUV almost knocked the doctor back onto the sidewalk, and he swore loudly, kicking the side of the vehicle. The door of the SUV immediately flung open, and Satu's smiling face appeared. Startled, the doctor took two steps back, trying his best to increase the distance between himself and the large, smiling man in the SUV.

"Doctor Bennett, please don't make this more difficult than it has to be," Satu said, still smiling while holding a gun with a silencer on the nozzle. "Get in the truck now! I promise you that I will not harm you if you don't give me a reason. I'm here as a concerned friend and citizen of Sudan. I feel you haven't received all the facts concerning the case against my general, Kronte."

Daniel looked around to see if anyone was watching this exchange, but everyone seemed to be preoccupied with the chaos unfolding around them at the airport. Swallowing deeply, the doctor decided he had no other choice but to get inside the vehicle. As he moved toward the door, another large man opened the front passenger door and climbed out, waiting for the doctor to get into the vehicle, and then climbed in after him, sitting in the seat beside him.

Satu tapped the ceiling of the SUV, and it sped off toward an unknown destination with the doctor inside. Satu smiled at the doctor while never taking his eyes off him. Once he was sure they were out of the airport, he began to speak . . .

Three hours later, a black SUV pulled up in front of Doctor Daniel Bennett's building. It sat there for about five minutes, and then the back passenger door opened, and Daniel stepped out. His eyes were crimson red, and he seemed burdened and subdued. He didn't even look back as the door closed on the vehicle, and it sped off into rush-hour traffic. Daniel looked up at the top of the building and shook his head. He began moving toward the front entrance but decided against it. He turned to the east and started walking as if in a trance. The doorman, sensing something was wrong, called out to him, but the doctor seemed oblivious. Still concerned, the doorman walked out onto the sidewalk and called out to the doctor again, but Daniel kept walking without acknowledging him. The doorman watched in horror as the doctor walked right out into oncoming traffic, almost getting run down twice, and even with multiple blaring horns and swearing drivers, he never lifted his head or acknowledged anyone. He just continued to walk on the crowded sidewalk like his mind and his body were on autopilot . . .

Manhattan, New York. Three days later . . .

Ayana sat alone in her downtown Manhattan office, staring off into nothingness. Her eyes were glossy, and her body motionless as she just stared at her office door in a trancelike state. It appeared she had a tornado of things twisting inside her head, but actually, there was relative calm where chaos used to reign. The only thought she had was Daniel and how much she loved and cared for him. She'd only been back in New York for a few days, and she was already going through withdrawals. The first night was the hardest, trying to sleep in her own bed again. Although her bed was equipped with the latest in Tempur-Pedic technology, the bed felt like she was lying on bricks and gravel. Only the doctor's warm, naked body and rhythmic breathing could cure her insomnia.

Suddenly, the phone on her desk began ringing, snapping her out of her daydream. She looked at the display on the phone and smiled brightly as she recognized the number that scrolled across the screen.

My baby!

She quickly answered, unable to stop smiling.

"Hello, hey, baby, I missed you so—"

"I'm in New York. I'm staying at the Waldorf. Meet me at eight o'clock tonight at the Bull and Bear. I'll see you then." As quickly as she picked up the phone, Daniel ended the call, leaving Ayana sitting at her desk, completely confused and beside herself. Every nerve in her body went into panic as she felt something terrible had happened, and this dinner date wasn't going to be pleasant at all. She slowly replaced the phone on its base and began rubbing her thighs frantically. Something had changed in Daniel, and she was terrified about what could've triggered that change. Suddenly, things began to take shape in her mind. Meagan called her back to New York because the UN Security Council had discovered that Kronte had several of his soldiers on US soil intimidating potential witnesses, including Dr. Bennett. When Meagan discovered that Satu, Kronte's second-in-command, had been following the doctor, she placed security details on both Ayana and the doctor. So, Meagan knew all about their *extracurricular* activities.

She scolded Ayana, but she seemed to understand their attraction for each other. She called them "two damaged souls" drawn to each other. However, she warned Ayana that things wouldn't end well between them once the doctor learned about her past, and now, somehow, she feared that time was upon them.

At 8:15 p.m., Ayana slowly walked into the elegantly appointed luxury Manhattan restaurant, in an equally elegant mid-thigh black dress that fit her like the passionate embrace of a yearning lover. She wore her dreaded jet-black hair in a ponytail tied with a black and gold metal ring. Her shapely and dark chocolate frame was held high on four-inch black heels that caused an already voluptuous back side to poke out even more. During her journey to the restaurant, she caused a few near fender benders as amazed drivers and pedestrians alike marveled at her appearance. She was stunning, and regardless of how heartbroken and angry the doctor was, he swallowed hard as his pulse quickened when he saw her being led to the table by the waiter.

The waiter pulled out Ayana's chair, and she slowly sat down across from Daniel, smiling while looking him in his eyes, trying to read him and prepare herself for the storm that she knew was coming. Daniel smiled back at her while looking her over hungrily and then turned away, grimacing as if in pain. After seating her, the waiter took their drink orders and quickly left them alone. Trying to lighten the heavy mood at the table, Ayana started a conversation that was light and impersonal.

"This place is beautiful. I've never been here before, but I've heard great things."

Looking around, trying to avoid looking her in her eyes, Daniel pretended to be taking in the luxurious atmosphere. Ayana could tell he was holding something in, and he seemed like a time bomb ready to blow. She felt any more small talk would set him off early, so she got right to it. It didn't make sense for her to sit here and have him waste hundreds of dollars on a meal that neither of them would enjoy.

"Daniel, I am so happy to see you, but I'm not feeling the same from you. So tell me what's up."

Daniel stared at her for about ten seconds without saying a word before he adjusted himself in his seat and began to speak . . .

"I find it hard to explain why I'm here because it's throwing me for a loop. I'm sure you have an idea about what got me on a plane and sitting here with you."

Ayana held her head down and began moving the fork back and forth on the white tablecloth. What she feared would happen was now a reality, and she was hoping a miracle would intervene and give her the strength to deal with losing the man she'd accepted could just be the love of her life. Stalling or pretending wouldn't help her, so she decided to voice the obvious.

"You spoke with Satu, correct?"

Daniel nodded and remained silent.

"And I know he would only speak with you to let you know that a long time ago, I was once the wife of the man that tortured, raped, and murdered your daughter."

Daniel violently slammed both hands down on the table, causing the glasses and tableware to rise off the tablecloth. The loud boom of his hands striking the tabletop startled a few diners, and their waiter quickly made his way to their table in an attempt to divert more disruptions in this upscale establishment. Seeing the waiter getting closer, Daniel looked directly in his eyes and without saying a word, warned the waiter against his plans, stopping him in his tracks. He immediately turned back in the opposite direction. Looking around at everyone staring at him with disgust and fear, the doctor decided he'd better leave soon before someone called the cops. The last thing he needed was a run-in with NYPD.

"I'm not going to ask you why you didn't tell me, because it's obvious. What I *will* say is I don't ever want to see you or hear from you again. I won't be used as a pawn for your personal vendetta against a man that took everything from me. You want him to pay for whatever he did to you . . . well, you're gonna have to do it on your own. Goodbye, Ayana."

Ayana felt the muscles in her chest tighten, and her back started to feel like someone was twisting her spinal cord. She was trying to hold herself together as the words of heartbreak exploded out of Daniel's mouth with a whisper that cut deep into her soul. Then suddenly, she looked up to watch him stand and toss a hundred-dollar bill on the table and start to leave. A war was now raging in her mind: a war between her pride and her emotional dependency on the love she felt for Daniel.

Should I let him leave? Let my anger at the fact he was willing to believe a mass murdering bastard over the woman I let him see, feel, get to know, or do I see things from his view? Would I stay if he did the same to me?

The war continued to wage in her head as he looked at her for one last time before turning away with eyes filling with tears from the pain of betrayal. He moved toward the door, and each step felt like one step closer to his own death. It was hard walking away from her, but he knew if he stayed, she would take advantage of him, and he couldn't bring himself to love the wife of the man that took Victoria from him in the most brutal and grotesque way. As much as it was hurting him to leave and having to face a life of loneliness, he felt he had no other choice. If he couldn't trust her, he couldn't love her.

As he walked out, the waiter walked toward him with his eyes almost bulging out of his head. His mouth was wide open while he pointed at a spectacle that soon caught the entire restaurant's attention.

Daniel turned around to see Ayana standing in front of their table bent over, holding her stomach as if she were experiencing tremendous pain. She was sobbing loudly as she looked at him with eyes filled with regret and anguish. Seeing her like that pulled at him, but he fought his urge to reach out to her. Seeing his uncaring demeanor sent Ayana into a panic. She could no longer hold in the pain she was feeling and began yelling at Daniel about a life so full of pain, she brought the entire restaurant to tears.

"He raped me! I was only 12 years old when Kronte attacked my village, killing my parents, and raping me before claiming me as his wife. I was his prisoner and punching bag for years—forced to lie next to the man that murdered my family."

Seeing everyone's reaction to Ayana's revelation, Daniel tried to stop her, but she continued . . .

"I was 16 years old when he decided to give me as a one-night reward to one of his soldiers, who blew up an entire school filled with children. He wasn't as brutal as Kronte, so for a 16-year-old girl with no experience in life but pain, he was my savior. I fell for him and continued to see him in secret after that night. Then I got pregnant, and Kronte knew it wasn't his because he can't have children due to an injury he received during his early career as a soldier.

"That monster beheaded the father of my child and then chained me up like a dog until it was time for me to have my baby. He let me see my baby one time, then took it away, commanding one of his soldiers to drown it. I don't know if it was a girl or a boy. All I remember is my baby's eyes. So, yes, I have a personal vendetta against Kronte, but my vendetta has nothing to do with you or how much I love you. Now, you know everything! Does it make you trust me more?"

Ayana was now on her knees, brought there by the pain of hearing her ordeal as a child through her own voice, echoing throughout the restaurant, exposing her inner demons with the love of her life and strangers alike, attempting to prevent losing the first man in her life that actually treated her like a human being and not a piece of meat. Daniel stood there, feeling like the biggest asshole money and stupidity can buy. He never considered when Satu told him at gunpoint that Ayana was Kronte's ex-wife, that maybe her holy matrimony wasn't so holy. He was so caught up in his own pain and anger that it never dawned on him that a man who could rape and murder a 5-year-old girl was incapable of being a loving husband. Everyone in the restaurant was now looking at the doctor with disgust and surprise at his attitude toward the beautiful woman weeping on her knees.

He didn't know what to do. He was frozen in place, because he was so wrong for his judgment of Ayana, and he allowed Satu to poison his feelings for her. He didn't know how anyone could come between them with the strong feelings they had for each other. Suddenly, everyone just faded away, and all he could see and hear was Ayana. Daniel couldn't take seeing her that way any longer, so he rushed to her, lifted her in his arms, and carried her out of the restaurant. The frigid night air didn't seem to affect him as he walked down the busy Manhattan street, carrying Ayana in his arms like a weeping child. Ayana kept her head down on his shoulder, refusing to look at anyone who was looking at them as if they were insane. Daniel maintained a stern and rocklike look on his face. His expression startled onlookers and kept any probing questions at bay. They feared this physically intimidating man in the dark grey suit, carrying a grown woman like a baby, may be just as crazy as Ayana looked in his arms.

When Daniel was satisfied they were far enough away from the restaurant, he stood along the curb and began to probe the oncoming traffic for a cab. Usually, when the doctor visited New York City, he would have an exasperating time trying to get a cab, but on this unusually tragic evening, he found himself stepping into the cab with Ayana in less than three minutes. It was a good thing too because Ayana was starting to get heavy, but he felt so horrible, he refused to let her touch the ground again after spending several minutes on her knees back at the restaurant, crying her heart out to him. She deserved better, and he was determined to give it to her if she would still have him because, after tonight, he wouldn't be the least surprised if she decided to break things off with him.

Damn, I really fucked up tonight.

Ayana moved over to the other side of the backseat and leaned her head on the cold and foggy window, looking outside at the city continuing with its nightly chaos, oblivious to her most recent ordeal. As the cab pulled off, Daniel came out of his suit jacket and gently placed it over Ayana's shoulders. Seeing the distance she placed between them, he decided to sit toward the other side of the cab to avoid any more conflicts. He would periodically look over at her, watching her trace her fingers along the window, drawing shapes on the glass like a bored child on a long road trip.

The traffic conditions were considerably light during this holiday shopping season. Once the cab pulled in front of Ayana's high-rise building, Daniel was sure he would be making his return to his hotel room alone and without Ayana in his life. Ayana looked up and noticed she was home, climbed out of the cab, and made her way around to the sidewalk in front of her building. Daniel watched her attentively from the cab's window, filled with regret for how he behaved at the restaurant. He wanted to get out of the cab and wrap his arms around her and never let her go, but he was afraid she would reject him. Looking forward, Daniel instructed the driver to take him back to the Waldorf. Suddenly, he heard a loud tap on the window and saw Ayana yelling at him to get out of the cab.

"Get out! Why are you still in there?"

Stepping out of the cab Daniel, looked completely confused. Seeing his reaction, she forced a smile and tapped on the top of the cab, letting the driver know he could leave. Daniel momentarily watched the cab speed down the street before turning to Ayana, still bewildered with the fact he was standing outside her building instead of heading back to his hotel.

"I got on my knees for you in public. You ain't getting off that easy, Danny. As much as I can't stand you right now, I can't deny how much I need and want you in my life. So let's go upstairs. It's freezing out here."

The elevator ride to her apartment was silent and awkward, and Daniel figured Ayana would unleash the beast once they were behind closed doors. To his surprise, once they were inside her apartment, she pleasantly asked him to have a seat; then she went down her hallway to her bedroom. Seated on her outlandishly comfortable couch,

Daniel looked around, surveying his surroundings. Ayana was from Sudan, and her pride in her African culture bled through every inch of her apartment. There were elaborate African artifacts on almost every wall. The décor throughout the living room accented the cultural theme that seemed to transport Daniel back to Sudan in the middle of Manhattan.

He nodded his head in approval at her eclectic yet tasteful style in decorating her home. He then noticed that there wasn't a television installed on the built-in entertainment area on the largest wall in the living room. Instead, the elaborate and massive area was filled with so many books. It looked like it would explode in a tidal wave of paper and cardboard if another book were forced inside of it. Ayana walked into the living room and stood, silently watching Daniel stare at her wall of books. He was so engulfed in looking over the wall that he hadn't noticed her standing there.

"I love to read."

Her voice startled Daniel, and he jumped like a kid caught with his hand in the cookie jar.

"I see. How many books are there?"

"I would say around four hundred books . . . maybe more, and I think I've read them all at least twice."

"Wow, that's a lot of reading."

"Not to me. I have many other books I would love to read but don't have the time anymore. As more conflicts erupt around the world, my job has become too demanding for me to read as I once did. You are welcome to borrow a few if you want. Just make sure you give them back."

She then walked over to the couch and sat next to him. Sitting this close to each other sent a sexual chain reaction through both of them, and they both inhaled each other's scent at the same time. Noticing the other's reaction, they both straightened up their postures, clearing their throats.

"Daniel, listen, I'm sorry I didn't tell you about my connection with Kronte. When I first met you, I didn't see a reason why I should share that with you. I mean, you were a real piece of work, and I didn't like you very much. Then when we became closer, I wanted to, but I still wasn't sure. The night before I came back to New York, I wanted to tell you everything, but then you told me about Victoria, and as much as I wanted to tell you, I believed it was the wrong time."

"Yeah, telling me that night would've been the wrong move. Now that I think about it, I'm not sure when it would've been the right time to tell me that. Kronte is a very touchy subject for both of us. I had no idea how much pain he's caused you. I do know he's a common denominator, which fuels our connection. I just wished we trusted each other more."

"Me too. I don't know what to do, Danny. I love you so much, but I have so much anger inside me, and tonight, it all came out of me at the restaurant. I'm sorry about embarrassing you like that."

"It's okay. You don't have to apologize. The menu was too expensive anyway. A hundred dollars for a steak? Who raised it? Jesus Christ?"

The two lovers laughed together, which lightened the mood and gave Daniel the confidence to reach over and pull Ayana closer to him. Feeling his arm around her relaxed her immediately. She lifted her legs onto the couch and lay her head on his chest. Ayana inhaled deeply and began to go into detail about the day that changed her life forever, the day she met Kronte "The Terror" Kroma.

"I was born in a village not far from the border that now divides Southern Sudan from Northern Sudan. My father was ex-military, and when things got really bad, he decided to use his military experience to help our village. The people made him chief, and he trained all the men in the village how to fight so that they could protect the village. A few years later, Kronte rose to power, and my father had another evil to fight besides the Northerners. He had over two hundred well-trained villagers at his command, and they were able to keep our village safe, despite the constant attacks and threats from enemies on two fronts.

"Kronte tried several times to destroy my village but was driven back by our fighters. He knew that rich in oil deposits lay under our village, so he convinced my father to have peace talks and broker a land deal that would benefit our village. I can still remember that day as if it were yesterday. I was playing out near the water pump when I saw the dust cloud in the distance, created by Kronte's motorcade of Jeeps. My father, believing Kronte was a man of his word, didn't rally the men to arms, and once Kronte and his men were in the center of our village, they began to slaughter my people like animals.

"They saved my family for last, raping my mother and sisters, forcing my father to watch every agonizing second. They saved the youngest of us for dessert."

"You," Daniel responded, with deep sorrow in his voice.

"Yes, me. Kronte raped me repeatedly and then cut my family's throats one by one, forcing each of us to watch our loved ones choke on their own blood. I can still smell the heavy alcohol on his breath, the stench of it seeping through his pores as he sweated like a horse. I can still see his fat, hairy gut exposed and bouncing from his opened camouflaged shirt as he moved from one person to the next, running the edge of his blade across their necks. Each time they fell to the ground, arms tied behind their backs, eyes wide open and gasping, their blood pouring from their necks, Kronte and his men would celebrate as if someone were taking birthday shots of liquor. When he was done, he turned to me. He looked me over like a hungry beast, trying to decide how he wanted to make me suffer. Suddenly, he smiled at me and instructed his second-in-command at the time and soon-to-be my baby's father, Samir, to take me to his Jeep.

"I was forced to sit in the back of that Jeep, covered in blood, sweat, and Kronte's semen, and watch those animals burn my village to the ground. I thought that day was the worst day of my life, but I was so wrong. Each day after that, for the next seven years, felt like the worst days of my life. I was raped, abused, tortured, and forced to sleep with any man that made Kronte proud. I was looking for a way out, and I believed Samir was it, but after Kronte murdered him for impregnating me, I decided I had to devise my own escape. So, after years of fighting, I pretended I had accepted my role as Kronte's wife and whore. He soon began to train me and take me with him on raids and massacres. I was there the day they slaughtered all those Christian people that came from the US to help."

"I remember that! That was years ago. They said they couldn't find the bodies or something along those lines. What was the televangelist's name that led that group? Bill . . . Will—"

"Fellows. His name was William Fellows," Ayana replied, sinking deeper into Daniel's arms, hoping his embrace could squeeze away the shame and guilt she felt running through her. "He killed all those people to prove a point to me about whose god was more powerful. I was raised Catholic, and Kronte was brought up in the teachings of Islam, and he hated that I held on to my—"

"Wait, Kronte is a Muslim?" Daniel asked, his voice becoming loud and aggressive.

"Don't ever call Kronte that!" Ayana protested, sitting up and looking Daniel directly in his eyes. "If there was ever a poster child for the term 'infidel,' Kronte is it. I've known many Muslim men and women in my life, and none of them are as sadistic and evil as Kronte. He may call on the name of Allah, he may pray toward Mecca and wear the attire of a practitioner of Islam, but he is *not* a Muslim. He is a demon, plain and simple. And just in case you *are* wondering, I am not a Muslim either."

Surprised by her reaction, Daniel apologized, kissing her softly on the lips. The tension and anger immediately subsided and dissipated like mist in the wind when she felt his lips on hers. She smiled with her eyes closed and returned to her original position, wrapped in his arms.

"He tortured and mutilated those people, forcing them to pray to Jesus while he and his men chopped them to pieces with their machetes. He mocked God *and* my religion that day. After that, I knew it was only a matter of time before he would turn his madness on me and murder me in my sleep. So, one night, during one of the many drunken sex orgies they would have after a successful massacre, I drugged him and his guards and escaped. I ran all night long, never taking a moment to rest. He searched for me for weeks as I jumped from village to village until I was able to convince the British Embassy to take me in. I worked in the embassy as a maid for a few months before getting the opportunity to leave Sudan and live in England.

"During my time in England, I underwent extensive psychological treatment to repair the damage that Kronte had done to my mental stability. Only the hand of God and my faith could've brought me through it. There were many times I wanted to take my own life and end it, but something always gave me hope. But it's been years since I've had any hope, until now. I have hope again, and my hope is tied to my love for you, and I don't want to lose it."

Feeling his heart breaking inside his chest as he listened to Ayana, Daniel began to understand just how strong and special the woman that lay in his arms was. There was no doubt in his mind that he would never find another woman like her, and he made a promise to himself to cherish her always. The two lovers continued to talk until the sun rose over the Manhattan skyline, revealing the most devastating details of their ordeals in Sudan and the years afterward.

Chapter 17

Unhappy Holidays

A couple of weeks later, Ayana and Daniel were standing at the door of his parents' Beverly, Illinois, home. Ayana was immediately impressed by the large, majestic, grey-stoned home that Daniel's parents lived in. It was elevated above the street on a small hill surrounded by a well-maintained stone stairway leading up to the large, dark mahogany front door. They were both nervous as Daniel rang the doorbell and waited to see which one of his family members would open the door. He silently hoped it wasn't his loud, foul-mouthed sister, Lisa. She made it a lifelong purpose to stay "turned up" at all times. Within seconds of him ringing the doorbell, the sound of the locks being unlatched echoed outside, and then the seemingly celestial smile of Daniel's mother greeted them. Ayana's mouth almost dropped to the ground as she realized where the doctor inherited his incredible looks.

Mrs. Diana Bennett was a dark, mocha-colored woman who was short in stature, yet a beautiful titan. Although she was an older woman, her skin was smooth and vibrant. She wore her hair in a natural, large, curly Afro with a headband. Although she was in full holiday cooking attire, she still was an intimidating sight, and

Ayana immediately understood why the doctor adored her skin tone.

"There's my baby! Get in here," Mrs. Bennett screamed while reaching up around her much taller son's neck. Daniel lifted her in the air as she yelled, playfully hitting him on his chest.

"Put me down before your father comes out here and jacks you up."

Then from inside the house, a deep and commanding voice could be heard saying, "I know that boy ain't lifting my woman in the air again!"

Daniel smirked and waved playfully in the direction of his father's voice.

"Mom, this is—"

"Ayana? We know who she is. You can't stop talking about her. Welcome, Princess, and Happy Thanksgiving."

"Thank you, Mrs. Bennett, for having me and Happy Thanksgiving to you as well."

Hearing Ayana's voice and accent sent an uncomfortable chill through Diana. She seemed to momentarily lose her place in time, before coming back to herself and ushering them into the family room where everyone else was playing board and card games. Ayana looked around the house and smiled at how elegantly it was furnished and decorated. It was the definition of what the American dream was all about. The family room was large and well lit, with a massive flat-screen television on the far side of the room that surprisingly wasn't on. Usually, Ayana's experience on Thanksgiving was food, family, and football, but she soon learned that in the Bennett household, the television stayed off, and the family enjoyed other forms of entertainment to pass the time while waiting for Thanksgiving dinner to be served.

The room was teeming with excitement with children and adults laughing and having a good time. When Diana walked into the room with Daniel and Ayana, the excitement quickly subsided as everyone stopped what they were doing to watch the attractive couple. Ayana forced a smile. She felt very uneasy as the entire family seemed to be looking her over, examining her appearance and maybe even deciding if she were the right woman for their Daniel. The silent standoff seemed to drag on until Lisa jumped up from the card table, almost knocking it over with her arms outstretched, yelling her brother's name.

"Danny! Come here, big bro!" she yelled loudly before throwing her arms around him and embracing him tightly. Then without missing a beat, she reached over, yelling Ayana's name and repeated the same embrace and greeting.

"Y'all need to stop acting like y'all ain't seen one of Danny's girlfriends before," she scolded her family.

"Not at Thanksgiving dinner we haven't," Daniel's little brother, Byron replied, while covering his mouth playfully. The entire room erupted in roaring laughter at Byron's comment, and suddenly, the fun-filled atmosphere returned to the room.

Hmmm, I'm the first woman he's brought home for the holidays? Nice.

As if she were looking at an older clone of Daniel, a man that was clearly his father got up from his large leather recliner and walked over to them. He wobbled a bit before gaining his balance and continued strolling toward them. Daniel's father was just as tall as his son but had a much lighter skin complexion. Even though their skin complexions didn't match, Ayana could still notice all of Daniel's facial features reflecting on his father's face. He was an attractive, older man that appeared to be in his early to mid sixties, but despite his age, appeared to be in great shape, devoid of a belt buckle hiding mounds of flesh most men his age carried around like a badge of honor.

"Welcome, Ayana, to our home. God bless you, my sister. I'm Donald, the father of the heathen standing next to you," his father said, before embracing her like his own daughter. When he was done, he turned to his son and looked him up and down while leaning away with his arms down at his sides. Daniel, in return, took a step back and gave him the same look. Both men appeared serious and unhappy with the other, and Ayana looked on, worried that something was seriously wrong, but then his father laughed and wrapped his arms around Daniel.

"Get over here, boy. Don't get too grown. You know I'll still take a rod to that behind."

"Yeah, right, 'Pastor Pacification.' Good luck with that. I'm not little anymore," he responded, still hugging his father.

"Whatever, Danny. The only thing you'll do is run like you did when you were younger. That boy could never take an ass—oops, I mean butt whooping," Lisa said, while playfully covering her mouth. "He would always take off running. Oh, and, Daddy, don't start acting like you were the warden of Englewood back then. How many times did you whoop any of us? Once . . . maybe . . . but that little firecracker in the kitchen, Mrs. Bennett, aka NYPD Blue, aka One Time? Now, *that* woman would beat us like she had a badge *and* warrant. You would never believe a person so small had that much butt-whooping talent deep inside them. She was the real deal Holyfield back then," Lisa teased, while she returned to her seat.

Mrs. Bennett, hearing her name and Lisa's recollection of their childhood, ran into the family room with a cook's spoon and potholder in her right hand. She gave Lisa a nasty look, and with eyes wide with surprise, began to defend herself.

"Lisa, stop lying to that woman! I didn't beat y'all like that! Actually, I didn't beat *you* enough with your wayward behind."

All of her children looked at each other and smiled before responding, "Yeah, you did, Momma."

"But I agree you should've got Lisa more," added Byron.

"Whatever, Byron. You were a runner, just like Danny."

"Heck, yeah! What you think? I'ma just lie there and take it like you did?" Byron responded.

Throwing her hands in the air, Diana grunted and stormed out of the family room, mumbling something under her breath no one could understand.

Daniel watched his mother leave the room before taking Ayana's hand and walking her around to meet everyone there. He started with his siblings. Terry, who was the oldest brother, followed in order by Paulette, Byron, and Lisa. All the boys in the family were very attractive men, with their mother's skin complexion and a mixture of both of their parents' features. Byron looked the most like his mother, and Terry, of course, looked more like their father. The girls, on the other hand, possessed their father's lighter skin complexion, their mother's facial features, and "brick house" body structure. Lisa was the odd ball of the girls, because she was just as tall as her brothers, with curves that would cause any man to crash and burn. Her voice didn't match her model-like appearance as it bellowed and traveled far and loud every time she opened her mouth.

Despite the glaring physical differences between the siblings, they were still a very close-knit family with roots in the Baptist church before their father decided to break away from the traditional religious practices and established his own nondenominational ministry. On the surface, it would appear that the family prospered from his ministry, but unlike other church leaders, their father didn't take one cent from the donations from his "prayer warriors." Long before he began his ministry, he was a successful businessman, with several construction companies and major roadway contracts for the states of Illinois, Iowa, and Indiana. The fruits of his labors paid off big dividends in the form of a beautiful home in a prominent south suburban neighborhood, five college graduates, all with great-paying careers, seven grandchildren, a beautiful forty-year marriage, and a huge, ultramodern prayer facility that was paid for in full.

They were a proud family, and Ayana could feel their love and pride flow in the room like an electrical charge. After meeting the remaining family members, Ayana and Daniel walked into the kitchen to speak with Diana, who was stirring a large bowl of mashed potatoes vigorously.

"Mom, how many times do I have to tell you to use the electric mixer we got you years ago for Christmas?"

"A lot more! I like to stir it myself. It's how my mother taught me, and I'm gonna keep the tradition going. Besides, it keeps my arms nice and toned," Mrs. Bennett responded, smiling.

"Now, get out of my kitchen and show her around the house, silly. Dinner will be ready soon."

Daniel gave Ayana a very detailed tour of the house, and he would periodically take her to a secluded corner and kiss her passionately, and then move on to the next room. Ayana noticed that the house was much larger than the exterior revealed. Eventually, they came to a large wooden door that seemed to suck the joy out of Daniel. He stood there staring at the door without moving, and when Ayana looked at him, he seemed to be holding his breath.

"Baby, what's in there?"

Daniel seemed oblivious to Ayana's question, and suddenly, a large hand landed hard on his shoulder, startling him out of his daydream.

"Still jumpy, huh, son?" Mr. Bennett joked while squeezing his son's shoulder playfully.

Then both of them stood at the door, appearing afraid to open it. Ayana feared some kind of monster or ghost was trapped behind that door from their reaction. Mr. Bennett snapped out of his own thoughts and moved to open the door.

"What's in there?" Ayana asked, still worried about how they behaved.

"It's a study and the family's history. Every picture we could find of our ancestors and all the generations since. We try to keep a visual account of our family tree so that we don't forget what was done to get us here, and what needs to be done to get us further."

Ayana smiled with pride at his response. She was really impressed with Daniel's family and secretly imagined being a permanent part of it. The door opened with an uncharacteristic squeal that seemed out of place from the rest of the well maintained home. Walking into the room felt like walking into a time warp. All the furniture in the room seemed to be at least a hundred years old, with every wall covered in many framed pictures. A large wooden desk stood in front of a window with a small couch to the left of it. The room smelled like old wood and an earthy-smelling fragrance similar to frankincense and myrrh.

Ayana's eyes were wide with wonder as she looked around the room like an excited little girl in a toy store filled with her favorite dolls. Smiling at her response, Mr. Bennett reached for her hand and led her toward the largest wall in the room.

"Start from here and then go to your right to see our family history, from hundreds of years ago up to today."

Nodding and smiling brightly, Ayana began to look over each framed picture and photo. Daniel watched her, smiling as she jumped from one picture to another. There were pictures of family members dressed in yesteryear's fashion. The color combinations and facial expressions on their faces made her giggle. Then she would move on to the next picture, and her eyes would widen when she looked at another picture and then turn, looking at both men, comparing them to a family twin from long ago. Soon, the smile on Daniel's face disappeared as Ayana moved through time until she came to a wall of photos he spent years trying to forget.

After Victoria's death, the family dedicated a large portion of one of the walls to her and all the memories. Instead of starting from the time she was a baby until her untimely death, they decided to go backward in time in an attempt to better deal with her passing.

Ayana paused when she realized who she was looking at, and her heart rate quickened immediately. Daniel's description of Victoria, although detailed, did her no justice whatsoever. She was a gorgeous and vibrant young girl, and looking over all the pictures, Ayana noticed she was smiling in every one, including a picture of her on the ground next to her bike after falling and scraping her knee. Her dark African skin glowing in the sunlight on the picture caused her beautiful smile to jump off the image in almost 3D resolution. Ayana tried not to let her emotions get the best of her. She moved through each picture as Victoria got younger and younger, and then, before her eyes, was the earliest picture of her. It was the largest picture of them all. It was a black-and-white photo of just her head. She was facing the camera, exposing a toothless smile so bright, it seemed to bring the sun into the room, although it was dark outside.

Her smile was so beautiful, intoxicating, and inviting that Ayana just stared at it for over a minute, before moving her gaze toward the girl's eyes. Daniel was now seated on the couch next to his father, looking toward the floor, too afraid to look at the pictures that would cause him to relive the love and loss of Victoria. Then his father tapped him on his arm and pointed toward Ayana, who was now on her knees shaking uncontrollably. She seemed to be under a spell brought on by pain so deep that she didn't appear in control of her own body. Daniel took a closer look and noticed the largest picture of Victoria was no longer on the wall. She was holding it in her arms close to her chest. He jumped up and ran over to her side, trying to pry the picture from her grasp, but she wouldn't let it go. Mr. Bennett slowly stood up and placed his hand over his mouth as he watched Ayana fall deeper into her clutch of pain.

"Son . . . son . . . Danny! Stop! Let her be."

Daniel turned toward his father with rage in his eyes. No one was allowed to take Victoria's pictures off the wall, not even the woman he loves, and he wanted her picture back on the wall.

"Son, relax . . . Talk to her. Softly . . . Get her attention."

Daniel didn't want to be gentle. He wanted Victoria back on the wall and out of Ayana's arms. However, he knew his father was right, so he began to whisper Ayana's name while gently rubbing her arm. Soon, her sporadic breathing and shaking stopped. She turned and looked Daniel, and tears immediately poured out of her eyes like rivers of sorrow.

"My baby."

"Huh? Ayana, what are you talking about?"

"Victoria, she's my baby."

"Wait . . . are you saying . . . that? Oh no! No, it can't be!"

"I'll never forget her eyes. Never," she screamed.

Daniel collapsed, falling on his back, weeping uncontrollably next to Ayana. Soon, their weeping grew louder, until they were both wailing, causing everyone in the house to come rushing into the study, looking on in amazement. Seeing his son in so much pain got the best of Mr. Bennett, and he flopped down on the couch, placed his head in his hands, and let his emotions flow. Diana stood frozen, unable to decide if she should console her husband or her baby and his girlfriend. It was too much to handle, and she started to cry herself, overcome by the sorrow invading the room.

It took the family almost an hour to calm Daniel and Ayana, but once they were calm, Mr. Bennett decided to speak to both of them alone in his office on the other side of the house. Ayana was still clutching Victoria's picture in her arms, hugging it as if her baby were actually there.

After gathering himself, Mr. Bennett sat across from them and began to speak.

"How is it that neither of you knew that Victoria was also Ayana's daughter?"

Despite his hesitation, Daniel decided to tell his father the details of their relationship and all the drama that transpired after his "talk" with Satu. After he finished, Mr. Bennett got up from his chair and paced around the room for a few moments before returning to his seat.

"You know, when I was much younger, I had the pleasure to meet Malcolm X twice— once when he was at the pinnacle of his career with the Nation of Islam, and again when he returned from Mecca. Being a die-hard Baptist, that was a miracle in itself, but my father was a supporter of Malcolm X, even though they disagreed on a few topics. The Malcolm X I met before his trip to Mecca and the one afterward were two entirely different men—both great men with a fire for justice and greatness but with different motivations.

"The militant Malcolm was steadfast in his beliefs, and he had very little tolerance for anything that didn't come out of the mouth of Elijah Muhammad. However, the Malcolm X I met later on was a changed man, and he told me something that stuck with me, even to this day. He said a man has to be humble enough to unlearn a lie in order to find himself, no matter how old he is or respected by his people. Son, I am saying the same thing to you. You have to unlearn the lie that has taken hold of your life since your ordeal in Africa."

"And what lie is that?"

"God no longer exists after Victoria's passing."

Ayana turned and looked at Daniel, surprised at what Mr. Bennett was saying about him. She knew he wasn't a religious man, but she had no idea his ordeal turned him into an atheist.

"Regardless of what may happen in this world, God must always be the center of our lives. Always. Before I turned my life and beliefs around to a doctrine of tolerance, love, and understanding, I would've never accepted my son as an atheist. Now, he's still a heathen, but he's *my* heathen, and as a man of God, I must humble myself to understand the pain of those that may not understand as I do and lose faith. What you endured over there was the definition of hell on earth. Anyone, and I do mean anyone, would question God's existence after experiencing that kind of evil. To be honest, I can't say if faced with a similar situation that my faith wouldn't waver.

"No one knows what someone would do in a situation unless they've lived through it, and as a person striving toward righteousness, I must show patience and empathy for that individual. That's what tolerance is. Doesn't mean we accept deviant behavior and make excuses for people's wicked lifestyles. It means although we may not agree with it, we try to understand the root of such behavior. The problems of your relationship, Ayana, are deeply rooted in my son's lack of faith in God and humanity. When you also consider the fact your relationship started with sex, you can see why things aren't open and transparent between you two. One minute, you can't stand each other, and the next, you are rolling around in the sheets, professing your love for each other.

"That isn't love. It's lust, attempting to cover up the pain you both feel in a physical connection. Because if it were true love, you would've discovered that the two of you had a connection much deeper than you could possibly comprehend. With knowledge comes trust. No relationship can last and grow built on lies, sex, and secrets. As the man, son, you have to be an example of strength to your woman. There isn't a stronger man than a humble man. It takes great strength to admit you are wrong and correct those wrongs. That level of humility will inspire your woman to be just as strong as her man.

"I don't subscribe to the belief that a woman is a weaker vessel than her man, and seeing the strength that's inside Ayana proves my point. She is an incredibly strong woman to endure everything she's gone through and still find a reason to smile. Very few people have that kind of inner strength. You two are also each other's strength *and* weakness, and you have to right this ship before it sinks. There is no doubt in my mind that you and Ayana are meant to be together. Only God could bring you two together with neither of you knowing of the other's connection to Victoria. There is hope for this relationship, but it's time for you two to stop being afraid and let this love flourish. Now, I could say stop fornicating, but I'm a realist, and I know making you promise that would be inviting you to lie to my face. I *will* say this . . . It's time for you two to start dating each other because what you've been doing *wasn't* dating.

"Son, I'm proud to see how far you've come. I've always been so proud of you, but since you've come back from Africa, I don't know the man I raised any longer. It's time for you to accept God and love back into your life. Because if not, this relationship won't work, and that will be another tragedy you can add to your anger against God."

Mr. Bennett then got up and left them both in the office without saying another word.

Ayana exhaled deeply and without looking at Daniel, asked, "Did you love her? Did you love her like she was your own?"

"I loved her like she was my life and the only thing that mattered. She *was* my own, and I'm sorry I couldn't keep her safe. I'm so sorry."

"You did your best, and it wasn't your fault. None of this is. I want to thank you for giving my baby happiness and love for the short time she was on this earth. For that, I am eternally grateful."

Daniel remained silent as he replayed his father's advice to both of them. Everything his father said was true, even the most hurtful parts, and Daniel knew that unless he regained his faith, he would lose Ayana, and there was only one way he felt he could accomplish it. He turned to Ayana and held her so that he could look her directly in the eyes and said, "I'm going to testify."

Chapter 18

Prepare for the Worst . . .

A week later, Daniel and Ayana traveled to New York to meet with Meagan and update her on Daniel's decision to testify. After briefing Meagan on all the details she wasn't aware of, Ayana held Daniel's hand tightly as they sat next to each other facing Meagan. Meagan sat behind her desk, trying to calm her nerves and hold back the long list of obscenities she wanted to blast out at both of them.

Finally, calming herself to an acceptable level, Meagan decided it was time to break the silence in the room.

"You two have created a heaping helping of holiday shit, and you could've ruined this entire investigation with your lack of self-control. However, regardless of the unprofessional nature you two went about it, we still got the desired outcome and more. Doctor Bennett, I want to thank you for making this sacrifice to bring that monster to justice, and please make no mistake, this *is* going to be a huge sacrifice.

"This trial is going to be a media circus, and now that we have an American that can testify and place him at the scene of a massacre, the madness will intensify quite swiftly. As soon as word gets out, your life will no longer be yours. You will become public property, and any slipup or actions that seem biased will make prosecuting Kronte more difficult than it's already gonna be. So, I know you two know what's coming next, right?"

Daniel and Ayana nodded together. They already assumed that Meagan would advise them both to refrain from their "extracurricular" activities until the trial concluded. Meagan shook her head while looking away from them. Although they seemed aware of what she was about to say, she decided to tell them anyway. Just to make sure everyone was on the same page.

"You two are going to have to stop seeing each other romantically until the trial is over. With a trial this big and so much at stake, I can't tell you that it will be over quickly. Usually, trials like this can last anywhere between six months to six years. So—"

After hearing the time frame, Daniel's heart and the lower region went into panic mode, and he nearly leaped out of his chair.

"Now, wait a minute! I understand what's at stake here, but telling me I have to wait six years to be with the woman I love is pushing it!"

Meagan had prayed silently that neither of them would object to her demands, allowing all those obscenities that were so eager to be let loose into the world to be locked away in her mind. But the doctor's loud protest sent her mental controls on a tailspin, and her lips trembled as she tried to hold back her anger.

"Doctor Bennett, please calm down," she warned.

"No, I will *not* calm down! Who do you think you are? We are not children. You can't tell us when and where we can see each other."

At that very moment, Meagan had decided she'd had enough and jumped out of her chair, her voice blaring through the air.

"If you would stop thinking about your dick for once in your life, you would see why you two can't see each other! You are testifying for more than your own personal desire to see justice served to that monster. You are testifying to prevent that man from going free and intensifying his efforts to eradicate an entire nation of people! Now, I'm a white woman, an American white woman at that, and judging by this country's history, I shouldn't even be involved in African affairs. I shouldn't even care if Africans kill each other, but I do! This man has murdered tens of thousands of men, women, and children throughout his campaign in that region.

"His influence and arrogance are so great that he had the gall to send his second-in-command on US soil to intimidate you. We captured Kronte by sheer luck, and I fear if he goes free because you can't keep it in your pants, we won't get another opportunity. So, excuse me if I don't have sympathy for your temper tantrum because you won't be getting any more pussy from Ayana during this trial. I couldn't care less. Masturbate—hell, get a hooker if it's that bad! Under no circumstances are you two to see each other romantically or casually until this is over. I would hate for both of you to lose such great careers over something as basic as sex. If you can't wait for her, Doctor, then you don't deserve her. Now, if we can move on, there is something else I need from both of you."

Daniel's mouth and eyes were wide open as he sat there, listening to Meagan read him like a children's book. A small grin developed on Ayana's face as she gave Daniel the "side eye" wondering what would drive him to act out like that. Ayana knew just how foul Meagan's mouth could be, and she knew not to provoke it. She wasn't happy about not being able to see the doctor until the trial was over, but she understood what was at stake. She knew that if Kronte went free, he would try to get rid of both of them to make sure no one with credibility could testify against him in the future. It was date nights, orgasms, and arguments . . . or life. The choice for Ayana was easy, but apparently, it wasn't for Daniel. After Meagan's tirade, things started to sink into the doctor's head, and he retreated within himself as he slumped into his chair.

He wanted to defend himself and make it known that his concern wasn't the lack of lovemaking with Ayana, but his fear that with her away from him, the anxiety of the upcoming trial and a trip back to Africa might make his nightmares return and be more dangerous than before. However, he knew it wouldn't make a difference. Meagan had already labeled him, and no words would change her view of him, only actions, so he decided to remain quiet and listen to what else she had to say.

Seeing that the doctor was now hearing her instead of just listening, Meagan smiled and calmly sat down in her chair.

"For us to place Kronte at the time and location of Victoria's death, we will need you to be as detailed as possible. Don't leave anything out. The more confident you sound, the more the council will believe your testimony. I understand from your testimony with the American Consulate, Doctor, you claimed that Kronte also participated in Victoria's rape, correct?"

Hearing Victoria's name in the same sentence as Kronte shook the doctor to the core, and he braced himself for a roller-coaster ride of anger and pain as he tried to find the words to respond. Ayana, on the other hand, wasn't so reserved, and she immediately started weeping. Meagan's emotions began to get the best of her, seeing her friend in so much pain. She wanted to stop, but she knew they didn't have much time, and she needed both of them focused.

"Listen, I know this is difficult for both of you, but without your detailed accounts of that day, it's going to be hard trying to prove you were there. Even if you, Doctor, are an American."

"What does my nationality have to do with my credibility?" the doctor asked while looking down at the floor, afraid to lift his head and see Ayana overcome with grief. He wanted to be stronger for her, but he knew he would lose that battle if he caught just one glimpse of her in such a state.

"The International Court of Justice feels testimonies from foreign nationals of Sudan are more credible than those that are from the locals. Call it prejudice or unfair bias. It's been a thorn in our side for years, but this time, that prejudice could, in fact, help our case against Kronte. But your relationship with Victoria as her adopted father and Ayana being her mother can damage our case if we don't have other hard evidence. I know DNA was taken after the incident, but forensics have advanced since then, and we need to employ all the advancements at our disposal to take that man down. Kronte's lawyers will try to discredit your verbal testimony by using Victoria's murder against you, saying that you want someone to pay for her death, and Kronte is the most famous face you could find.

"And make no mistake, they *will* find out Ayana is her mother, and if the two of you continue to see each other, it will look even worse. You have to understand that

Kronte's so-called freedom revolution is a $600 million a year weapons business for some of the most powerful arms dealers in the world. That's a huge account for them, and they won't let him go down without a fight. There are also rumors of Kronte working with some very powerful people that have their eyes on the oil under that country. It's believed that all the land that he's taken from the villagers he's massacred has massive oil veins running under them."

"How anyone could sell that man weapons, knowing what he's doing with them is beyond me," Daniel stated.

"It's because no one really cares about the plight of Africa. As long as his weapons kill Africans, no one cares. Yeah, some celebrities may make a documentary, donate money that only 15 percent of it will actually go to the people, or give a shout-out while they accept an award, but that's it. Why do you think no one pursued him after he attempted to kill you and killed Victoria? Remember, Victoria was an American citizen too, because you adopted her. He attacked two US citizens, leaving one dead, but just like you, she is a person of color, and the international community doesn't take your suffering seriously."

Daniel looked up at Meagan with his eyebrows crumbled and head slightly turned. He couldn't believe the words that were coming out of her mouth. A white woman was saying things that most white people would deny, giving validation to many people of color's gripe about how those in power disregard their suffering and the injustices they face daily. Meagan noticed his confusion and giggled. She knew her statement would more than likely catch him off guard, but she meant every word.

"Doctor, I can't spearhead this trial if I don't accept what's real and what's fantasy. I refuse to lend my intellect and talents to the notion that racism is dead and a conspiracy theory like Elvis and Area 51. Racism is definitely alive and well all over the world, and the fact that genocide is allowed to continue in Africa without UN intervention is a clear indication of that. Maybe this trial and Kronte's conviction could help change that. Maybe when we present everything and then bring you into the equation, people will listen and take notice. I know more than likely they will notice temporarily and then move on after all the media coverage dies down, but for once, I would like the world to take things like this seriously. Just once, it would be an amazing thing. However, I know more than likely, it's an impossible dream. But a girl can dream, can't she?"

Daniel shrugged his shoulders, still looking down at the floor and rubbing his hand on Ayana's back, trying to console her.

"I know this is a lot," Meagan continued. "But we need both of your permissions to continue. We need more forensic evidence from Victoria."

Daniel and Ayana remained silent, neither of them able to open their mouths and give Meagan permission to disturb Victoria's grave. It was a horrible decision to make, and neither wanted to be the first to speak. Seeing their state of mind, Meagan decided to leave the office and give them time to decide. As she began to move from behind her large desk, Ayana nodded silently while squeezing Daniel's hand so tightly that he could feel his bones in his hand grinding together. Gritting his teeth from the sudden sharp pain, he looked over just in time to see her nodding her head in agreement. He wanted to scream "No" and go on an office-destroying rampage. He wanted to curse Kronte, God, and everyone that remained alive while his baby girl lay lifeless in the ground. He wanted to do so many destructive things, but he decided against all of them. Instead, he closed his eyes slowly and nodded his head in agreement. Meagan watched them both in unified pain, and it broke her heart. She couldn't even imagine the pain and confusion going through them.

She also admired their bravery. She knew what she was asking wasn't an easy request, but it was necessary. Before leaving the office, she wanted to ask them if they wanted to be present during the exhumation but decided against it. She didn't want to upset either of them any further. It was going to be a long, hard road ahead, and the last thing she wanted was to throw another boulder on their shoulders.

A few weeks later, Daniel's life immediately began to tailspin into a media madhouse. As soon as the word got out about the American doctor that would be testifying against one of the world's most notorious warlords, his phone became a never-ending portal of talk-show invitations and interview requests. It'd gotten so bad that Meagan appointed a publicist for him. At first, the attention was overwhelming, but soon it became his new normal, and sometimes he found himself enjoying it. Meagan and Ayana made sure they coached him on how to answer or not answer certain questions concerning his intentions and expectations on the upcoming trial.

Christmas and New Year's came and went. Daniel was preparing himself to go on his first nationally televised talk show, with one of America's most popular talk-show hosts. It was a very important interview because it would be the first time the world would get to hear about his ordeal in Sudan and his life after his miraculous recovery. With all the media attention, Daniel was able to cope with his emotional and physical torture of not having Ayana around. His only form of contact with her was either through email or the brief, occasional, "How are you holding up?" phone calls from her. He wasn't sure if Ayana was suffering as much as he was. He was grateful that the nightmares didn't return, but his bed was now a soft desert of loneliness, and he decided to sleep on the couch until he could get used to sleeping alone again.

Meagan advised him that a lot was riding on this interview, and he needed to campaign for the public's sympathy and outrage about the events that led up to the death of the young American-Sudanese girl. The week-end before the interview, Daniel and Timothy decided to have a guy's night out on the town to lighten the mood and maybe get Daniel to relax. Daniel didn't want to be bothered, feeling exposed and out in the open for more media ambushes or insincere attention from people that simply wanted to get their few seconds in the spotlight. But Daniel owed Timothy so much, and he felt it might be fun to go out with his friend and have a good time like they used to.

It'd been months since Daniel had been out in the nightclub scene, and it seemed like they were opening new clubs just as fast as they were closing schools in the city of Chicago. Timothy decided they'd go to one of the newest clubs in the city that boasted a more sophisti-cated crowd than the run-of-the-mill twerk factories that dotted the nightlife landscape. Sitting at the bar, Daniel took in the ultramodern décor of the club. The sounds of the mid-'90s and early 2000s music blasted through the speakers, while the LED lights changed color according to the intensity of the bass and the mood of the music. Nodding his head while forming a slight smile on his face, Daniel looked on in satisfied approval.

Timothy chose a great spot.

Before long, both men were laughing and bobbing their heads to the music at the bar and having a great time, while the bartender kept their glasses filled with their choice of drinks. The club was full of women who seemed eager to dance to the incredible music the DJ was spinning on his electronic turntables. Looking at Daniel smiling while he watched everyone on the dance floor have a great time, Timothy grinned, satisfied that so far, the night was a success. He hadn't had much time to spend with his friend. He could tell Daniel was changing, and he was praying that the change wouldn't be so drastic that he couldn't recognize his friend of over a decade.

"Danny, it's great to hang with you, bruh."

"Likewise. This is a great spot, dude. You picked a winner," Daniel responded, yelling over the loud music.

"I'm glad you like it. Now, get out there and dance! I didn't bring you out here to sit at the bar. There are a lot of fine-ass women out there, dude, and a few of them been staring you down. You should go out there and see what's up."

Daniel shook his head, unwilling even to entertain the idea of bumping and grinding on a woman that wasn't Ayana. Timothy, seeing his reluctance to go out on the dance floor, placed his hand on his shoulder and shook his head in disapproval.

"Dude, I'm not trying to hear no sad stories about your lovesick puppy ass. Get out there and have fun, bruh. Tomorrow, you go on national TV, and after that, you may not get a chance to do this again, because you will be a local celebrity. I know none of these women out here can hold a candle to Ayana. I'm not asking you to sleep with any of them. I'm just saying go dance."

"Fuck that shit! They're dancing like they're fucking," Daniel responded, laughing uncomfortably. "I don't need the temptation. It's been a minute."

"It's been a minute. Maaaaan, don't get me started. You've only been without sex for a couple of months. I had to endure an extended period of 'Sahara Dick.' So, excuse me if your slight drought doesn't move me. Get your ass out there before I go get the ugliest bitch in here and tell her you want to dance with her."

Danny turned, shocked at Timothy's threat.

"Oh no, you wouldn't!"

"Try me!"

"Aw, dude, that's fucked up," Daniel complained while he took one last sip of his drink and stood from the bar stool.

"Call it what you want, but I see your ass getting out on that floor."

Daniel slowly moved out on the dance floor, and after taking a few steps, he felt a warm yet familiar hand firmly grab hold of his. He looked down at the dark, coffee-colored hand and looked up to see Ayana's beautiful and vibrant smile. His heart almost jumped out of his chest as he smiled brightly like a kid at Christmas, looking at a tree surrounded with an endless number of elegantly wrapped gifts. Ayana placed her index finger over his lips and pulled him close to her and into the dense dancing crowd.

Timothy smiled brightly once he noticed his plan worked flawlessly and turned around to the bartender to order another drink. He wasn't here to dance or have a good time. He was here to watch his friend's back and make sure anyone's prying eyes that might recognize the lovesick couple wouldn't disturb their night.

Time paused as the two lovers passionately embraced, dancing to the music. Their clothes soaked with sweat from the heat of the crowd and their passionate choreography. They refused to look away, afraid to lose one second in each other's eyes. Neither of them spoke a word as they continued to dance and kiss. Daniel missed everything about her, but he absolutely missed her perfectly rounded backside, and he caressed and massaged it like a man caught in a lustful trance. Her skin was so soft. She smelled like the fragrance of heaven, and he secretly prayed that he could make love to her tonight. He needed to be inside of her and feel her thighs trembling around his head as he devoured every inch of her.

Ayana saw the lustful look he was giving her, and she smiled while biting her lip. She didn't know how this night would go, but she was excited that so far it was going perfectly. Being this close to him and feeling him caress her and hold her close to his body caused her to tremble like a deep-sea earthquake, and she didn't care who caught them. She wanted him right here and now. Pulling him away from the dance floor, Ayana began to lead him toward the back of the club where the bathrooms were. Usually, in a club this packed, there would be a line leading into the bathrooms, but it seemed fate was working in their favor, and there wasn't one soul standing outside waiting to use the facilities. Forcefully opening the men's bathroom, Ayana stepped inside with Daniel in tow. He quickly turned and locked the door behind him, and before turning off the lights, he noticed the bathroom was uncannily clean and well decorated.

The darkness momentarily startled Ayana, but before she could jump, she felt Daniel spin her around, forcing her body up against the cold, tiled wall. The doctor was forceful, and his aggression should've frightened her, but surprisingly, it excited her, and she immediately felt the moisture of her excitement sliding down her thighs. She then put both her hands on the wall and forcefully pushed her ass up against him. He grunted loudly as her sudden push out sent vibrations of lust through him. He quickly lifted her midthigh dress around her waist, and Ayana closed her eyes in anticipation of feeling his large, rock-hard, and pulsating muscle of pleasure drilling deep inside of her. Instead of feeling his dick, she moaned loudly when she felt his hot and wet mouth engulfing her excited center, licking wildly on her clitoris and lips. His head seemed to disappear inside her ass as he pushed forward, still licking and lapping at her sensitivity as if the cure for all his ailments were buried deep inside of her, and he needed to lick, nibble, and eat his way to it.

Suddenly, there was a loud banging on the door as someone tried to force their way into the bathroom. Ayana expected the doctor to stop, but he didn't miss a beat as he kept at it, with his tongue in full motion. The person continued to bang on the door, and the more they banged, the wilder the doctor's lust became. Just when Ayana felt the orgasmic explosion building up, the doctor jumped to his feet and forced every inch of himself inside of her, moaning loudly in her ear. Ayana screamed as she felt the veins and grooves of his manhood sliding across her G-spot.

Soon, a crowd of curious people could be heard outside. Ayana became nervous, and before she could turn around to protest, the doctor placed two fingers over her mouth and whispered, "Shut up and take this dick," in her ear.

Moaning loudly, she complied with his demands and lifted herself on her tiptoes so the doctor could get a much better angle as he continued to pound her hard and fast. Unable to contain herself, she moaned loudly each time he took a long, deep stroke inside of her.

I guess if I'm going to get arrested and lose my job, I better enjoy every moment of this, she thought to herself.

The doctor was now entranced in his own need to reach his climax, and he began to intensify his thrusts, until each time he dove deep inside of her, the force would lift her entire body off the floor, and her face would knock up against the wall. They were yelling and moaning so loudly that the crowd outside began to cheer while security scrambled around, trying to break up the building crowd and find the keys to open the door. Ayana's body began to shake and convulse as she felt her body detonate all of her built-up passion. Knowing they didn't have much longer before the door was unlocked and this scene exposed, Ayana arched her back while squeezing her walls around Daniel's invading muscle in her. The sudden tightness caused the doctor to roar and release himself inside of her. His leg muscles began to tremble as he immediately stumbled backward, but he still held on to Ayana's waist, pulling her back from the wall with him. The sound of her six-inch heels scraping across the tile jolted the doctor out of his climactic bliss, and he quickly braced himself to stop them from falling to the bathroom floor.

Ayana immediately started to fix herself as Daniel pulled up his pants, trying to prevent anyone that might come in through that door from seeing him in such an exposed position. Ayana, now presentable, reached toward the wall and turned on the light to expose Daniel standing in his black dress pants, completely covered in her juices. It looked like he'd just peed himself, and her mouth flew open while she pointed at him. Looking down, Daniel swore and allowed an uncomfortable laugh to come out of his mouth.

"Baby, that's bad. I'm so sorry. I didn't know I came that much."

"It's okay. At least I know I did my job."

"Oh, baby, yes, you did. I want to go lie down and sleep right now, and my legs are still shaking. I can barely stand up in these heels."

"Damn, I want some more," Daniel complained while he looked her over lustfully.

"Well, you can't get more in here. We got to go right now!"

They both exhaled deeply as Daniel walked ahead of her and undid the lock. As soon as the door opened, two large security men were standing there with keys and flashlights in their hands. Behind them was a loud and eager crowd, excited beyond comprehension to find out who was in the bathroom having sex. The look on the security guards' faces made it clear that their night here was over, but the crowd felt differently, and seeing them both caused them to erupt in a championship-winning cheer. Ayana began to giggle behind a nervous Daniel, and before he could turn around to see what she was giggling about, she was fist pumping and stirring up the crowd's excitement. She started cheering along with them and laughing wildly.

Daniel couldn't believe her reaction. He thought she would be embarrassed, but then again, she was the one that led him into the bathroom. It was at that moment his father's words replayed in his head about neither of them knowing the other. Not wanting her so engulfed in the amusement of the crowd, Daniel pulled her and quickly began to lead her out of the club with both security guards in tow. As they quickly moved past the bar, he caught a glimpse of Timothy shaking his head wildly, while laughing till tears were running down his eyes. Daniel didn't find anything funny or amusing.

Those two are something else . . .

Chapter 19

The Interview

Daniel sat in front of the mirror in his dressing room, staring at himself blankly. He seemed disconnected from the chaos happening around him as Meagan talked a mile a minute, giving him all the dos and don'ts concerning his interview. Meagan knew this host was an expert at ambush journalism and would try to sidetrack the doctor away from the important points of the interview and his reasons behind testifying against Kronte. Meagan was talking so much that she didn't notice the doctor's blank expression until she paused for a second to straighten his tie.

"Doctor Bennett! Are you listening to me?" she yelled into his ear.

The doctor jumped before turning toward her loud mouth and giving her a nasty and annoyed look. Meagan shrugged and continued to talk, now that she was sure he was paying attention.

"Remember, don't let him bait you into any discussions concerning your mental stability or how you feel Kronte should pay for his crimes. You don't want to come off as crazy or self-righteous. You are strictly here to tell your side of the story, the events of that day, and how it's changed your life since then . . . well, minus your night terrors. Understand?"

Daniel nodded and turned to look at a smiling yet nervous Ayana staring at him. She was secretly hoping Meagan would leave the two of them alone in the dressing room long enough for her to hug and kiss him. She smiled, thinking about his arms wrapped around her and the warm feeling it caused to vibrate through her body. She felt like a little girl around him, carefree and open for any and everything. The thought of mounting him right in this room even crossed her mind, and she tightly pressed her legs together to try to diminish the sudden heat that began to warm her inner thighs. From the way Meagan was drilling him, she knew she wasn't going to leave them alone for one second. She should've been ashamed that Meagan had to treat two adults like teenagers going through puberty, but she wasn't. This was the first time in her life anyone had ever made her feel this way, and the way the doctor aroused her body . . . only God knew how sprung she was on him.

Soon, there was a knock on the door. One of the young interns stuck her head in the door to let them know Daniel had five minutes before showtime. When the chirpy blond woman looked in the mirror at the amazingly handsome reflection of the doctor in his three-piece beige suit staring back at her, she immediately cleared her throat and ran her hand through her hair. Ayana noticed the intern's flirtatious demeanor and rolled her eyes, folding her arms. She wanted to say something, but she couldn't. Otherwise, their relationship would be known, and she felt the intern wouldn't hesitate to alert the host of this new development.

So, despite her burning urge to set the young girl straight, Ayana remained quiet while the intern lingered at the door, still staring at the doctor, hoping for a sign he was interested.

I bet she's stuffed a lot more than submarine sand-wiches in that big-ass mouth, Ayana thought while looking the blonde up and down. *If she thinks she's got a chance with trying my man, she's gonna have a rude awakening and an ass whooping to match. He's mine, bitch. Keep your distance.*

As if the girl could read Ayana's mind, she walked toward the doctor, placing her hand on his shoulder and began rubbing it softly. She continued to smile brightly while asking him if she could get him anything. He looked at her, smiled, and shook his head. Appearing disappointed, she turned to leave and caught a glimpse of Ayana staring at her and grinning. She could tell Ayana was on to her, and she rolled her eyes while walking out of the room.

Silly rabbit, tricks are for kids.

Daniel stood behind the wall leading out to the stage, inhaling deeply while opening and closing his hands. Then the moment arrived, and the stage manager gave him the cue for him to walk out on stage to the thunder-ous applause of the studio audience. Daniel could feel his palms sweating as he forced himself to smile and wave at the welcoming audience. After greeting the host, Peter Spelling, Daniel took a seat and braced himself for whatever Mr. Spelling had in store. Everyone in America knew just how drastic and unforgiving Peter Spelling could be if he smelled one ounce of bullshit from his guest, and he was notorious for ambushing guests with secrets they thought they had hidden away. Daniel si-lently prayed that he didn't have anything on him tonight that could derail their plans.

The objective was to get the international public to be sympathetic to his story and tragedy, which would raise awareness of what's going on in Sudan, sparking an international outcry over Kronte and his war crimes. With the backing of a compassionate public, the International Courts of Justice would take his testimony more seriously, which could help in Kronte's conviction. If there were a platform that could skyrocket the awareness, Peter Spelling's show was it. His show was syndicated and broadcasted in over thirty countries. Peter was more popular than the president, so if he endorsed their cause, it would be a heavy blow to Kronte's legal defense.

Peter sat across from Daniel smiling brightly, exposing his set of ultra white teeth. If his smile were an attempt to ease any anxiety, it wasn't working, and Daniel began to feel like Peter would eventually attack him with all those pearly whites like a human piranha. After reading a brief greeting on the teleprompter, Peter began the interview.

"Welcome, Dr. Bennett, to the show. It is an honor to have such a brave individual like yourself tonight. What made you decide to testify against Kronte, knowing there have been several failed attempts to bring him to justice? What is it about your testimony that's different from the countless others?"

Daniel was bewildered by Peter's question, but he knew this was a one-time opportunity, and if he blew it, there would be no coming back from this. He inhaled deeply and prepared himself.

"My testimony isn't any different from the other testimonies of the people that have suffered under Kronte's reign of terror. We all have suffered and experienced great loss because of his actions. I am just the only person alive that can identify him at one of the many massacres he's carried out over the years."

After hearing Daniel's response, Peter sat up in his seat as his eyes widened, and he licked his lips as if he were thirsty for more of Daniel's juicy dialogue.

"Now, that's very interesting, because I've done my research and what you say is absolutely true. It seems he's been able to keep himself away from any of the crimes he's accused of. So, your testimony could be damaging to his defense."

"That's what we are hoping."

"We?"

"Yes, I'm not acting alone. I am working with some amazing and dedicated people at the United Nations, and they are just as committed to seeing justice served."

"I understand you lost someone very dear to you during the massacre of the village that you were volunteering in—your adopted daughter, Victoria."

Daniel clinched his hands into a fist, attempting to calm his emotions after hearing Victoria's name. He then nodded his head and leaned forward. Seeing his reaction, Peter placed his hand on Daniel's shoulder and looked into the camera with a solemn and determined look.

"I know this is hard for you, Dr. Bennett. Please take your time."

Daniel then sat up straight and smiled before he began to go into details about the events the day Victoria was taken from him. Fifteen minutes later, the majority of the studio audience and stagehands were wiping away tears of sorrow after hearing the doctor's horrific ordeal at the hands of Kronte and his soldiers. Even the host had to fight back genuine tears, and when Daniel finished speaking, Peter remained silent for several seconds before he continued the interview.

"That . . . tha . . . That is a harrowing account of that day's events. I can't even begin to imagine how that has affected your life going forward. You not only lost your daughter, but you were almost killed. How have you been able to cope with such loss and tragedy for all these years?"

"My practice, my family, and close friends have been supportive in my pursuit of some kind of normalcy. But it's an ongoing battle for me. I will never forget what happened, but I'm hoping that helping to bring Kronte to justice can give closure for me and others who have suffered greatly at his hands."

Peter immediately jumped to his feet and began to clap wildly as the audience rose to their feet and joined him in applauding Daniel's bravery. After a lengthy round of applause, Peter settled the audience and returned to his seat.

"So, what are you expecting to happen if . . . and that's a strong *if* . . . because like I said, Kronte has been able to avoid conviction several times before, if he's convicted? What type of justice do you feel would justify his actions?"

"I'm no judge or jury. I trust the International Court will bring about a just sentence for him."

Peter leaned back, looking at Daniel with a slight smirk while shaking his head. Daniel could see the host wasn't buying his politically correct response. He wanted something real from him, and Daniel knew that if he stuck to his guns, Peter would peel away any emotional layers he had and expose his bullshit to the rotten core. Leaning forward again, Peter tapped Daniel on his knee and nodded.

"Come on, Doctor, really? After everything this man has done to you? After everything he's done to that country? Tens of thousands . . . Some would even say *hundreds* of thousands of men, women, and children slaughtered. You expect me and the world to believe you are fine with the International Courts dealing a just punishment? Hasn't the International Court's lack of transparency and not taking these allegations seriously allowed him to continue his genocide against the people of Southern Sudan?"

"Yes, you are correct."

"So, as a human being, as a doctor that had to deal with the wounded and dead, as a father that lost his little girl in such a barbaric manner, what do you feel should be his just punishment?"

Daniel's left heel began to tap repeatedly on the floor. Rubbing his hands together, he looked down at the floor and closed his eyes. Although the studio audience was deathly silent, Daniel could hear a loud ringing in his ears. He tried his best to find an answer that could side-step the question. But why should he? Why should he sugarcoat how he felt about the man that took everything from him and the woman he loved? Why should Kronte get the respect of his restraint? As the ringing in his ears became as loud as a bullhorn, Daniel's full lips retreated in his mouth, and he shook his head in response to the questions in his head.

"Anything less than life imprisonment or death would be an injustice."

"Yeah! *That's* what I'm talking about!" Peter yelled gleefully, jumping to his feet while clapping and nodding his head in approval. The audience went insane as they screamed, howled, and cheered at the doctor's response.

The interview lasted another twenty minutes, and by the time they were signing off, Daniel was smiling and waving happily at the cameras. According to the news analyst the next day, the interview was a slam dunk, and soon, Google searches about Kronte, Southern Sudan, and the atrocities were peaking at over two million an hour. Social media exploded with the hash tag #JusticeforVictoria# going viral, and the doctor's interview had over ten million views on YouTube.

It was a great victory, but the battle was far from over, and soon, those in opposition to their efforts to bring Kronte to justice devised their own assault, and it began exactly one week after the doctor's interview with Peter Spelling. Daniel was back at work and having a fairly good day in the ICU with very few violent crimes victims. There were mostly injuries from car accidents or construction site mishaps due to the recent blizzard that blew through the city. As he was signing another patient chart, he felt someone tap him on the shoulder, and when he turned around, he was face-to-face with a solemn-looking Timothy.

"What? What happened? Is it your research?"

"I wish it were that simple and private, but no, there is a video circulating the net, and now it's on every major news channel in the country."

"What video?" he asked, taking a step back.

"I think you know which one."

"Oh shit! No! Inside?"

"No, but they recorded about four minutes of the two of you howling and moaning like porn stars. They also got you guys walking out of the bathroom, and Ayana fist pumping like she was a revolutionary or something. You know, after seeing you two together, they decided to dig deeper, and now they know she's also Victoria's mother. They are claiming that your intentions are not as genuine as you made it out to be. That the two of you are looking for revenge on anyone, and Kronte seems to be the most famous face to place blame."

Daniel felt the good vibrations he had all day leave his body, and he suddenly felt like a little child caught with his pants down, exposed, and limp.

"I know you guys were floating on cloud nine after last week's interview, but you had to know Kronte has supporters too. I know you told me Ayana would lose her job if Meagan found out you too were seeing each other, so I know this is gonna sting big time, but you got to get in front of this immediately, before it spirals out of control, and you lose all the support you just got from the public."

Daniel remained silent, walking away toward his office to clock out and face the music that was playing outside the hospital to the tune of countless media cameras and reporters . . .

Chapter 20

Crucifixion

Daniel sat in his living room, watching the news coverage of the newly labeled "Bathroomgate." Reporters and legal analysts were cruel and disrespectful as they described Ayana as an out of control, sex-crazed, vengeful woman, willing to use her body and beauty to get what she wanted, which was Kronte, her ex-husband, to pay for leaving her with nothing. They painted a picture of Daniel as a weak and easily influenced man willing to do anything to keep such a beautiful and wild woman in his life. The fix was in, and Daniel watched as fire as hot as the sun burned deep in his soul. He wanted to smash the television into pieces, but that wasn't going to solve anything.

He was angry with himself more than he was angry at the news broadcasts because it was his moment of weakness and lack of proper thought processes that allowed this to happen. He wasn't thinking with the proper head, and now, the aftermath was devastating. His phone has been ringing nonstop since the broadcasts began, with calls from his family, and a never-ending string of blocked calls he assumed was from reporters wanting a statement. No matter who the call came from, he didn't answer any of them, other than the call he received from an irate Meagan. She called screaming, advising him that she would be in the city tomorrow, and he'd better make time to meet with her. She didn't mention Ayana's name, so he assumed she'd already made good on her promise of ending her employment with the UN. The thought of Ayana losing her career and her reputation sent his nerves into an earthshaking frenzy. He buried his head in his hands, trying to cope with the oncoming migraine.

Pastor Donald Bennett sat in his large armchair in the dimly lit family room, surrounded by most of his children and his wife Diana, who was seated on his lap, leaning back with his arms wrapped around her waist. Everyone was watching the news broadcast as it replayed the video of Daniel and Ayana's embarrassing romp in the nightclub's bathroom. The coverage was brutal, and tears flowed down Diana's face as she watched in horror the media's slaughtering of her son's and Ayana's reputations. The pastor was fuming. He could barely breathe, as he would periodically look away every time someone would say something negative about his son he knew wasn't true. However, what could he say? His son was hardheaded and refused to listen, and now he'd placed himself and Ayana in a terrible situation.

They'd been calling his son nonstop all day, but the pastor knew his son, and it was unlikely he would pick up the phone. Since he was a little boy, he was terrified of disappointing his parents, and he would avoid any contact with anyone until he built up enough nerve to face them. He was always the overachiever of the family, because of a need to impress those he cared for, and so, he was certain when the doorbell suddenly rang, it wasn't Daniel. He tapped his wife on her thigh and got up to open the door. Diana reached out and held his hand, preventing him from moving forward. He smiled and silently wiped the tears from her eyes. She smiled too and sat down in the recliner, placing her hand over her face trying to hide her pain.

As he walked toward the front door, the pastor prayed that it wasn't another reporter, because if it were, he was afraid he would lose his restraint and revert to his days on the streets of Englewood, before he found his faith.

Peering through the peephole, the pastor was shocked to see Timothy's face staring back at him. Opening the door, he smiled, shaking his hand warmly.

"Hey, Timothy! Come in. Long time no see! How you been? If you're looking for Danny, he's not here."

"Yeah, I know. I didn't come here for him. I came to talk to you and everyone else in the family. Danny needs our help, and I have the perfect way to do that. There's no way I'm gonna let that animal get away with what he did to Victoria."

The pastor nodded and walked him into the family room to speak to everyone else . . .

4:35 a.m. Fox News Chicago. Chicago, Illinois

The lobby was teeming with activity and the raised voices of people bellowing out demands for information and coffee. The sound of all the chaos bounced off the ivory-white walls that surrounded the lobby, playing on Timothy's anxiety. With a quiet disdain, Timothy looked at the Fox News Chicago logo on the wall behind the receptionist. He'd called every news station since yesterday evening, and only the program director at Fox News agreed to meet with him. However, his window of opportunity was very small, and he needed to be front and center at 4:30 a.m. To make sure he wasn't late, he'd arrived at 4:00 a.m. and looking at his Rolex, it was now 4:35 a.m., and still, no one has come to get him.

It's only been five minutes—no big deal.

Then he heard a loud gasp directly in front of him, and when he looked up, he almost choked on his saliva. A woman stood before him with her blond hair tied back in a ponytail. She was dressed down in jeans, a white blouse, white boots, and wearing a look of shock and extreme anger. Timothy felt instantly mortified when he realized it was Julie Gates, the woman whom he'd had a racially fueled battle on social media last year after he'd insulted her by calling her a bitch. Timothy took several steps back and considered turning and running once he heard "Security" yelled from Julie's mouth. Timothy was so disconnected from the many women he'd encountered, that he'd totally forgotten this woman's name. However, he was on a mission, and not even Julie Gates and the memory of her calling him a "nigger" would stop him from accomplishing his goal.

Karma is a bitch, he amusedly thought to himself. Noticing Julie's intentions on leaving him standing there for security, he quickly reached out for her, gently holding her hand. Julie immediately snatched away from him.

"Don't you fucking touch me, you piece of shit," she whispered while leaning closer to him, trying to avoid anyone hearing her angry reaction to him being in her lobby. Still not deterred, Timothy took another step back, raising both hands in the air.

"Listen, I know I'm not your most favorite person in the world right now."

"That's the understatement of the year," she snapped back.

"Hey, I didn't come here for any trouble. I came here with a story, a video that no other news station has of Dr. Daniel Bennett . . . Something that could change the game for you guys here at Fox. But, well, if you don't want that kind of exclusive news, that's fine. I'll go to NBC with it."

He slowly started to turn toward the exit, and Julie grunted loudly before grabbing ahold of his arm.

"Okay, stop. What video?"

Looking around, Timothy noticed six large security guards were waiting to pounce on him at Julie's command. He swallowed hard while looking at each of them with an uncomfortable grin.

"Call off your gladiators first."

Without uttering a word, Julie nodded at the security guards, and they all retreated to their previous posts. Once Timothy was sure they were gone, he exhaled and took a step closer to Julie, while looking in her eyes. Julie's aggressive stance relaxed the moment their eyes met. Suddenly, she felt his strong, yet pleasantly soft hands hold her own.

Goddammit, this man is fine!

Noticing his charm working on her, he whispered in her ear that they should speak in private, and she smiled brightly while leading him to her office down the hall. The receptionist looked on, shaking her head while laughing. She knew Timothy was working Julie, and it was amusing to see her always aggressive boss being softened by a man that she clearly didn't have a great experience with. Once they were in Julie's office, she sat behind her large mahogany desk, and Timothy took a seat in the chair on the opposite side of it. Still smiling and blushing, she relaxed in her chair and gestured for Timothy to speak.

"As I said, I have video footage of the doctor that no one has."

"Is it dramatic footage?"

"Oh yeah, it's pretty dramatic, and I'll give Fox the exclusive rights to it, but you have to agree to interview his entire family and me on your panel this evening."

"Wait. You're cutting it pretty close. We already have someone lined up for that panel."

"Cancel them and put us in that slot."

"You want me to cancel on the governor of Illinois?"

"Yep. I bet the governor won't be as dramatic as this video and what we have to say. I can guarantee it."

Julie began to consider Timothy's proposition while rocking back and forth in her chair. After a minute of silence, she stopped rocking and looked at him with a determined stare.

"Okay, but that depends on what's on that video. I need to see it now before I make that call. If I make this call, I need to make sure I'll still have a job tomorrow morning."

Nodding, Timothy pulled out his cell phone and leaned over her desk, giving her a good angle of the screen. Having him this close to her and smelling his cologne caused her body to warm, and she felt her lower back muscles vibrate as if her chair's massaging feature were turned on. Timothy pressed *play* on the phone, and as soon as the video began, Julie's eyes widened, and her mouth flung open. She never asked during her brief viewing how he got the video. She didn't need to know why a friend would expose something so damaging, and after only watching one minute of the five-minute video, she reached for her phone to advise her team to contact the governor and reschedule his appearance on their evening panel discussion.

After discussing the particulars of the family's interview, Timothy got up to leave, relieved that he was able to accomplish the impossible despite the obvious obstacles. However, Julie wasn't satisfied with the feeling that suddenly came over her that Timothy was using her yet again. She decided it was time for him to make amends for his previous transgressions against her.

"Tim, before you leave, there's one more thing I need from you to seal this deal. I need a public apology about what you said to me."

Stopping in his tracks, he turned, puzzled by her request.

"Public?"

"Yep, during the interview, I want you to apologize to me. No specifics, just something sweet and genuine."

Timothy almost exploded into a tirade of anger, but he knew there was too much at stake, so he agreed to her demands and quickly left before she asked him for something else that he wasn't willing to give up . . .

same thing, "Bathroomgate." Soon, she
o Fox News, and she dropped the remote
he recognized the smiling face covering
ty inches of high-definition real estate. It
n TV, smiling while comfortably sitting
several other African Americans. The
the room had an uncanny resemblance
nd it didn't take long for her to conclude
amily who was also being interviewed at
n by the Fox News tyrant Kelly Dewitt.
r hands in the air, she turned to Daniel,
yeah, what a friend indeed you have in
otherfucker is a turncoat! I can't believe
worse?"
ere answering her question, a video
n the screen, showing one of Daniel's
ght terror attacks. The video was highly
niel screamed, and his body convulsed
he bed onto the floor with a loud thump.
d back in her chair and appeared to be
ideo played in its entirety.
desire to jump up and turn off the TV,
d closer to him and held on to his arm.
r, and she smiled. She wanted him to
rted and how far he's come since those
es. It was time for him to start seeing
r instead of a victim. Daniel reluctantly
but fire burned in his chest for Timothy,
betrayal was not extinguished. He
r a visual and verbal fucking by those

after the video ran its course, Kelly
narrative with such emotional vigor

Chapter 21

Resurrection

Daniel watched as Meagan and Ayana walked through his condo's door with worried anticipation. Ayana's posture seemed weak and subdued, while Meagan strutted into his condo with long, quick strides. She dropped her purse on the floor, glaring at Daniel like a hawk staring down a mouse. He slowly closed the door and walked over to the living area.

"Would any of you like something to dri—"

"No, we won't be here long," Meagan snarled back. Ayana was already seated on the couch, and she refused to look Daniel or Meagan in the eyes. Daniel became concerned and walked over to her, but Meagan suddenly cut him off.

"Dr. Bennett, now is not the time. Please, have a seat!"

At that moment, Daniel had reached his fill of Meagan's aggressive nature and decided to set her straight.

"No, *you* have a seat. You are in *my* house, and although we made a mistake, you will *not* speak to me like a child. *I* pay the mortgage here, and you won't make me feel uncomfortable in my own shit. So, sit your rude ass down. Let's get this over with, so Ayana and I can move on with our lives together."

Taken aback by the doctor's response, Meagan immediately sat down, looking puzzled. She was used to ordering people around, including men, and very few of them had the balls to stand up to her. She believed that the doctor wasn't confident enough to stand up to her, and his reaction threw her off completely. Hearing Daniel's proclamation and aggressive stance made Ayana look up and smile. Noticing Meagan's compliance, Daniel sat down in the recliner and stared, waiting for her to begin. Clearing her throat and gathering her confidence back, Meagan leaned forward, preparing to give Daniel and Ayana the latest public polls concerning the trial.

"Things are bad. No, things are *beyond* bad. After your interview with Peter Spelling, the public's support was at 98 percent, and now we are sitting on a tearjerking 12 percent. A few new hashtags are going viral, like, '#AYANASASS#' and '#bathroombandits#,' and let's not forget '#hornyhoax#.' Now, no one is taking this trial or either of you seriously. Your testimony will be as valuable as ice to an Eskimo. At this point, it's not far-fetched to assume Kronte will go free again. All because you two couldn't stay away from each other. How fucking selfish! I just can't believe it!

"You are adults having sex in a bathroom in a crowded nightclub. Are you *purposely* trying to ruin this trial?"

Daniel and Ayana remained silent, unable to muster up one logical reason for their actions. They were in love, and whatever they did was driven by thoughtless impulses.

"You have nothing to say for yourselves? Ayana . . . nothing? You gave up everything for a few moments in a dark bathroom and a fist pump? Now, I have to replace you in this case, just to salvage some legitimacy going

forward. You
go back to Er

"What do y
That wouldn
fan of long-d

"Oh yeah,
she'll have t

"And ther

"Nothing!

"Meagan,
cern here? C
Because I w
than cowor
friend neve

"Really?
about our
bathroom.'

"Actuall

"Doctor!
you tried i
should I?"

"Becaus
care."

Meagai
ing her lip
from his c

"What
about?"
screen m
televisior
Meagan
brown le
from one

be covering th
made her way
control when s
the entire sever
was Timothy o
in a room with
other people in
to the doctor, a
that it was his f
a remote locatio

Throwing he
screaming, "Oh
Timothy! That
it. Can it get any

As if God w
began playing
more violent ni
disturbing as D
until he fell off
Meagan collaps
weeping as the v

Daniel felt th
but Ayana move
He looked at he
see where he sta
terrible nightma
himself as a vict
remained seated,
and his family'
braced himself f
closest to him.

Immediately
Dewitt began he

that it almost seemed like she were taking what she just saw personally.

"Now, this is a revealing and disturbing video of the man that everyone claimed was a hero and fit to testify before the International Courts. But it's obvious he is in no shape to testify nor fit to be a doctor with people's lives in his hands daily. How many people have lost their lives because this doctor isn't mentally stable to do such an important job properly? There are so many variables here, but they all point to lies and dangerous secrets.

"Dr. Avers, it was you that brought this video to our studios, and I want to thank you personally for exposing this fraud of a hero. And Dr. Bennett is your friend, correct?"

"Yes, Kelly, Dr. Bennett and I have been close friends since college."

"If that's so, why would you expose this disturbing video of your friend? What did the American people just watch?"

"I brought it to the American people's attention so that the *entire* truth can be known. No more secrets or half-truths about my friend and his relationship with Ayana. And what we just saw on the video is just one of the many violent nightmares Dr. Bennett was experiencing since his return from Sudan."

"Did he seek professional help to deal with these 'night terrors'?"

"Absolutely. He saw around four or five doctors and psychologists, and none of them could help him. It got so bad that one day, I walked into his office to find him lost in a daze, pointing a gun at his head. It was a frightening sight, and I'm just happy he's made it thus far without taking his own life."

Kelly's eyes widened the more she listened to Timothy tell it all. She became so excited that she almost leaped out of her chair in triumph.

This is so much better than interviewing that boring-ass governor.

"So, basically, what you are saying here today is the doctor is mentally unstable and, in fact, could be a liability to the trial?"

"Well, I wouldn't—"

"C'mon, Dr. Avers, I know he's your friend, but as a doctor and the leading researcher in cancer treatments, you have to admit your friend's mental instability is more of a danger than what he let on the other night. Then when you add on this secret relationship between himself and the UN representative that just so happens to not only be his adopted daughter's biological mother, but also the ex-wife of Kronte himself, it just stinks of scandal, cover-ups, and personal vendettas. He attempted to defraud the public's sympathy, and while everyone was championing his cause, he was in some shady nightclub having sex in a public bathroom like they owned the place.

"No, Dr. Avers, you may not be brave enough to call a spade a spade, but I am, and I'm calling it as I see it. This whole thing is a sham, a farce, and the truth needs to be told today, no matter how uncomfortable it may be. You opened this door by revealing this video and talking to me here today, so it's best you reveal all the skeletons in that dark bathroom. The American people deserve no less!"

When Kelly was done, she looked into the camera with pride, waiting for Timothy's response. She was used to exposing people and tearing them down to nothing. Today wasn't going to be any different. She wanted Timothy and Dr. Bennett's family to know she had a home court advantage, and there was no way they were going to leave with the victory here this evening. When she was done with them and the lying Dr. Bennett, they wouldn't be able to walk the streets without being heckled and ridiculed.

Timothy seemed to be uncomfortable as he continuously readjusted himself in the chair he was sitting in inside the Bennetts' family room. There were bright camera lights everywhere with cameramen and makeup artists standing around waiting for his response. He appeared to regret doing the interview, but suddenly, he looked up at the ceiling and smiled. Exhaling deeply, he looked into the cameras and began to speak with a confidence that wasn't present at the beginning of the interview.

"Well, Kelly, I want to thank you for encouraging me to be more forthcoming concerning Dr. Bennett's condition. So, here's the truth. During the time I recorded that video, Dr. Bennett was definitely a liability and unstable. And it was during that time when Ayana and other UN representatives approached him, and he declined to assist them."

"But—"

"I'm not done, Kelly," Timothy interrupted. "After that night, I contacted Ayana Burundi because she's a crisis counselor for survivors of war and massacres. At first, they couldn't stand to be around each other, but after I explained what the doctor was experiencing and that his life was at stake, she agreed to help him, even though he'd already declined to help them. For her treatment to be effective in such an extreme case of survivor's remorse, she had to move in with Dr. Bennett.

"During this time, neither of them knew of the other's past, and Ms. Burundi didn't tell Dr. Bennett of her previous so-called marriage to the warlord Kronte. Truth is, Kronte murdered her parents in one of his many massacres, and he raped her as a young teenager, repeatedly, and claimed her as his wife—no ceremony, no ring, no honeymoon. I don't know a woman on the planet that would call that a marriage and run around telling every man she dates—not one.

"The two of them became close, of course, while living under the same roof, and as the relationship blossomed, she began to reveal her past connection to Kronte. This past Thanksgiving, both of them found out the baby that Kronte took from her arms the night she was born was actually Dr. Bennett's adopted daughter, Victoria. In this room, I have several witnesses that can attest to her reaction after seeing Victoria's photos and discovering that she was, in fact, her child. Now, why didn't the doctor reveal that on the show? Who would? Do you want to turn on the television and hear about *your* child's death repeatedly? I don't think anyone wants to endure that every day, all day."

Kelly looked at the camera with her head slightly turned, and her mouth twisted to one side of her face. Shaking her head, she exhaled and pointed at the camera angrily.

"Dr. Avers, are you *seriously* trying to make me believe that these two were brought together through some kind of hocus-pocus destiny or something? Nothing happens that way in the real world—*nothing*. Things are planned, and this has careful planning written all over it."

"Sorry, Kelly, but I don't think anyone can plan this kind of connection. The UN has recorded conversations and sessions between the two of them. Oh, trust me, it doesn't get any more real than this. Now, on the topic of the doctor's mental stability, Ayana did what five other doctors couldn't, and the man in the video isn't the man that everyone saw during that interview. Before Ayana's help, he couldn't even say his daughter's name, let alone talk in detail about the events of that day. Now, he can. As previous interviews with his coworkers revealed, they all have seen a sudden, positive change in him, and the fact that he was free within himself enough to be in that bathroom that night speaks volumes of his progress. Let's not judge about their choice of location, because I'm sure there are very few sexually active people in this city that haven't found themselves having sex in unconventional places."

"I don't know what you're talking about, Doctor. I'm a native Chicagoan, and I've never—"

"You're telling me you've never had a secret rendezvous on the lake, Kelly? C'mon, Kelly . . . c'mon, now," Timothy interrupted with a mischievous grin on his face. His grin and tone of voice made Kelly blush and giggle. "No self-respecting Chicagoan can say they didn't," he continued.

"Moving on," she said, clearing her throat, "we can delve into odd places to have sex on a different night. Tonight, we are talking about your friend, Dr. Bennett, his girlfriend, and their irresponsible behavior."

"I agree they can be irresponsible, but 'frauds' and 'insincere' are inaccurate. They are more dedicated than anyone I know to this case and trial."

Then from behind Timothy, the deep and intimidating voice of Pastor Bennett chimed in. His voice demanded attention, and every camera in the room turned in his direction.

"I would like to add that although I may not condone my son's choice in places to be intimate, I can say that this union between my son and Ayana is divine intervention. You are a God-fearing Christian woman, aren't you, Kelly?"

"Yes, I am," she responded with pride.

"Great, so you understand that sometimes a higher power is the orchestrator of our lives. For the two of them to find each other at this time in their lives and fall in love isn't a coincidence. This is destiny, and I don't think the American people would want any other group of people to spearhead the task of bringing down a monster like Kronte, than two people in love who have shared in Kronte's treachery. Of course, it's personal, and even if they didn't see each other romantically, it would *still* remain personal. Kronte has done a terrible thing on this earth, and he needs to be brought to justice and prevented from continuing his reign of terror. His evil ways took our grandbaby from us, but it also brought her birth mother into our lives. She saved my son's life and asked for nothing in return—no monetary compensation or pat on the back.

"My son was just an empty shell until Ayana helped him to cope with his guilt and remorse. He'll never be the same man he was before we lost Victoria, but now he is free to feel again, and for that, we are eternally grateful to her. Now, *that's* the truth, and you can do with it as you will."

Kelly looked down and smiled, realizing what just happened. She just lost home court advantage in a manner of minutes. It was a well-planned ambush, and she walked right into it. They let her tear the doctor down, make him a threat to himself and others, and then they used Ayana to build him up. They wanted the public to see how his relationship with Ayana was a blessing and that their relationship was the best thing that could happen for this trial. By the time the interview was over, Kelly was certain that the viewing public would also be convinced. It was a masterful coup d'état, and although she was furious, she was also impressed. Her producer also noticed what she did, and when she was removing her earpiece, he walked over to her looking angry and confused.

"What the fuck was that?" he asked while pointing at the cameras.

"That, Bill, was a family. A *real* family, and they just turned this thing around for the doctor and the UN. At this point, those two could have sex in the Daley Center courtyard in broad daylight, and no one would care. In fact, they might actually cheer them on. People love drama, but what people love even more is a story of redemption, and they gave the viewers both tonight. Damn it! I should've seen that coming!"

"Yeah, but Dr. Avers played the part very well. He opened the door for you, and I don't know anyone that would have left it alone. He made it so easy. And to think we cancelled the governor for that. Although it was a great show, it wasn't what we were going for. Someone's gonna lose their job over this."

"Yep, that silly bitch, Julie. I heard she was all 'lovey-dovey' with Dr. Avers earlier."

"Yeah, I heard the same, but I doubt she knew what he was up to."

"Doesn't matter. That bitch set this up, and this interview was supposed to be the nail in the coffin, but it looks like their image has been resurrected, and they used her to do it. Fuck me! Those fuckers were good!"

"That Dr. Avers was a fine specimen, wouldn't you agree?" Bill asked while waving his hand in front of his face, fanning himself, as if he were getting hot. Kelly jerked around and looked at Bill with a disgusted frown on her face, shaking her head.

"Bill, one thing you should remember is I am actually a God-fearing Christian woman, and although legally I have to work with you, I don't want to hear about your sinful lifestyle and lust for other men. Get away from me with that foolishness!"

Bill looked down at Kelly and let out a quiet "humph" before spinning around like a ballerina and storming toward the far side of the studio.

That man has more bitch in him than I do, she thought while watching Bill prance out of the room.

Back at Daniel's condo, everyone just sat there in silent amazement after the broadcast was over. Daniel and Ayana had experienced so many different emotions while watching the interview that they both felt dizzy trying to comprehend everything. Meagan was still in the chair with one hand covering her face.

"He's right, you know. This *is* personal, and destiny all rolled into one big mess," Meagan said, still appearing dazed by the interview.

"Meagan, you don't believe in destiny," Ayana declared, confused by her comment.

"A long time ago, I did. I believed in God, destiny, the Holy Trinity, and even the Easter Bunny. Experiences change you, and it definitely changed me."

Meagan then sat upright in the chair and looked at both Daniel and Ayana. Her eyes were now red and filled with tears.

"Daniel, you are right. I shouldn't have even considered leaving my friend out to dry. I wouldn't have gotten this far without her. But like your father said, this is personal for both of you and also for me."

Ayana was confused and looked at Daniel as if he might have an answer, but all he did was shrug his shoulders, looking just as confused as she.

"How is this personal for you, Meagan? I don't understand."

"I wasn't born Meagan Quinn. My maiden name is Fellows, Meagan Fellows. I am the daughter of the televangelist William Fellows."

After hearing Meagan reveal who she really was, Ayana gasped and covered her mouth. She immediately started to tremble, and Daniel could hear her beginning to wail in sorrow. Meagan became alarmed by her reaction, not having a clue why grief overcame her so badly. She turned to Daniel, and all he could do was shake his head, refusing to look her in the face. She then looked over at Ayana, searching for answers. Meagan believed that Ayana was devastated by her deception, so she began to plead her case to her friend.

"Ayana, I'm so sorry for deceiving you. I have no excuse for my actions, besides wanting to make the man who killed my father pay."

"So, you did all this to avenge your father's death?" Daniel asked, trying his best to hide the fact that he knew something that could possibly change Ayana and Meagan's friendship forever.

"Not just his death but forty-three other volunteers from my father's church," she yelled back, trying hard to fight back the tears.

"I was a true believer, not because my father was, nor because it's been a family tradition, but because in my heart, I believed there was a God, and as long as we did his will, he would protect us. My father was a good man. He wasn't perfect, not by a long shot, but in his heart, he was a good man who wanted to help people, so he and forty-three other volunteers decided to go to Sudan to help the people there. I was fresh out of college then, and my mother and I didn't agree with them going over there. We'd heard the stories, and we knew it wasn't safe, but my dad kept saying God would protect them.

"Well, after being over there for less than a week, they all 'disappeared,' and to this day, no one has heard from them. A few days after their disappearance, the US Embassy confirmed that the village where they were stationed was attacked and burned to the ground, no survivors. The US didn't do anything about what happened, saying it was a 'sensitive' situation, and if they sent in troops, it could turn into an international incident. After I discovered God wasn't willing to protect my father, I decided I wasn't willing to believe in him any longer.

"My mother committed suicide about a year later, and I decided to dedicate my life to seeing that monster pay. I knew if I tried to join the UN Security Council under my maiden name, it would be a dead giveaway, and they wouldn't have hired me as the liaison to Sudan. You know, that whole thing about conflicts of interest or being too close to the situation. So, I got married and divorced about a year later, but fought to keep my ex-husband's last name. After they hired me, I dove right in, going after Kronte, but after several failed attempts, I discovered that some very powerful people were profiting from his genocidal campaign, and they were protecting him.

He purchases over six hundred million dollars' worth of weapons annually, and all the land he's stolen from his victims is rumored to have oil, which skyrockets the earning potential of anyone that's in league with him. He's a multibillion-dollar business to many greedy and powerful people.

"Then I met Ayana, and her input and dedication brought us closer than I've ever been. So you must understand my frustration when I felt we were gonna lose again. Daniel, you have an amazing family, and your friend, Timothy, is nothing short of a genius. He handled Kelly Dewitt as if she were a child, and he was her teacher. That was beautiful. They just revitalized our efforts and made it so the two of you can be a couple without hiding your feelings from the public. Absolutely amazing! I will have to thank him personally when this is all said and done."

While Meagan was talking, Daniel constantly rubbed Ayana's back and shoulders, trying to calm her down, but she was overcome with guilt, and the longer Meagan talked, the more hysterical she became. Meagan became alarmed and attempted to walk over to her, but Daniel raised his hand, stopping her.

Meagan became more concerned the longer Ayana carried on, and Daniel knew it was only a matter of time before she would start asking questions that no one wanted to be answered. He leaned over, whispering into Ayana's ear, attempting to calm her down, but it seemed she was oblivious to the sound of his voice as she continued to cry in agony.

"OK, I know what I've done was bad. But the way Ayana is crying, something else is going on. Daniel, what's wrong with her?" Meagan asked, looking at the two lovers suspiciously.

"It's just been a really emotional day, that's all," Daniel responded, still refusing to look Meagan in the face.

"No, no more lies or secrets," Ayana wailed through her cries of pain. "I was there, Meagan. I watched the entire thing," she screamed.

Sitting up in the chair with her head slightly turned to the right, Meagan asked, "You were where, Ayana?"

"There! When Kronte killed your father and his followers. I was there, and Kronte made me watch the entire massacre! It was a game to him, proving to me that Allah was the one true god, and the god of the Christians wasn't real! I'm so sorry, Meagan, I didn't know. I swear, I didn't know. Otherwise, I would've told you years ago!"

Meagan's lips began to tremble, and her eyelids fluttered as she processed the devastating revelation Ayana just told her. All these years, she hoped in the deepest recesses of her mind that Kronte held her father and his followers prisoner. That one day, he would use them as leverage to demand something from the US. She hoped against all the evidence that somehow her daddy was still alive. Now, that hope was taken from her, the truth coming from the mouth of the most unlikely yet reliable of sources. Her father was dead, and her best friend was there to watch every terrorizing minute.

Meagan's entire body went numb as she flopped back into the recliner. She began shaking right before she covered her face with both her hands, screaming her pain into them. Daniel sat there feeling useless as he watched these two strong and heartbroken women sink deeper into their emotions.

Ayana kept repeating, "I'm sorry," as she rocked back and forth on the couch, holding herself around the waist as if she had a stomachache. Meagan slowly removed her hands from her face and stared at Ayana for almost a minute. Her face was wet with tears, eyes red, and flooded.

Daniel inhaled deeply, finally building up the nerve to look Meagan in the eyes, expecting to see an unbridled rage burning in them. But what he saw was compassion and deep sorrow for Ayana as she remained in a trance-like state of pain. Shaking her head, Meagan got up from the chair and walked over to Ayana. Standing over Ayana for about ten seconds, Meagan looked down at her as she rocked back and forth, repeating the same two words and hoping they would rescue her from her guilt. Daniel watched Meagan with deep concern. He didn't want to have to confront her physically, but if she attacked Ayana, he wouldn't hesitate to protect her.

His anxiety grew the longer Meagan stood over Ayana. Then Meagan reached down with both her arms, wrapped them around Ayana, and said, "It's not your fault." Ayana's eyes widened as she felt Meagan's loving and warm embrace, and she responded by embracing her back, causing Meagan to cry again. Unable to move, Daniel sat in silence as he watched Ayana and Meagan share a much-needed cry together . . .

Chapter 22

Let's Get Ready to Rumble

Forty-eight days later. Beverly, Illinois

A few days before their departure to Sudan, Daniel's family decided to throw a going away party for him and Ayana. The house was filled with Daniel's coworkers, friends, family members, and reporters that wanted to cover his journey to what the media was calling "the trial of the century." Everyone seemed to be having a good time, and Daniel decided to pull Timothy away from the noisy crowd to have a man-to-man.

"Tim, I can't thank you enough for everything you've done for me over the years. If it weren't for you, I wouldn't be where I am today, Ayana wouldn't be in my life, and I could've lost my practice because of a dumb decision in the heat of the moment. You've been a much better friend to me than I've been to you, and I thank you from the bottom of my heart, bruh."

Timothy looked at Daniel and smiled. Daniel had no idea how much Timothy looked up to him and saw him as a big brother and role model. He admired his strength and resilience after everything that's happened to him.

Everything he did was to show Daniel just how much his friendship meant to him. He wanted to say so much to him, but he knew too many words would ruin the moment, so he simply raised his glass and responded, "You are welcome."

"By the way, how did you do that to Kelly Dewitt?"

"You mean Kelly Nitwitt? Dude, that bitch was so transparent, I saw through her arrogance as soon as the cameras started rolling, and her ugly mug appeared on the monitor. I knew she wouldn't be able to resist tearing down you and Ayana. I'm almost certain they were instructed by some very powerful people to smear you guys all over the wall. I couldn't have that. People keep forgetting I'm a genius. They keep looking at me as just a simple black man, and I used that to my advantage."

"I bet she won't be interviewing you again."

"Who knows? Maybe she'll call me back to talk about a secret rendezvous on the lakefront," Timothy said while shrugging and taking another sip of beer out of his bottle.

"Wait, would you bang Kelly Dewitt?"

"Hell yeah! She's good and ugly, but she's a freak! I could tell by the way she reacted when I challenged her about the lakefront. Oh yeah, she could get it, because I know she'll be a lot of fun in the sack."

Daniel leaned back on the wall behind him and laughed until his sides hurt.

"Tim, to be such a genius, you make some really questionable decisions when it comes to women," he said, wiping the tears from his eyes.

"True, but even Superman has Kryptonite. I got Pussy-ite."

Daniel spat out the remaining beer in his mouth and began roaring with laughter . . .

Four days later. Juba, South Sudan

Daniel, Ayana, and Meagan arrived in Juba, South Sudan, accompanied by a contingent of UN and South Sudanese security personnel. Daniel stepped out of the plane, and emotions, as well as the dry and intense African heat, immediately overcame him. It felt like several lifetimes ago since he'd stepped foot on African soil, and the feeling of pride and fear immediately filled him. As soon as they stepped out, they were greeted with cheers from a crowd of thousands, while concussive and hypnotic African drums played with such emotion, it almost brought the doctor to tears. It felt like he were home after years of being lost in the wilderness, and the people of Southern Sudan missed him dearly. It took the group almost thirty minutes to get into the armored vehicles as the awaiting crowd rushed forward to get a glimpse of the man that could change their future.

Inside the vehicles and heading toward the hotel, the South Sudanese UN Representative in Juba, Patrick Wek, began to brief the group on the particulars of the trial and the dos and don'ts while they were in his country. One thing he kept reiterating to the group is no matter the circumstance, Daniel should never leave the hotel without his security detail. After he mentioned Daniel's confinement to the hotel for the fourth time, Daniel became increasingly nervous, because something was telling him there may be a bounty on his head in this country. They were less than a week from the start of the trial, and

Meagan wanted them to visit the site where the massacre occurred, in hopes of jarring any other suppressed
details Daniel may have hidden deep in his memory.
Daniel didn't feel too comfortable visiting the place that
held so much pain and death attached to it, but he knew it
was a part of the judicial process.

Daniel's heart, as he looked outside the vehicle's
window, sank to the depths of his chest as he took in the
aftermath of a country still struggling to find its place in
the world. The country was hopelessly underdeveloped,
and the people looked beaten and torn after decades of
war and famine. He used to love this country and its
people, and he suddenly felt ashamed that after Victoria's
death, he refused to keep himself abreast of the events
that shaped the newly independent nation of Southern
Sudan. The country of Sudan was divided into two
nations: Sudan and Southern Sudan, to end decades of
war. People believed that by separating the two warring
factions, both sides would be able to move forward in
peace, but it seems the people ran from their northern
aggressor . . . right into the arms of Kronte, and he was
just as brutal.

It was an hour-long drive that seemed like a tour
through the land of the lost, and by the time they pulled in
front of the hotel, grief had overcome Daniel. Although
the vehicle's air-conditioning was working overtime,
sweat covered him. Meagan decided that all three of
them should share a two-bedroom suite to reduce the
risk of having security spread too thin, guarding multiple
rooms. She thought the two sex-crazed lovers would
protest her decision, but they agreed without hesitation.
They understood this wasn't a vacation. They had a job
to do. It wasn't going to be easy, and everyone needed

to be focused. They were in enemy territory, and they couldn't relax one second while they attempted to put away the most powerful warlord on the African continent. Despite it being a third world country and lacking many necessary services, the hotel was elegantly appointed, and the room was decorated in a regal and luxurious fashion. Daniel gritted his teeth at the irony and stormed into the bathroom to calm his nerves.

"What's up with him?" Meagan asked, confused with the doctor's anger.

"It's been so long. So many things have changed, and most not for the better. I think he blames himself for not being involved," answered Ayana, staring at the closed bathroom door with sadness.

"But it's not his fault how things are," Meagan protested, still confused by the doctor's reaction to the state of the country.

"Our daughter was Sudanese, and Danny feels a direct connection with my country because of her. So, even though it's not his fault, he still feels responsible as do I."

Meagan nodded and turned to go to her room to unpack and contact her supervisor so that they could get their schedules in sync. Ayana wanted to knock on the bathroom door but decided against it. She knew Daniel needed some time so that he could get himself together to deal with a very emotional time ahead. She walked into their room and began to unpack her bags and wait for further instructions from Meagan and the UN legal team.

Three days after their arrival, a convoy of armored vehicles pulled out from the front of the hotel at three in the morning. The UN legal team was heading out to the massacre site that claimed Victoria's life. Being confined to the hotel almost drove Daniel mad, and although the trip to the site was going to be a hard experience, he still welcomed the change of scenery. It was going to be a very long trip to the far northern border of Southern Sudan. There were concerns that they may meet opposition from the Northern Sudanese border patrol, so the UN decided to send extra security and advise the northern country of their intentions since they would be that close to their southern border.

The ride was bumpy, uncomfortable, and after four hours, everyone in the vehicle was ready for a break, so Patrick decided to make a stop in a small village for a while to stretch their legs. Stepping out of the vehicle, Daniel felt as if his legs were made of wet noodles, and moving too fast would result in him collapsing on the dry, cracked earth beneath him. Holding Ayana's hand, Daniel walked toward what appeared to be a small store and bar. Seeing them moving toward the store, Patrick silently signaled for two security personnel to follow the couple. They immediately rushed toward the doctor and Ayana, following them into the dimly lit makeshift store.

They walked into the store, and their noses were immediately met with the nasal-burning stench of funk, mildew, and strong alcohol. Daniel and Ayana seemed unbothered by the rancid odors, but Meagan immediately placed her hand over her nose and coughed slightly. Daniel turned to her, silently signaling her with his eyes to "suck it up." He didn't want the owner of this store offended by her reaction and refuse them service. Daniel doubted they would find another store for another five hours, and he was thirsty beyond madness.

He walked up to the counter and greeted the old man that possessed a skin tone so dark that it was hard to make him out in the dark shade behind the counter. Short, grey hair covered his head. He scratched repeatedly before extending his hand, smiling brightly to greet the doctor and Ayana. He displayed rows of uncannily clean and well-maintained teeth that caught Meagan off guard, and she gasped without thinking about it. Daniel looked down, shaking his head and praying the nameless barkeep wasn't offended by her reaction.

"Hi, my name is Daniel Bennett. Do you have any soft drinks for sale?"

The barkeep immediately jumped up and began screaming in his native dialect, while pointing at the doctor as if he were some kind of alien. The armed guards immediately sprang into action and rushed toward the bartender with their automatic rifles pointed at him, their fingers on the trigger. Without thinking, Ayana leaped in their path, holding up her hands and leaning backward toward the bartender, shielding him from any attacks.

"Ms. Burundi, please move out of the way," one of the soldiers demanded in his heavy accent.

"No, he's not a threat. He's excited to meet the doctor. Nothing more."

"How do you know that?" the soldier asked, still refusing to lower his weapon.

"Because I speak the dialect he speaks. This is my tribal land. I was born about an hour west of here. He was simply saying, 'I can't believe it's you.' There is no threat here, Soldier. Lower your weapons."

From the doorway of the bar, Patrick yelled, "Lower your weapons and back away!"

They complied and returned to their positions on either side of the door leading into the bar. The bartender was now hiding, stooping behind the wet, wooden counter, so Daniel leaned over the counter and tapped the man on his shoulder. He looked up at Daniel, who was smiling and gesturing for him to come out. The bartender hesitated for a few seconds and then rose to his feet.

"Do you speak English?" Daniel asked, smiling.

"Yes," the bartender answered. "My name is Jean Paul. I am greatly honored to meet you, Doctor. How can I help you?"

"We need something to drink. Not alcohol, but something more refreshing."

"Oh yes, yes, I have soft drinks! I have Coke, Fanta, Sprite, and Dr. Pepper. Which one would you prefer, sir?"

Daniel turned around and asked everyone in the bar, including the two soldiers, what they preferred, and after taking everyone's order, Jean Paul reached behind the counter into the cooler to pull out the drinks. As soon as he disappeared behind the counter, the soldiers lifted their weapons and aimed them in the direction of the bartender. Daniel stopped them before they got up close and personal with the bartender again. Jean Paul returned within seconds, smiling with his hands and arms filled with several different colored glass bottles of soft drinks. When he noticed the aggressive stance of the soldiers, his smile disappeared, and he forcefully placed the drinks on the counter, sucking his teeth.

Ayana immediately walked toward the bartender and began speaking to him in their native tongue, attempting to explain the soldiers' actions, but it appeared the bartender wasn't easily convinced. Once Daniel informed the soldiers, once more, that there wasn't any danger, he turned around toward the bar to pay for the drinks. As he got closer, Jean Paul began to speak to him.

"I hope you can make a difference because we've been under these kinds of conditions for as long as I can remember. Always a gun in our face, always a soldier afraid of civilians even though *they* have weapons, and all we have is our black skin and pride. I hope that after Kronte is gone, none of these armed men will take up his empty slot and restart the clock. We believe in you, Doctor, and we are praying for your success, but please understand that Kronte isn't just a man. He's a mentality. He's a way of life, and those men that are guarding you are products of that way of life."

Daniel turned and looked back at the two soldiers to see if they were listening, and judging by their dark stares in his direction, they were. Leaning forward, he placed his hand on the bartender's hand, trying to calm him down, but it wasn't working, and the tension continued to build. Daniel began to understand just how bad things had gotten since the last time he's been here. He then understood that even if they could accomplish the impossible, the tensions between the people and the government were so high, another war was bound to spark again if something wasn't done. It was a heavy realization, and it made him feel like no victory could be had here. Just like in the bar, if someone didn't back down, no amount of outside interference could prevent a disaster.

"Let's go now," Daniel demanded after leaving a US hundred-dollar bill on the counter. He immediately grabbed hold of his drink and stormed out of the bar with the soldiers quickly following . . .

The motorcade, pulling into the desolate ruins of the village, came to a halt, and everyone slowly stepped out of the vehicles. The air tasted foul and burned like fire entering the lungs, causing everyone to cough and spit. The clouds covered the sun, preventing its warm and revealing light from penetrating the dusty and dry terrain. The lack of sun and dry, blowing wind sent a depressing vibe through the group as they walked toward the village of Talasidada that was once the home of over three hundred souls. Now it was merely a scorched and dead patch of land. It appeared the earth itself mourned the evil that happened here, and it refused to allow even one blade of grass to grow there again.

Not much left of the village besides flattened clay walls and old, rotting timber. Everything else that made this place home was either burned or looted by Kronte and his troops. Daniel slowly walked toward what used to be the center of the town where his life changed forever, and he immediately fell to his knees, overcome with the torture of the memory of losing everything in one short afternoon. Ayana joined him on the ground, holding him while she cried, looking at the ground where she imagined her baby met her death in the most inhumane way. Meagan couldn't hold back the tears as they ran down her face, watching the two of them thrown into a time capsule of pain and remorse.

Patrick, unmoved by their display, sucked his teeth and ordered the soldiers to secure the area while he walked over to them.

"Doctor, we don't have much time here. The longer we stay out in the open, the more dangerous this trip becomes. I need you to go through that day with us here today so that we can assess the validity of your testimony."

"Hold on! Wait a fucking minute! What you mean 'validity of his testimony'?" Meagan asked, pulling on Patrick's shoulder, making him face her.

"Thousands of people say they saw Kronte in person, but none of their testimonies add up," he responded, pulling away from her while looking at his shoulder where she touched him. "We need to confirm everything the doctor said is true. Otherwise, if there is one inconsistency in his story, Kronte will go free. So, as the head of this investigation, I am obligated to take whatever steps needed to ensure we are not made a fool of in front of the courts."

Meagan was about to protest further, but Daniel held up his hand and nodded his head.

"I was in the medical facility, preparing for another busy day. Many of the villagers had come down with yellow fever, so I'd been extremely busy for the previous two weeks. I could hear a few of the village children playing right outside of the window, and I remembered smiling because it had been awhile since any of the children were well enough to play. The children seemed to be having a blast, so I stuck my head out the window to see what they were doing. That's when I saw the dust cloud made by oncoming vehicles from the west of the village. Any other day, I wouldn't have made much of it, but this dust cloud was massive, which, when you live in this region, you already know what that means. Run!

"I immediately ran to sound the alarm at the guard post, but someone struck me from behind, knocking me to the ground. I must have been out for a few minutes because when I came to, all I could hear was the screams of the villagers and bodies . . . So many bodies were lying all around me. Once my head stopped spinning, I looked around, and whoever hit me had left me there alone, so I jumped up looking for my daughter, who I left sleeping in our hut. Our hut was right over there, about twelve feet from the medical building. I looked for her, but she wasn't in the hut, so I made sure I stayed out of sight of Kronte's forces as I moved from structure to structure, looking for her.

"I was about to double back when I heard her screams coming from the middle of the village. Her screams . . . they were so . . . I could feel her pain through her screams. It made my blood turn cold. I rushed toward her screams, not caring about who saw me. I didn't care about the violence that was going on around me. I just wanted to save my baby. I saw a group of Kronte's soldiers standing in a circle, looking down at something. They were cheering, and a few of them were unbuckling their pants."

Daniel then sprinted away from the group toward a pile of mud bricks . . . The only thing left standing of the medical facility he helped build. Looking down at the cracked earth, he wailed in agony as he collapsed to his knees and seemed to lift an invisible body from the dirt. "Oh, my baby. Look what they've done to my baby. I'm so sorry. I'm so sorry, baby."

Ayana placed her hand over her chest and began to weep. Kneeling next to him on her knees, she wrapped her arms around him and whispered in his ear, "It's OK. Let it out. Let it go."

It took Daniel another hour before he concluded his verbal recollection. Then the group packed up their gear and headed back to their vehicles for the long ride back to the hotel . . .

Chapter 23

First Round Knockdown

Wednesday 5:00 a.m., Juba, South Sudan. The mood in the room was a mixture of excitement and fear as Meagan, Daniel, and Ayana packed up everything they needed for the trial. Today was the day, and no one had gotten any sleep the night before. Daniel was to ride alone with a heavily guarded motorcade, and Meagan and Ayana would travel in a different motorcade. Ayana wasn't comfortable being away from Daniel, but she had no choice. There wouldn't be any room in the vehicle for anyone besides Daniel and the many armed soldiers who would be acting as human shields, just in case a sniper tried to get a clean shot. The human shields would not have been necessary, but the armored vehicles were pulled from their security details due to an uprising in a village toward the east, and the government needed to transport some delegates out of the area before things got out of hand.

Meagan pleaded with the American Embassy in Juba for some assistance in security, but they declined her request. They were at the mercy of the Southern Sudanese government forces, which she didn't trust one bit, but she had to work with the hand she was dealt.

"When you get into the vehicle, turn this on and don't turn it off," Meagan said, handing Daniel a small black box similar to a pager.

"What is this?" he asked, looking over the device with confusion.

"It's a solar-powered GPS tracking device. It uses satellite triangulation technology, and it can track you in any structure, even underground, up to twenty feet below the earth's surface. It has a seventy-two-hour standby battery life, just in case you are in a location without solar energy."

Nodding, Daniel began to place the unit in his pants pocket, but Meagan stopped him before he could complete the job.

"No, don't put it in your pocket."

"So where should I put it?" he asked, turning his head slightly to the right and looking her up and down.

"No, silly boy, not there," she replied, giggling. "Here, use this," she said, handing him a carrying case with a strap attached that would wrap around his thigh.

"Damn, I just put these pants on," he playfully complained, before walking into the bedroom to put the unit on.

When he was out of sight, Ayana walked over to Meagan, still keeping her eyes on the bedroom door to make sure Daniel didn't come out before she said what she needed to say.

"Meagan, what's going on? You don't trust Patrick Wek?"

"Hell no! I don't trust *anyone* here. There are too many 'coincidences' occurring since we've arrived here. The uprising in the east was the last straw for me because there hasn't been one news report about it on local or international channels, and when I asked the embassy for help, they turned me down without an explanation. Something isn't right about how they are handling things, and I'm not taking any chances."

"Then call off the trial. Postpone it! Ask for a change of venue and get Daniel out of here, Meagan," Ayana pleaded, now alarmed after listening to Meagan explain her suspicions.

"I tried that too. No flights available until next week," she replied, flopping down on the couch and burying her head in her hands and screaming. "I placed us all in danger, Ayana, and I'm not sure if any of us will get out of here alive. I just hope I'm overreacting, and everything goes as it should. Should we tell Daniel?"

Ayana looked down at her and remained silent. Suddenly, she heard movement behind her, and there stood Daniel, looking at both of them, worried about the expressions on their faces.

"What's up? Is everything okay?" he asked while reaching out to Ayana and pulling her closer to him.

"Yeah, just a little nervous about today. We want to make sure everything goes as planned," Ayana lied while forcing a smile. Just then, a loud knock vibrated through the room from the door, and they heard Patrick Wek's voice advising Daniel it was time to go.

Smiling, Daniel held Ayana tightly, kissing her gently on the lips and then walked toward the door. Before walking out the door, he looked back, smiling, and said, "I love you." Ayana collapsed on the couch next to Meagan once the door closed behind him, fearing it could be the last time she would see him alive . . .

Outside, Daniel stepped into a large military vehicle already occupied by at least six soldiers, and once he was seated, six more soldiers followed him inside and closed the door. Patrick peered into the window, smiling slyly while looking directly into the doctor's eyes, sending a cold chill up his spine. He then tapped on the side of the vehicle, and it pulled away. Once they were on their way, Daniel looked around the interior of the vehicle and introduced himself to the soldiers, who, in turn, warmly introduced themselves. Daniel's eyes moved from each dark-skinned face to the next and quickly noticed he didn't recognize any of the soldiers. Because of his previous experiences in Africa, he made it a point to remember every face assigned to his personal security. Taking a closer look, Daniel shook his head as he noticed they were all very young, appearing to be no older than 18. The uncomfortable feeling of being set up began to cloud his mind, so he decided to see just how bad of a situation he was in. He began to ask them each their ages and how long they've been in the armed forces.

His anxiety intensified when he discovered all of them were fresh out of boot camp and were given this detail a couple of days ago.

What the fuck is going on?

Although he should've been afraid of the men surrounding him, he didn't feel like any of them meant to do him harm and were genuinely concerned about his well-being. Then one of the men pulled out his cell phone and began playing the infamous bathroom video to the amusement of all in the vehicle, except the doctor. The soldier with the cell phone noticed the doctor's anger and leaned toward him, smiling and saying, "I meant no disrespect, Doctor. It's just that Ms. Burundi is like a celebrity here, and for you to be her husband . . . well . . . That's impressive. Also, what you are doing for our people is incredibly brave. You didn't have to be here, but you are, and we will give our lives to make sure you make it to that trial."

Despite his anxiety, Daniel began to smile. Seeing him relax gave some of the soldiers the confidence to start telling jokes to lighten the mood.

"Doctor Bennett, a man asked one hundred women what shampoo they preferred, and do you know what they said?"

Shaking his head, Daniel chuckled and said, "I don't know. What did they say?"

"How the hell did you get in here?"

Another chuckle escaped Daniel's mouth as nodded his head and said, "Good one."

Seeing that the doctor was entertained, the soldier decided to tell another joke.

"Dr. Bennett, the other day, I was having sex with a married woman when her husband came home early. She told me I'd have to use the back door and said I'd have to be quick. On reflection, I should have just left, but it's not every day you get an offer like that."

The vehicle erupted in laughter, and Daniel and the soldiers leaned over on each other laughing hysterically. As everyone tried to catch their breath, the jokester held up his finger and said, "One more, eh?"

Wiping the tears from his eyes, Daniel nodded and said, "Yes, one more."

"Why is girlfriend one word and best friend two words?"

"I don't know. Why?"

"Because your best friend gives you space when you need it!"

Everyone started to laugh again, and the jokester was preparing for another joke, and his audience was all too eager to hear it.

"I asked my wife if I was the only one she's been with. She said, 'Yes, the others were sevens or eights.'"

Daniel pointed at the soldier and laughed gingerly. As the rest of the soldiers continued to enjoy the entertainment, Daniel looked out the front window of the vehicle right . . . before the concussive blast from the exploding land mine went off, sending the vehicles in front fifteen feet into the air and shattering the glass around his vehicle.

Immediately, the soldiers began fumbling with their weapons and screaming in their native tongues. A number of them jumped on top of Daniel to shield him while the rest of them lifted their guns in preparation for an attack. Without warning, a hail of bullets penetrated the vehicle, tearing through the driver's body and sending vast amounts of blood spraying everywhere.

"What's going on?" Daniel yelled from under the pile of soldiers. One of the soldiers yelled for him to remain silent and stay down. Then the entire truck began to shake violently, and he suddenly felt a surge of extreme heat as his stomach felt like he was going down the steep plunge of a roller coaster. Everyone in the vehicle was upside down, banging on the ceiling of the truck, and then the truck leaned backward, sending everyone toward the back of the vehicle and on top of the doctor. The weight knocked the air out of him as he tried to scream, but nothing came out. He was suffocating fast, and then in the next moment, the vehicle leaned forward, crashing into the hard dirt road, smashing the front of it, and sending glass and metal toward the back.

The hail of bullets returned, cutting through the soldiers covering the doctor. He could hear them screaming in agony and felt their blood splatter all over his face. The assault went on for over three minutes, and then as suddenly as it started, everything stopped. The young soldiers still alive, yet mortally wounded, were either screaming in pain or whimpering out their last breath. The damaged side door flung open, and Daniel got a glimpse of the shooters. It was déjà vu from many years ago. The men that peered inside the vehicle looked just like the boys that lay on top of him.

"Where's the doctor?" one of the men asked a barely conscious soldier. The boy remained silent, holding a large, bloody wound on his side. The attacker didn't ask again as he raised his rifle and fired several bullets into the boy's body. He then began to push aside the bodies, looking for the doctor, now buried deeper beneath bodies, metal, and rubble.

"Is he in there?" asked another voice from outside the vehicle.

"I don't see him, and there is so much shit, I can't tell if he's among the dead or even in here at all."

"I need to inform Mr. Wek immediately," yelled the voice outside the vehicle.

"Fuck that! I'll throw a grenade inside: that way, we know for sure he's dead. No need to inform Mr. Wek of anything. He'll become vexed and try to cheat us out of our pay!"

Daniel began to shake in terror at the thought of a grenade going off inside the vehicle. That would surely kill him. He closed his eyes tightly and held his breath as he prepared himself to feel the heat and shrapnel of the exploding grenade.

"No! No grenade, you imbecile! If you throw a grenade in there, we won't get physical confirmation. Just empty another clip into the vehicle, and let's go. Our job is done here. He *was* in this vehicle, and as far as I'm concerned, the doctor is dead, and if not, he'll be dead soon enough."

"No, I don't care about physical confirmation! I just want to make sure he's dead!"

"Soldier, I am giving you an order. Do *not* throw a grenade in this vehicle!"

Daniel heard the double click and the loud cracking sound of the rifle spewing death throughout the vehicle. The bodies on top of him shook violently as they were torn to pieces by the multitude of bullets that ripped through the damaged truck. Then he felt it . . . The burning, penetrating, agonizing pain of a bullet tearing through his right thigh. He wanted to scream, but he put his hand over his mouth . . . right before feeling another bullet pierced through his left side that seemed to reopen an old wound. The pain was indescribable, but the doctor remained silent, trying to fight back the need to scream out in agony. It seemed like the attacker had an endless number of bullets because he appeared to go on and on without reloading. Then suddenly, the loud cracking stopped, and the attacker slammed the door and ran off.

Daniel could hear other men yelling and the sounds of several vehicles pulling away in the distance. He listened for another five minutes before he removed his hands from his mouth and yelled out in pain. He placed his hand on his wounded side, feeling his blood pour out of it like thick syrup. He tried to move, but the pain in his side made it difficult for him to brace himself to push the bodies off him, so he decided to lie there silently and wait for the calming veil of death to overtake his consciousness . . .

Chapter 24

The Countdown

Ayana collapsed in Meagan's arms after the smug and unconcerned Patrick Wek delivered the news that Daniel's motorcade was attacked, and he feared that he was one of the many casualties. Meagan looked at Mr. Wek searching for answers in his eyes, but all she saw was a coldness that seemed almost inhuman. The court-room went into panic mode as the news of the attack on the motorcade spread like wildfire. Meagan glanced over at Kronte and his legal team, and the look on Kronte's face said it all. He was all too pleased with himself, and he couldn't hide it. The longer Meagan looked at him, she discovered he wasn't trying to hide his satisfaction with the news. Then in classic Kronte fashion, he smiled while looking in the women's direction and made a shooting gesture toward them.

Meagan adjusted herself to contend with the added weight of Ayana leaning on her and rolled her eyes at his antics. Although all common sense should tell her she should be terrified of Kronte, she wasn't. For a few seconds, she considered trying to reach for one of the security forces' guns and taking justice in her own hands, but she knew it wouldn't give her or anyone affected by the man's evil reign of terror one ounce of justice.

"Ayana, pull yourself together. We have to address the panel in a few minutes, and we need to ask for a continuance until we can confirm Daniel's death. There's still a chance he's *not* dead."

Ayana looked up at her, shook her head, and then continued to wail in agony. Kronte was becoming more excited and aroused by the pain Ayana was feeling, knowing her boyfriend was dead.

Stupid bitch. Should've never tried to cross me.

He then leaned over and began to whisper in his lawyer's ear. The lawyer immediately got up and headed out of the courtroom's massive double doors, into the white, marble-covered hallway. Outside in the hallway, Patrick was addressing a group of reporters, and the lawyer stood by waiting for his interview to be done. Once Patrick addressed the last reporter, he fixed his tie proudly and turned around to address the lawyer.

"What is it?" he asked in his heavy Sudanese accent.

Without saying a word, the lawyer nodded and walked back inside the courtroom. Rolling his eyes, Patrick pulled his cell phone out of his grey suit jacket pocket and placed a call. The background noise of a noisy engine and the loud, chaotic chatter of multiple voices shouting and vying to be heard blasted in his ear when the person picked up, and he quickly pulled the phone back.

"Hello? Mr. Wek?"

"Report!"

"Everyone is dead, sir."

"I need visual confirmation that the target was silenced."

"Sorry, sir, we don't have visual confirmation. There were so many bodies on top of him, so we decided to shoot up the entire vehicle again to make sure."

Patrick gritted his teeth and quickly moved out of sight and hearing of anyone that may be standing at the door leading into the courtroom.

"You fucking idiot! I told you visual confirmation is the only way you will get paid. Now, take your incompetent ass back to the vehicle and get visual confirmation. Do it now!"

"But, sir, the area is crawling with government security forces now—"

"I don't care! Get it done," he grunted into the phone and abruptly ended the call. Looking around to make sure no one was nearby, he quietly swore through his teeth before heading back into the courtroom. Once inside, he quickly looked over at the lawyer who was seated next to Kronte and shook his head. Kronte's entire demeanor changed when he noticed Patrick's response. Meagan was watching both men closely, and their actions confirmed what she already knew—they were all in league with one another. Once she noticed Kronte's change in confidence, she quickly moved toward the front of the large courtroom to discuss her options with the court judges.

"Your Honors, please excuse my intrusion, but in light of the current events, I would humbly request a continuance until we can confirm the fate of Dr. Bennett."

Before the head judge, a dark, heavy man wearing an old-English white wig could lean forward to respond, Kronte's lawyer sprang into action, trying to prevent the judge from deciding before he had input.

"Your Honor, I move to have this charade stopped now, and my client allowed to go free! Their so-called star witness is believed to be dead, and we can't wait for him to be raised from the dead. A report from the area says there were no survivors. Without his testimony, the UN Security Council has nothing on my client, and I request he be released."

The judge's face immediately turned sour as he stared at the rude lawyer making his way up to the panel with a calm, yet apparent, disgust.

"Counsel, I don't know how they do things in Europe, but in Southern Sudan, we don't just blurt out orders to a panel of judges, nor do we call these proceedings a 'charade.' The charges against your client are serious. These are not mere traffic violations or petty theft. Your client is accused of murder, rape, genocide, and a demon's basket full of other evils. It's either the miracle of stupidity or maybe intoxication that would lead you to believe I would even entertain releasing that man before this trial is concluded or the prosecution drops all charges."

Hearing the judge's response, the lawyer stopped in his tracks and retreated to Kronte's side. Meagan looked down at the floor, smiled, and then looked up to wait for the judge to give her an answer for her request. The judge kept his eyes on the lawyer, shaking his head. Then he looked down at Meagan, widening his eyes and shaking his head, annoyed by her presence.

"What is it?"

"The continuance, Your Honor?"

"Oh, that," he responded while throwing his hands in the air. "You people are asking too much today. But because the defense was so rude, I will grant you seven days to gather whatever evidence you can against Kronte."

"Your Honor, that's not enough time to find out if . . ."

"Ms. Quinn, there is very little chance your Dr. Bennett is alive, so let's not go over that again. Seven days and not a day more. Come back here with a solid case, or we will have to call it a mistrial and, unfortunately, release the accused. Am I making myself clear?"

"Yes, Your Honor," she responded, exhaling deeply.

"Good, now have a good day," he yelled, slamming his gavel.

Back at the hotel, Ayana went into her room and closed the door without saying a word. Meagan sat down on the couch and looked off in the distance in a daze. Then an aggressive knock jolted her out of her daydream.

"Yes?"

"It's Sergeant Edwards, ma'am."

"Are you alone?" she yelled from behind the door while looking through the peephole.

"Ma'am?"

Rolling her eyes, she opened the door and forcefully pulled him into the room, then looked down either side of the hallway before closing the door.

"What are you doing here, Sergeant?"

"The Canadian and French ambassadors sent me and three platoons of Special Forces personnel, ma'am. They heard about what happened to the doctor, but when the UN Security Forces went to search the vehicle, his body wasn't there. It appeared someone dragged him out. We tracked a vehicle headed toward the west side of Juba. We believe he's alive and in the company of friendlies, but he's not out of the woods yet. If we know he might still be alive, so does Kronte's men."

"Listen to me, Sergeant, Patrick Wek is a rat, and he's on Kronte's payroll."

"How do you know that, ma'am? Do you have solid intel you can share to back that up?"

"No, I don't," she replied angrily.

"Then we can't use that, but we will keep that in advisement while we move out to go search for the doctor. You and Ms. Burundi should remain at the hotel. I am leaving a platoon here for your protection."

"You can leave whomever you want, but we are *not* staying here."

"Ma'am?"

She moved aggressively toward the soldier and began to whisper in his ear. After about a minute, he nodded and immediately left the room without saying a word . . .

The smell of blood, alcohol, and an unfamiliar, earthy, and organic smell filled Daniel's nostrils, causing him to jerk and shake. His eyes shot open; then the pain from his wounds caught up with his consciousness, and he began to cough and squirm. He looked around to take in his environment, which appeared to be a red mud hut with a burning fire on the far right side of the structure. A pile of bloodied white towels lay near the fire, as well as a couple of empty bottles of rubbing alcohol. The roof of the hut was made of small tree branches sewn tightly together that effectively kept the storm raging outside, where it belonged. He felt exhausted, thirsty, and starved, but he closed his eyes, thankful that he was still among the land of the living.

The sound of movement behind him startled him, and he called out to find out who was sharing this hut with him. A strained and deep accented voice answered, "My name is Barry."

"Your name is Barry, and you are Sudanese," Daniel said, trying to twist his body so he could see to whom he was speaking.

"Yes, Barry. Don't worry about how misplaced my name is. Barry, Barry, Barry, Barry, Barry," the man kept repeating while clapping his hands. "My name is the least of your troubles, Dr. Bennett."

"You know who I am?"

"Of course. Otherwise, I would've left you out there to die."

"That's kind of cold," Daniel whispered while clearing his throat.

"Ha! I have a village and family to think about. The last thing my people need is for Kronte's men to come here and set it—and us—on fire."

"You're the chief here?"

"Correct."

"Why would you risk your village and family for me?"

"Because whether Kronte's men come here today or tonight or next week, they *will* eventually come, and so far, you are the only person that has the power to stop him. So I brought you here to heal you and then help you get to the courthouse so that you can do what you came here to do."

"Are you the village doctor?"

"Oh no, Gregory is the village doctor. But after everyone finds out I brought you here, I might end up being the village idiot."

There go those out-of-place names again.

"So, Gregory and Barry saved my life?"

"Correct."

"Thank you."

"Aah, don't thank us yet, Dr. Bennett. We have yet to figure out how we are going to get you to the courthouse alive."

"Why take me there? Just get me to the hotel."

"To be a doctor, you aren't very bright."

"Hey, what's that supposed to mean?"

"Doctor, the hotel is a private establishment with people that work there for a very small salary. It's clear Kronte has eyes everywhere. One sight of you there and his men will come there to finish the job. At the courthouse, you have a better chance, because that's a government building that also houses the UN Security offices. Although Kronte is an evil man, he isn't a stupid man. He knows attacking any UN soldiers or personnel will be displeasing to his sponsors. So, going to the hotel would end in your death and anyone that's with you. Therefore, it's the courthouse, so you can put that monster away for good and free my people from his treachery."

"Then are you are basically using me?"

"It's no different than how the Western world treats Africa and Africans. They use our land, resources, and the people. If we have no value to your own advancement, you toss us away like garbage."

"Not all people from the West are like that."

"Maybe, but none of you stand up to your politicians. You sit by and watch your governments destroy entire civilizations as if it's trivial entertainment. So, excuse my coldness toward your situation, outside of you testifying against Kronte."

"Then what's next?"

"Well, the word is your woman Ayana and Ms. Quinn were allowed seven days by the courts to either find you or bring more evidence against Kronte. You've been out for forty-eight hours, so we have five more days to get you healed enough to move you. You lost a lot of blood, but our doctor Gregory was able to stop the bleeding and remove the bullet from your side. He used some natural herbs that should speed up your recovery."

Hearing Meagan's name made Daniel subconsciously reach down for the device that he had strapped to his thigh, but he quickly discovered it was no longer there.

"If you are looking for that tracking and listening device, it's no longer operational. When the bullet went through your thigh, that device got damaged. Good thing, because it took most of the force of the bullet. Had it not been there, I'm afraid you may not have been able to walk again."

"To be just a village chief, you seem to know a lot about a lot."

"You Americans look at what a person has as a measurement of their intellect or self-worth," Barry chuckled.

"That's not who I am."

"Oh, you don't have anything to prove to me, Doctor. The fact that you are here, trying to rid us of Kronte, shows the kind of man you are. That's why you are in my home and not out there rotting on the side of the road. Enough talk. Get some rest. Someone will be along to bring you water and something to eat. It's not McDonald's, but it's all we have," he joked before walking out of the hut.

Daniel lay there, trying to gather his thoughts about the events during his ride to the courthouse.

All those young boys . . . dead.

At that moment and thinking about their sacrifice, Daniel decided that no matter what, Kronte wasn't going to stop him from testifying. Even if it meant his life, he would testify, and whatever he needed to do to get to the courthouse, he was willing to do it. Then his mind wandered to thoughts of Ayana and the pain she must be feeling, believing he was dead. Exhaling, he placed his hands on his head and tried to calm himself and prepare his body for an interesting trip in the next five days.

Chapter 25

The Comeback Kid

Patrick Wek, sitting in the backseat of his Mercedes, screamed obscenities to one of the soldiers-turned-assassin on his cell phone. They discovered that the doctor's body wasn't at the site of the attack, and, therefore, there was a good chance he survived.

He's like a fucking "cocka" roach.

They'd searched the area for any signs of the doctor, but couldn't find him, so they concluded someone might have helped him get away. Patrick knew that if the doctor were allowed to live and testify, he would be exposed, and Kronte would make sure his family would pay the ultimate price if he didn't close the loop. He turned his attention to his surroundings and noticed that the driver was driving much too slowly for him, so he reached forward, smacking the driver across the back of the head, screaming, "Step on it, you idiot!"

Racing through the night, Patrick was on his way to the hotel with a truckload of soldiers behind him. At this point, he was desperate, and he didn't care how it looked when he stormed the hotel and took the two women working for the UN. He needed some kind of bargaining chip, just in case the doctor showed his face at the courthouse.

Corporal Williams looked through his night vision goggles at the two speeding vehicles headed straight for the hotel and silently signaled his platoon to stay alert. Sergeant Edwards briefed them on the possibility that Patrick Wek was compromised and could attempt to kidnap the two UN representatives, Ms. Burundi and Ms. Quinn. His strict orders were "under no circumstances was anyone allowed inside the hotel." Corporal Williams knew what that meant. He and his team were locked, loaded, and ready to cut down anyone attempting to force their way inside the hotel.

The corporal swallowed hard as he braced himself for anything. Once the car and truck filled with about fifteen soldiers pulled up in front of the hotel, the UN soldiers stationed at the hotel's entrance stepped forward, attempting to stop the men.

"Hold on, Mr. Wek. The hotel is on lockdown. No one is allowed to leave or enter here until further notice," the soldier warned with one hand up and the other firmly holding his sidearm with the safety off.

"Get out of my way, Soldier. I would hate for you not to return home to your family," Patrick snapped back. His threat caused the other two UN soldiers hiding in the tall bushes on either side of the walkway leading into the hotel lobby to jump out and surround Patrick, with their weapons aimed at his head. Patrick's entire body froze in place as he found himself surrounded.

"Gentlemen, let's relax. For the safety of Ms. Burundi and Ms. Quinn, I was instructed to take them to a more secure location after what happened to Dr. Bennett."

"The safest location for either of them is here with us. No disrespect, sir, but if any of your men attempt to force their way inside the hotel, *you* will be the first to die."

"What! Do you *know* who I am?"

"Yes, sir, and I will kill you, all the same, if you or any of your men attempt to get past me."

Patrick gave the corporal an evil grin before he began backing away with his hands raised over his head.

"This isn't over. I will get inside that hotel and get what I came for."

"If a bullet in your brain is what you came for, then I agree, but if you try to get anything else, it may not work out as you planned. Now, clear this area immediately!"

Patrick continued to back away. After about five minutes of dead silence, the corporal noticed that the vehicles weren't leaving, so he backed away toward the front entrance of the hotel. The other soldiers, noticing his reaction, began to move in defensive positions as well, awaiting his orders. Corporal Williams placed his hands over his ear communication piece and advised his team to ready themselves for an assault, right before the first wave of bullets rang out toward them. The corporal immediately kneeled behind a large concrete pillar that held up the walkway's overhead cover and placed his assault rifle's night vision scope over his eye. Once he was able to locate his attackers, he yelled out, "Weapons free!" and his comrades began to return fire.

Hell erupted in front of the hotel as bullets tore into the concrete and shattered the massive windows that covered the entire front of the elegant, yet small hotel. Corporal Williams used his night vision scope to pick off one Sudanese soldier after the other with precision, making sure he conserved ammo while maintaining his position in front of the hotel. Patrick was hiding behind his vehicle, yelling out orders for his soldiers to push forward. In his anger, he didn't notice that their numbers were dwindling fast, and soon, only a handful of his soldiers remained on their feet, cowering behind the now-demolished truck they had ridden in. Still unable to see that he was overmatched, Patrick kept demanding the soldiers push forward, but they all remained in their hiding places, pretending they couldn't hear him over the gunfire.

Seeing that the Sudanese soldiers were retreating behind the truck, Corporal Williams silently signaled for his squad to advance to finish off the remaining soldiers and capture Patrick Wek. The soldiers posted on the roof of the hotel began to lay down cover fire so that the Sudanese soldiers couldn't peek out from behind their hiding places and notice the UN soldiers were advancing on their positions. Signaling for flanking positions, Corporal Williams ordered the team of five UN soldiers to move silently around Patrick and the remaining Sudanese soldiers. Once they had them directly in their sights, the UN soldiers aimed their weapons at the men's heads. Patrick, ducking behind his Mercedes, looked up just in time to see Williams's weapon next to his temple; then Patrick did something that startled the soldier for a split second. Williams was expecting an expression of fear or surprise on the traitor's face, but what he did, instead, was smile so brightly, Williams could see his ultra white teeth in the pitch-blackness of the night.

Then from the top floor of the hotel, multiple gunshots rang out, and Williams's communication earpiece erupted with the sounds of the remaining team members in the hotel, yelling what the corporal already knew. The frontal assault by Patrick and his soldiers was a distraction. Another force of Sudanese soldiers was storming the hotel toward their objective. Refusing to look away toward the hotel, Williams kept Patrick in his sights, while demanding an update from his second-in-command on the roof.

"How many are there, Soldier?"

"There are about thirty soldiers, sir. What is your situation?"

"We have Mr. Wek and five of his soldiers captive. We can move inside to assist."

"No, sir, there are a lot of these muthafuckers, but we'll give 'em hell, sir. If you assist, Mr. Wek will escape, and we can't have that. I'm going to move inside the hotel and assist."

Williams didn't want to lose any soldiers, but he knew they had to hold this position until morning, so he gave the soldier the okay, and he immediately fired a warning shot close to Patrick's head. The whistle and heat from the passing bullet caused Patrick to scream in a high-pitched tone that sounded like a hyena or whining puppy.

"Are you crazy? You almost killed me!"

"Almost don't count. Call off your men or the next one will."

"Kill me. Go ahead. It won't stop the obvious, and if you kill me, my men have been ordered to kill everyone in that hotel, and I do mean *everyone*. All you had to do was turn over the women, and no one would have to die. But since you provoked me—"

Williams fired another shot, and this time, it found its intended target, which was Patrick's right ankle. The pain and burn of the bullet tearing through such a sensitive and fragile part of his body sent Patrick reeling back onto the ground. Screaming and cursing, he rolled back and forth, holding his leg in agony.

"You fucking pig! How dare you—"

"I may not be able to kill you, but I will make you suffer if you don't call off your men. The next shot will go into one of your kneecaps. Now, if you want to be able to walk again, I would suggest you call off your hit squad. I won't ask you again."

"Fuck y—"

The loud ear-splitting crack of Williams's assault rifle going off shook the resolve of the other captured Sudanese soldiers, and they all jumped, while raising their hands even higher than they were before. Tears began to pour out of Patrick's eyes as the pain and visual devastation of his kneecap sank in. He began to feel faint as his body tried to cope with so much pain from two different locations on his body. Noticing Patrick losing consciousness, Williams quickly turned his rifle around and savagely struck him on his wounded ankle, springing Patrick back into consciousness.

"I can do this all night, you piece of shit! Call them off now!"

"You can't do this! It's against the UN rules of engagement! We are your prisoners," Patrick screamed while weeping in pain.

"I don't see any UN commissioners around, do you? You weren't quoting international rules of engagement when you attempted to murder Dr. Bennett, nor did I hear a peep about any code violations while you attacked us."

Then without warning, Williams fired another bullet in Patrick's other knee, tearing open flesh and shattering bone. Patrick was now out of his mind in agony, and he began to howl like a wolf, trying to get his body to comprehend the extreme levels of pain the corporal's torture put him through. With both knees damaged beyond repair, Patrick's lower body went limp, and he lay on the dirt as if he were in a casket, ready for burial.

"I got a full clip. You only have two nuts, and with this scope, I could hit them with my eyes closed."

Patrick's eyes grew to the size of silver dollars as the corporal's threat sent his body into a frenzy of terror.

"No, no, no, no, no, please. Enough! I'll call them off! No more! I can't take anymore!"

"You have five seconds."

"I'm in so much pain I can barely lift my arm to speak into my radio . . ."

"One . . ."

"Wait! Wait! Okay!"

"Two . . ."

Patrick began to slowly lift his walkie-talkie toward his mouth while staring at Williams, his eyes begging for compassion. Williams stared back coldly and unmoved. For Williams, each second could be another one of his team members getting wounded or worse, and he wasn't going to give Patrick any more time.

"Three . . . four . . ." and then Williams moved forward, stepping down hard on Patrick's thigh and pointed his rifle at his genitals, readying himself to fire another torturous shot.

"Stand down! Stand down! Drop your weapons now," he screamed into the radio while squeezing his eyes closed tightly, bracing himself for another round of horrendous pain. The sound of gunfire ceased immediately, and Williams could hear the familiar voices of his team ordering Patrick's men to get down on the ground.

"Report!" Williams yelled while activating his ear-mounted communication device.

"All threats have surrendered, sir, and are being detained."

"How many team liabilities?" he asked while swallowing hard, preparing himself for the pain of losing men under his command. The pause after his question increased his anxiety, and he braced himself for the worst.

"Four wounded, two critical, and six KIA, sir."

Williams stumbled slightly as the numbers sank in, and the realization that he would have to answer to the soldiers' families—men with wives, children, parents, siblings, and planned futures. All snuffed out too soon because the bastard squirming at his feet wanted more . . . It was always about more and not about who would suffer while they got more. Shaking his head, the humidity of the African heat seemed to make his head spin.

Patrick looked up at Williams while begging for medical attention, fearing he would bleed out and die. Williams was in a daze, and by the time Patrick's annoying whine snapped him out of his confusion, he'd already decided that Patrick wouldn't see another sunrise. He knew he couldn't kill him now, but he also knew he didn't have to save him. So, he turned around, heading toward the hotel and left Patrick bleeding in the dirt. The other UN soldiers that were watching him understood his intentions. No one said a word and pretended the wounded man on the ground was invisible.

All this death and the women aren't even in the hotel . . .

Chapter 26

Rumble in the Jungle

While Sergeant Edwards drove the Hummer toward West Juba, he periodically looked over with an uncomfortable amusement at Ayana expertly handling the AK-47. She was cleaning it and loading the clip with such ease that he wondered if she could take it apart faster than he could.

Damn, she's good.

Looking up, she caught the sergeant staring at her with his mouth slightly ajar.

"I was 'the wife' of a ruthless warlord. It was smart of me to pick up a few useful things," Ayana said while shaking her head. "I first learned how to clean the weapons, and then I learned how to shoot. By the time I was able to escape, I was a better shot than Kronte, and he used to be an elite sniper in the Sudanese army."

Edwards nodded while tilting his head. He was clearly impressed with her résumé, but he still wasn't comforttable with her and Meagan accompanying him to locate the doctor. However, once Meagan whispered to him that their room was bugged, he understood just how dangerous it would be leaving them there, so he reluctantly brought them along. He ordered Corporal Williams and the remaining men to keep all communications "dark" until the morning. He knew that Kronte's puppets would be monitoring all communication channels, and he needed time to get into the city undetected during the night. He prayed that Patrick wouldn't be so bold as to attack the hotel, but he knew desperation makes people do some insane things, and he dreaded getting the first update at sunrise.

Looking at his watch, he noticed it was just after one in the morning. They were almost in the city, so he decided it was time to brief the ladies and the other four soldiers he brought along with him.

"When we get into the city, we need to move quickly and silently. If we run into any opposition, we should seek to avoid conflict, but if we have no other choice, we need to take out the opposition as quietly as possible. That means I need everyone packing something sharp and shiny. Am I clear?"

"Yes, sir," the soldiers responded in unison.

Noticing neither Ayana nor Meagan responded, he looked at both of them awaiting their responses.

"Oh, yes, sir," Ayana giggled while playfully saluting the sergeant. Her playful and relaxed demeanor made him very uncomfortable, and he slightly adjusted himself in the seat while clearing his throat. Meagan tapped Ayana on the shoulder, trying to get her attention and find out what her problem was. Ayana looked at her friend, rolling her eyes while shaking her head. Meagan knew now wasn't the time to lecture Ayana about the dangers of the city, but she was hoping Ayana wasn't losing it. The last thing they needed was for her to get into the city and start acting as if she were Rambo.

"We are getting close to Juba Bridge. Everyone, get down now," announced Edwards, right before he began to accelerate. He didn't want to be moving so slowly that anyone walking by or standing alongside the road could see inside the vehicle and notice the precious cargo he was carrying. While leaning down, Ayana looked up at the top of the newly constructed Juba Bridge through the window. It was a sign that things were changing for her people, yet the fact they were traveling across it like smuggled contraband reminded her that much was still the same. The burn of determination was scorching her soul as she calculated the odds of her ever seeing Daniel alive again. The image of the doctor's mutilated body left to rot on the side of an unpaved, obscure road flashed across her mind, and she gripped the AK-47 in her hand so tightly, her wrists and arm muscles began to ache.

Before long, the ride became increasingly rougher as the sergeant maneuvered through the dense crowds of a city that appeared never to sleep. She could hear the chaos of the night seeping into the vehicle, and she yearned to see if her people were having fun or suffering. Then the vehicle stopped moving, and the sergeant quickly climbed out of it, shutting the door quietly behind him. After a minute, he gently tapped on the window, and everyone began to make their way out of the Hummer. Ayana felt the moist mud give way to her weight, and the sounds of insects and wildlife filled her ears. It was pitch dark, and her eyes needed a few seconds to adjust before she discovered the sergeant had parked the Hummer in the swamps near the foot of the Juba Bridge. There wasn't much light or dwellings in this area due to the insane amount of malaria mosquitos that made the still and muddy waters of the swamp their home.

Edwards raised his left hand in the air, pointed to a small group of dimly lit homes in the distance toward the western side of the city, and the group began to move quietly. Meagan was beside herself with anxiety and wanting to slap herself for being so stupid to suggest they tag along with the sergeant on this search-and-rescue mission. She was a boardroom warrior, having no place in the thick of things, and her trembling legs made it clear she was out of her element. Watching Ayana move through the swamp in front of her and holding her AK-47 with relative ease made it clear that Ayana was now in *her* element, and seeing her like this shook her to her very core. Suddenly, the sergeant held up his hand, making a fist, and everyone except Meagan immediately crouched down into the tall grass of the swamp.

When she finally noticed she was the only one standing, she dropped to her knees, making a lot of noise in the process. Ayana turned back to look at her, aggressively biting her bottom lip and shaking her head.

What am I doing here? Meagan thought to herself.

After several minutes, she heard the rustling of the rest of the group moving again in the darkness in front of her. After taking a few deep breaths, Meagan returned to her feet and followed, this time much closer while keeping a mental note of certain hand signals the sergeant made so that she could react correctly.

Soon, they reached the homes, and the UN soldiers split up, leaving the sergeant with Ayana and Meagan. They were stooping behind a makeshift outhouse, and the smell was unbearable. Several times, Meagan almost puked all over herself as she covered her mouth and nose, trying to keep the smell and her twisting stomach under control. The soldiers returned within minutes and began whispering things to the sergeant Meagan couldn't make out. Once they were done speaking, the soldiers walked farther in between the houses. Edwards made his way over to the women, smiling. Although the situation was far from a smiling matter, his smile warmed Meagan's heart, and she felt good news was coming.

"Some of the villagers said that they saw a Jeep carrying a man driving further west into the city. They believe they were friendlies, and the doctor was alive. They estimate the doctor's rescuers took him about two clicks west in a remote part of the city."

"That's great news, right?" Meagan responded, smiling.

"That he's alive, yes. Where he is, no," Edwards sighed. "That part of the city isn't too friendly to UN forces, and there has been fighting between supporters of two opposing political parties. So, if we—"

"If?" Ayana interrupted, staring at the sergeant as if he were insane.

"Sorry, I mean when. *When* we move into that area, we will more than likely be going in hot."

"Going in hot? What are you saying, Sergeant? That we will go in there guns blazing? How do we expect to get the doctor out of there, if we go in there shooting people? Does that make sense to you?"

"Ma'am, what do you suggest? We waltz in there with our UN patches on our uniforms, smiling and singing songs? If I can prevent anyone here from dying on this mission, I will do what I must."

"And we have to do what we must as well. We are the UN, not the marines or Secret Service. We are supposed to be here to solve the violence, not add to it."

"What do you suggest?"

"Let Ayana and me go in."

"No! No way! Not gonna happen!"

"Listen, trust me. I don't want to go in there, but two women will go over a lot better than a group of armed Europeans."

"In what world?" Edwards snapped back. "They would rather rape and kidnap you than listen to one word you say."

"We have to have more faith in my people," interjected Ayana, rolling her eyes. "The fact they kept Danny alive means they aren't as bad as you think. So Meagan's plan could work."

"That's a very weak 'could,'" Edwards responded angrily. Nevertheless, after carefully calculating her chances of success against his own, he concluded that although a big gamble, her plan was the most feasible if they wanted to reduce the collateral damage to the Sudanese and UN soldiers. Grinding his teeth, he nodded in agreement with Meagan's plan.

Meagan swallowed hard as she looked at Ayana and then down at the weapon she was gripping tightly in her hands. Ayana understood immediately what her friend was saying without uttering a sound. She wanted to make sure Ayana was willing and able to use the weapon if things went south, and she nodded back at her with a determined look in her eyes. Ayana was willing to do whatever was needed to ensure that they rescued her love and that none of them lost their lives while attempting the impossible. Satisfied with Ayana's response, Meagan tapped Edwards on the shoulder, and they began to move swiftly toward the last location the doctor was seen alive . . .

The searing burn of the fires seemed to cook Meagan and Ayana's faces as they walked past several burning homes and structures. There were countless bodies sprawled on the scorched earth, burnt and mutilated in the most grotesque way. The heat was almost unbearable, and it seemed to cook the tears that fell down Ayana's face as she looked around at the devastation and death.

"What happened here?"

"Satu happened here," a voice from behind them responded while he removed his weapon's safety, and the clicking sound echoed through the air.

Both women immediately turned around to face a wounded and angry villager pointing his rifle at them. There was an angry and heartbreaking look in his eyes as it became clear he wasn't a soldier, but a survivor from this latest massacre by Kronte's second-in-command.

"Who are you, and what do you want?" he asked, taking a step closer.

"We are here looking for the American doctor. We are his friends."

The man leaned forward, staring at Ayana; then he let out a long and relieved sigh before lowering his weapon.

"Ms. Burundi, it's you. I'm sorry I didn't recognize you in the dark. The doctor isn't here any longer. The village chief and doctor left right before Satu and his men attacked us."

"Do you know where they went?" Ayana asked with urgency.

"Yes. They are heading toward the city center."

Meagan's eyes widened as she realized exactly where they were taking the doctor.

They are taking him to the courthouse.

"Ayana, we have to get out of here now!"

Ayana just stood there in a daze infected by the disease of death around her. She was frozen and lost within her own memories of the days when scenes like this were commonplace in her life as a teenager. Meagan, anxious to leave before the angry villager decided to kill both of them, shook Ayana violently, trying to wake her out of her nightmare. Ayana suddenly swung her AK-47 in front of her chest, and in one swift motion, used it to push Meagan back. The forceful reaction almost knocked Meagan to the ground, but she found her balance before she lost complete control.

"Ayana, what the fuck is wrong with you?" Meagan screamed at her friend, who seemed like a totally different person.

"Don't touch me like that. Here is not the place to be forceful with me, Meagan," she responded, appearing unmoved by the pleading look in Meagan's eyes, begging for her old friend back. "You're right. We must leave this place now and go find the doctor before Satu and his men do. I'll push ahead, while you go back to inform the sergeant."

"Ayana, you shouldn't go after them alone."

"I won't be alone," Ayana responded while looking over at the villager that had now moved by her side. "We both have a vendetta to settle."

"He's no soldier. He's just an angry villager without any real training. No offense," she yelled back.

"None taken. You are correct, but I will join Ms. Burundi, nonetheless," he responded with a slight smirk on his face. Throwing her hands in the air and almost spinning around in a full circle, Meagan screamed while pulling her hair that now smelled like smoke and burnt flesh. Pointing at both of them, she bit down hard on her bottom lip and spun around, storming in the opposite direction toward the awaiting UN soldiers. Ayana watched

Meagan until she was out of sight, then turned to her new companion, nodding before the two of them began running in the direction of their targets . . .

Daniel felt like he was losing consciousness the more that he moved. The chief was helping him brace some of his weight on his wounded leg, but it seemed it wasn't doing much to speed up their escape. He could hear the frantic and purposeful movement of his pursuers not far behind them as they weaved and cut in between the buildings in the city. Every so often, Satu's men would fire shots in their direction, sending bullets whistling past their heads, causing them to duck or stumble, which was taking a harder toll on his wounded body. The doctor's body was overworked from trying to dodge people, bullets, and buildings. His heavy breathing made it clear to the chief and the village doctor that they needed to find a place to hide. Otherwise, the doctor might not survive the trip.

"Here, come here," a whispering voice commanded from their right. Turning, they saw a woman sticking her head out of the window of a makeshift storefront that was so torn down that it appeared it would fall to pieces from just a slight gust of wind. The chief swallowed hard. The structure's flimsy appearance made him nervous, but they didn't have any other choice. They moved inside the store, closing the door behind them and ducking down away from the windows. They could hear the loud banging sounds of the soldiers going door-to-door, forcing their way into people's homes and businesses, searching for the doctor and his helpers. Daniel felt cold and weak, covered in a feverish sweat as he lay on the dirt floor, listening to the chaos unfold outside. The woman stared at the doctor attentively, appearing oblivious to the sounds of terror and violence riding the winds of this hot and humid night.

She seemed unnaturally intrigued by him, and her gaze began to make Daniel's skin feel like it was covered in squirming maggots. He wanted to look away, but she was situated in front of the front door and window of the shop, and he didn't dare look away for fear of not seeing his pursuers walking by or peering into the window. Daniel glanced at the chief and village doctor to see if they noticed her staring, but they both seemed uninterested in her. He wanted to ask her, "*What is your problem?*" but he didn't want to make a sound, fearing his big mouth would give away their location. So, he decided to stare her down just as hard as she was staring at him. The stare down lasted for so long that Daniel felt like she was hypnotizing him, and although she was a much older and homely woman, she suddenly began to look like Ayana, then Victoria, and then Ayana again. The morphing started to make the room spin like a merry-go-round until he could barely keep his head steady or his eyes open.

"His wound has reopened," whispered the village doctor when he looked down at Daniel's side, noticing the steady stream of blood moving across the dirt floor.

So, she wasn't just staring at me. She was staring at me, bleeding out.

"Can you stop the bleeding?"

"I think so, but I'm afraid he's lost too much blood, and if we don't get him to a hospital, he will die. I can use a few things in my knapsack, but afterward, we are going to have to leave immediately and head to a hospital instead of the courthouse."

The chief sucked his teeth and looked up at the window, appearing to be in deep thought before agreeing with the doctor's suggestion.

"I hope he makes it because what Satu did to our village must be avenged. They must pay, no matter the cost."

"Then let's get him to safety and let the UN do the rest," responded the village doctor before he began to scrounge around the shop, looking for things that could help him close up Daniel's bullet wound. By the time he returned to Daniel's side, he had passed out again, which was a good thing for the village doctor. He didn't need Daniel screaming out in pain while he worked on his wound.

The darkness seemed to possess a hidden malice that froze the blood of the three men as they carefully stepped out into the night. Everything was still. Even the gentle breeze of the night was absent, afraid to be anywhere near these three that were being viciously hunted by evil men hell-bent on taking their lives. The streets were clear and completely dark, and for a city as large and lively as Juba, it was a chilling revelation that even while behind bars, Kronte's influence was still palpable.

Daniel, although experiencing an extreme amount of pain, was walking on his own with the village doctor and chief on either side of him. As soon as they cleared the shop's door, the woman immediately shut it behind them, leaving them out in the open and feeling naked to the night's watchful eyes.

"Let's move quickly," the chief whispered. His voice seemed to travel louder and much farther than any of them wanted.

"Let's not," a voice responded out of the darkness, right before a blinding light engulfed the entire area. The three men tried to back away inside the store, but their backs were met with a closed door and a woman on the other side refusing to reopen it. In front of them stood Satu, a host of men, and three military Jeeps equipped with giant strobe searchlights atop the roofs' bars. Satu's giant frame was much more intimidating in this blinding light, and the evil smile plastered on his face made Daniel shiver.

"Doctor Bennett, I must say, for a man who's been shot more than Tupac and Biggie combined during your lifetime and still standing, it's very impressive, very impressive indeed. But this is the end of the line for you and your two friends. This time, I will make sure you are dead so that you can't testify against my commander for raping and killing Ayana Burundi's little bitch. She was an embarrassment to Kronte, and as long as she drew breath, it tainted his legacy as a powerful leader in Sudan. Maybe next time, Ayana will keep her whorish legs closed and stay faithful to the man who owns her."

"She was a little girl," yelled Daniel with all the strength and rage his damaged body could muster. "She was innocent!"

"No, Doctor, no one is innocent—not even that little girl. No one escapes, not even an American with a conscience. Everyone dies. That day was her day, and today is yours. Enough talking. Shoot these cockroaches now," Satu ordered loudly while pointing at the three men. Immediately following his order, the loud, bloodcurdling sounds of multiple guns firing filled the air. Daniel and his two companions closed their eyes, bracing themselves to feel the flesh-piercing pain of the oncoming bullets . . . but no pain came. No feeling of death or screams bellowing out of the mouths of the man standing next to them sounded. The only sounds they heard were a continuous flow of gunfire, the sounds of multiple bodies dropping, and the familiar voices of the UN soldiers screaming orders of surrender.

When Daniel opened his eyes, many of Satu's men were lying on the ground dead or dying, and the remaining ones were on their knees with their hands above their heads, surrounded by a team of determined UN soldiers. Daniel exhaled deeply and slid down to the ground, exhausted by fear and pain. As he watched the UN soldiers conclude their victory over Satu's men, Daniel's gut began to tremble, and suddenly, he felt something was off . . . A major piece to this puzzle was missing—the biggest piece—and that piece was Satu. He wasn't one of the captured or dead. Daniel's anger suddenly energized his adrenaline, and he jumped to his feet, yelling for one of the UN soldiers to come to him.

"Yes, Dr. Bennett, medical personnel is on their way. Just hang tight."

"No no no . . . listen. Where is Satu Massamou?"

"Who?"

"Satu Massamou, Kronte's second-in-command, and the one leading this party of rebels you just captured," he responded, frantically looking past the soldier, desperately searching for any signs of the dangerous man that could continue Kronte's work if Kronte is convicted.

"Where's your commanding officer?"

"He's still out there searching for Ms. Burundi and some other villager she teamed up with to find you!"

"What the fuck did you just say?"

"Ms. Burundi . . . She's out here too. She separated from the team and went rogue, trying to find you. I wouldn't worry much, sir. She's armed, and from Edwards's description of her, she's more than capable of defending herself."

That may be true for a foot soldier, but against a fleeing Satu, she may not be skilled enough, Daniel thought to himself.

"Which way?"

"Sir, we have orders to secur—"

"Which fucking way, Soldier? If you want to secure me, I'd suggest you accompany or shoot me, but I'm going out there. She has no idea how dangerous Satu is. So, what's it gonna be, Soldier?"

"Sir, you are gravely wounded."

Daniel stared blankly at the soldier without saying a word. Understanding his silent response, the soldier replied, "Very well, sir. Stay behind me."

Satu was running toward the swamps at the foot of the Juba Bridge, hoping the tall grass and water would hide his escape route across the river. The anger he felt was indescribable, and he vowed to himself that if his commander is convicted and executed, he will dedicate his life to making those responsible pay the ultimate price. Although being in command of the rebels came with unbridled power and wealth, Satu felt insecure about stepping into such big shoes. He knew he didn't have the "smarts" or charisma to deal with the intricacies of running the rebels and all the resources they possessed, while constantly appeasing their international sponsors. He knew he was too blunt and cold to keep so many relationships mutually beneficial and peaceful, and because of that self-realization, he fought with everything he had to make sure Kronte was freed and allowed to run things.

Now, it appeared all his hard work would be in vain. *What was that?*

Something startled him, and he stopped in his tracks, tuning his ears to listen closely. Sniffing the air, Satu caught the sweet smell of women's perfume and the musty stench of a common villager. Both smells invaded his nostrils at the same time. Not too strong, just a whisper of a smell, letting the giant know that a woman and possibly a man were pursuing him. They were about ten seconds behind him, coming from the west, and they were closing in fast.

There is only one woman stupid enough to pursue me. Well, if I can't get the doctor, I might as well kill his bitch.

Satu quickly stepped to his right and ducked behind a pile of boxes and wooden crates. He moved one of the boxes slightly so that he could see his pursuers before they could see him. He then reached down to his side and pulled out an eight-inch blade, looking it over fondly as its blade reflected the moonlight on this deadly night.

Satu could hear their footsteps quicken as they believed they were gaining on him. He smiled as he prepared to ambush them. He momentarily relished the pleasurable thought of plunging his blade deep into Ayana's flesh repeatedly and watching the horror and pain explode across her face as the life left her eyes. Inhaling deeply and timing his attack perfectly, he quickly pounced from behind his hiding place, throwing wooden crates and boxes in every direction while growling like a great beast. Without even thinking, he lunged forward, extending his massive arm and burying his blade in the body of his unsuspecting victim.

His blade, sharp as a scalpel, penetrated flesh with sickening ease as he felt its entire length invade the body of Ayana's companion. The villager screamed in agony as the blade violated his body and essential organs. The force of Satu's attack pushed the villager into Ayana, forcefully throwing her to the ground, but the force wasn't strong enough to loosen her grip on her AK-47. As her body slid on the hard earth, she cocked her weapon, twisted her body, and aimed toward her attacker, pulling the trigger. Her sudden movement on the ground affected her aim, and she initially missed her mark: Satu's chest. However, the hail of bullets in his direction caused him to pause for a split second, and that gave her time to fire again, landing twice in his right leg.

The bullets tearing into Satu's leg caused him to roar in pain, pushing his massive frame back several feet. Looking at the damage Ayana did to his leg enraged Satu. He ignored the mind-numbing pain and stormed forward toward her. His movement and speed surprised Ayana, and she paused in awe, watching this violent giant stomp toward her. Her pause gave Satu enough time to reach her. Before she could pull the trigger again, a powerful kick from his left leg ripped the rifle from her hand and sent it flying off into the darkness. Her eyes opened in horror as she watched him reach down for her and lift her into the air effortlessly as if she were made of toilet paper.

When he had her at eye level, he pulled his head back, intending on head-butting her and breaking her nose. Before his strike could land, Ayana quickly placed her forearm in the path of his head and simultaneously landed an elbow strike on the side of his large neck. Her strike caused the nerves in his neck to send an unwanted message to his arms, and he unwillingly released his grip on her, causing her to fall to the ground. Ayana quickly got to her feet and backed away, creating a semi-safe distance from Satu's assaults.

"I forgot my commander trained you in unarmed combat," Satu growled while rolling his neck and shoulders, attempting to regain control over his limbs. "Too bad your friend over there dying with my blade still in his side wasn't trained as well," he continued to taunt. "Come. Let's finish this, you ungrateful bitch," he snarled, before rushing toward her.

Ayana decided to stand her ground and wait for Satu to make the first strike. When he was within striking distance, he threw punch after punch, which she carefully dodged and sidestepped. She was attentive not to try to strike back, for fear of one of his attacks getting through and knocking her unconscious. She needed to be smart about facing down this monstrously strong assailant. Although Ayana knew she was more skilled at hand-to-hand combat than Satu, she wasn't as strong, and one hit from him could end this confrontation immediately.

Then Ayana found an opening, and Satu paid with a hard kick to his injured leg. The pain caused the giant to stumble and fall to one knee. She quickly took advantage of his position and struck him across the jaw with her forearm, knocking out a tooth in the process. The feeling of her ripping his tooth from his gums sent shocking pain throughout his head, and Satu yelled out in anger and pain. Backing away quickly, Ayana moved to her right, waiting for the angry Satu to stand and continue his assault. But to her surprise, he remained on his knees, breathing heavily and staring at her like a violent predator.

Why doesn't he attack?

She stood there, puzzled by a man she knew prided himself on being a great combatant, a warrior, and who always looked down on women like they were worthless.

So, to see him accept defeat at the hands of a woman was a strange thing to witness. She momentarily lost concentration, and that's when Satu lunged forward suddenly, knocking her off her feet. Her back hit the ground hard, knocking the air out of her, and before she could regain her composure, he began pounding her with both fists like an enraged gorilla. Her body jerked and bounced on the ground from his vicious attack. Suddenly, blood began to pour out of her mouth, and her eyes fluttered uncontrollably as she began to lose consciousness and her grip on life.

Smiling with pride while he watched Ayana convulse and choke on her blood, he raised both arms in the air, readying himself for the final blow that would smash her windpipe. However, he suddenly felt a heavy body slam into him, knocking him from on top of his victim. He rolled over and looked up to see Dr. Daniel Bennett standing over him, his chest heaving heavily with a rage in his eyes that frightened Satu, and before he could respond, Daniel lifted his foot and sent it crashing down on Satu's face, breaking his nose and smashing four more teeth out of his mouth.

Falling backward from the force of the doctor's kick, Satu tried to brace himself, but the doctor wasn't done, and he sent a sweeping kick across his jaw. Satu's fall changed trajectory, and he fell on his side, coughing out his teeth and a mouthful of blood.

"You piece of shit! Look what you did to her," Daniel screamed before everything seemed to turn red, and he began to attack Satu with a rage that made him appear he'd gone completely insane.

The UN soldier, having seen the horrors of war himself, was shocked by the viciousness of Daniel's assault.

He ran over to stop him. But when he got within range, Daniel quickly snatched the soldier's rifle from his hands, turned, and opened fire on Satu, filling his body with every bullet in the rifle's clip. Satu's body trembled as if it were jolted with several thousand watts of electricity as the bullets riddled his body like a rag doll. After the rifle stopped firing, Daniel, still in a daze, continued to squeeze the trigger, not satisfied with the violent death he'd just sentenced and carried out against Satu.

The soldier, now beside himself with anger and shock, took the doctor down with a sweeping leg kick. He then jumped on top of the doctor, prying his weapon from his hands before pushing his face down toward the dirt and returning to his feet.

"What the fuck is wrong with you, Doctor? Do you know I could've killed you?" he yelled, shaking his head at the doctor who was now on the ground, seemingly in a trance. "Do you hear me?"

Within seconds, the rest of the UN soldiers surrounded the entire area. They were drawn to the sudden gunfire. Meagan stepped from behind a group of soldiers, crying uncontrollably at the sight of her friend dying on the ground.

"Medic," Edwards yelled behind him as he rushed over to Ayana's side.

Daniel snapped out of it and crawled over to Ayana, his eyes filled with tears as he held her hand in his, kissing it repeatedly while pleading with her to hold on and stay with him . . .

Chapter 27

The Final Bell

Six months later. Manhattan, New York

Meagan glanced outside the large window behind the UN ambassador's desk and took in the luminous sunlight and clear skies, smiling.

"Are you listening to me, Ms. Quinn?" the ambassador asked, annoyed by her wandering eyes and smile. This wasn't a smiling matter, and her lack of seriousness was beginning to anger him.

Snapped back from her daydream by her boss's question, she nodded and returned her attention to him. Satisfied, he continued, "Juba was a complete and utter clusterfuck!

"Yes, sir, I do apologize about how everything got out of control, but we weren't left with any other choice."

"I understand, and although you broke almost every UN protocol, I am proud of you and your leadership in such a hostile situation. Many powerful people will feel their pockets lightened, and they won't be too happy about it."

"I'm sorry, sir. I didn't know that was a concern of the UN."

"No, it isn't," the ambassador chuckled, shaking his head at Meagan's sarcasm.

"Were we able to convince the International Courts on a change of venue?"

"Yes, sir. After the events on that night, they didn't want anything to do with Kronte's trial, so they agreed to a change of venue."

"Where will Kronte's trial be held now?"

"London, sir."

"That's a semi-neutral location," he responded, frowning slightly.

"Not as neutral as Juba, perhaps, but it will do, sir."

"Touché," he responded, smiling.

"And what of Doctor Bennett?"

"His health has improved, and he'll be ready to testify when the trial starts. We also have video footage of Satu confessing his commander's direct involvement in the massacre that claimed the doctor and Ayana's daughter, Victoria. The old woman that sheltered them recorded him from inside her old store, so with the doctor's testimony, the video footage, and DNA evidence, our case against the warlord is the strongest it's ever been."

"And how are you dealing with—"

"I'm taking it day by day, sir. But I'm confident Ayana will awaken from her coma before the baby arrives."

"When is the baby due?"

"In three months, sir."

"Do we kno—"

"No, sir," Meagan responded.

The ambassador stood up and began to pace back and forth, unnerved by the details of one of his most valued UN representatives.

"Ms. Burundi has always been a strong woman, and she possesses a soul that just won't quit. We must make sure she's getting the best care. Period. And pray that she and the baby will be healthy."

"I agree, sir. I've never met anyone quite like her," Meagan agreed, clearing her throat while attempting to fight back her emotions. "Is there anything else, sir?"

Looking over at Meagan, trying to remain professional and strong in front of him, the ambassador smiled and shook his head. Meagan quickly stood up and made her way out of his office closing the door behind her . . .

After several months of waiting religiously by her bedside, Daniel nervously waited for the doctors to emerge from the operating room with news of his new baby and Ayana. He continuously rocked back and forth, holding his hands in front of his mouth as if he were suffering from frostbite. There were concerns that Ayana may awaken from her coma during the procedure, and that could pose a serious risk for her. Daniel wanted to be present, but the doctors advised it was best for him not to be in the operating room until they were done. His mother and father sat on either side of him, watching him with concern. Every seat in the waiting room was filled with people that cared about the couple, and the stress of uncertainty filled the air, making it hard to relax or breathe easily.

"Everything is going to be fine, son. Just believe that God is watching over Ayana and your baby," Mrs. Bennett said, rubbing her son's back as he leaned forward as if he had a stomachache. She hated to see her son suffer as much as he has since he went to Sudan, and sometimes, she wondered why God allowed him to suffer so much. What was the message or point? Daniel's father kept a stern and concentrated look on his face, trying his best to appear unmoved by the emotional energy in the room, but he was, just like everyone here, filled with anxiety. He prayed repeatedly for a positive outcome for everyone involved.

Timothy paced back and forth with a cup of coffee in his hand that he constantly kept refilling. He'd had so much coffee that the caffeine started to make his vision blurry, but he refused to have a seat. The last thing he wanted for his friend was another tragedy, and he hoped that life didn't deal him another devastating blow, because if it did, it would be completely unfair in Timothy's book. After everything he'd endured, Timothy believed Danny deserved an extended vacation from bad luck.

Suddenly, the waiting room door opened, and the doctor walked in, gesturing for Daniel to join him out in the hallway. Everyone watched as Daniel rushed out of the room with desperate anticipation.

A couple of hours later, Daniel walked into the waiting room smiling brightly, holding his son in his arms. His face was drenched in tears as his son quietly slept, wrapped tightly in white hospital blankets. Everyone rushed over to him, filled with relief and excitement, anxious to see the new addition to the Bennett family. What they beheld was the angelic face of a child of two nations, possessing the striking beauty of his mother and the skin tone and strong male features of his father. The sight of the baby immediately brought everyone to tears, seeing the pain and love of both his parents in the newborn.

"How is Ayana?" Daniel's father asked through his tears.

"She's still in a coma, but the doctor says she's stable. They are hoping that now that she's given birth, it will be easier for her to wake up. But it's a long shot. I was hoping she would be awake before I leave for the trial."

"Yeah," his father responded, looking down at the floor. "There's still time, son. You're not gone yet. Have you spoken to her?"

"To whom?"

"Ayana."

"Dad, she's in a com—"

"Hear me out, son," his father interrupted, raising his hand. "Just because she's asleep doesn't mean she can't hear you, son. Sometimes, you have to give people a reason to wake up. You have to understand just how much she's been through. Her spirit is weary, son. Just like yours, but I can see your son has given you strength, and maybe talking to her about your child may do the same for her. By the way . . . What's my grandson's name?"

"Timothy Barry Bennett."

Timothy was playing with the baby's fingers when he heard the baby's name. He quickly turned to Daniel with eyes filled with tears. He was searching his friend's eyes for answers. He couldn't quite understand why he would name his first son after him, and Daniel smiled, seeing his friend's confusion.

"It was because of you, I survived that night you broke down my door, and that led to Ayana and me falling in love. I owe you everything, and it would be an honor for my son to carry your name."

Timothy broke down, reached over, and embraced his best friend.

"Okay, although I'm salty that you didn't name him after his grandfather, I'm confused about the middle name. Barry?" Daniel's father teased.

"One of the men that pulled me out of that vehicle in Sudan. He risked his life to get me to safety. His name was Barry, or so he told me. I don't think his real name was Barry, but that's the name he gave me, so I'm giving it to little Timothy. My son is the product of the most beautiful and traumatic times of my life, and every day I see him, I want to remember God's grace and mercy that allowed me to survive it all."

"Amen," his father and mother responded in unison.

"Thank you, brother, for naming your son after me. One thing, though. I wouldn't advise telling him when he's older where he was conceived. Telling your boy he was conceived in a nightclub's bathroom to the cheers of a listening crowd might not go over too well."

"Knucklehead." Daniel's father chuckled while playfully popping Timothy upside the head. Everyone began to laugh and continued to woo over baby Timothy Barry Bennett.

After everyone left the hospital, Daniel remained at Ayana's side, holding their baby in his arms. The room was quiet besides the sound of the life-monitoring machines connected to Ayana. It was also mostly dark, besides the small overhead light from the headboard of her hospital bed. Daniel sat there holding his son, watching him sleeping as he pondered the words of his father. He felt silly even considering what he advised. Yes, many people claim to hear and feel while they are in a coma, but there wasn't much scientific proof behind those claims, and as a doctor, he couldn't afford to place stock in hocus-pocus and tall tales. After his most recent ordeal in Southern Sudan, however, Daniel began to understand and believe that sometimes, things can't be explained, like love and his faith that Ayana would one day awaken, still in love with him and still the same woman. He closed his eyes, lowered his head, and despite how silly he felt, began to talk to her.

"Ayana, I've never been the type of man to rely on anyone. Even before going to Sudan, I've always done things on my own. I didn't want to rely on anyone. That's always been who I was.

"Now, things are different for me, and I'm irreparably broken without you, Ayana. I smile, but it isn't real. I live, but it isn't life. Nothing, and I mean nothing, makes sense without you. Looking at our son sleeping in my arms just makes this day even more tragic for me, because you've given me everything, including your own life, because you loved me so fiercely, and it's unfair that now I'm unable to return the love you've so selflessly given to me. Even when I was horrible to you, you still found a reason to have faith in the man that I could become. The man you knew I should be.

"I know without thinking twice, I don't deserve you, but I still want you anyway, and I hope one day that I can change your life as much as you've changed mine. I love you, Ayana, and I pray to God that you come back to our baby boy and me. We need you."

After he was done talking, the only response he got was the hissing sound of the ventilator and the constant beeping of her life-monitoring system. He raised his head, looked at her with a torturous yearning, and a tremendous need for her to respond. She remained inanimate and asleep, seemingly oblivious to his pleading for her to wake up. Daniel immediately became upset with himself for being taken for a ride on his father's religious roller coaster.

Have faith, my ass, he thought, leaning back in the chair, still holding li'l Timothy while he slept as quietly as his mother did. Sighing loudly, he closed his eyes and allowed his exhaustion to take over so that he could sleep . . .

Scheveningen: The Hague, Netherlands
Two weeks before the trial date . . .

A man in his midthirties calmly strolled up to the check-in desk at the ICTY UN Detention Facility. A bright yet out-of-place smile plastered itself on his strikingly attractive face. The guard's facial muscles immediately tensed at the sight of his smile in a place as dark and gloomy as this special tribunal detention center. The man leaned forward while running his hand through his mid-length dark brown hair as if he were in a photo shoot for a top modeling agency. This infuriated the guard further, and when he got a closer look at the teal, tailored suit that covered his athletic frame, he mumbled an obscenity under his breath. The well-dressed man's eyes looked up at the guard immediately after he was done insulting him and smiled even brighter.

"That wasn't very professional, now, was it?" the man teased in a prominent Scottish accent that seemed to add another level of attractiveness to someone who could've been a world-class model. The guard impressed and annoyed by the man's ability to hear that well, rolled his eyes, forcefully pushing the sign-in sheet toward the stranger.

"Who are you here to see?"

"Kronte."

"Kronte who?"

The stranger blankly stared at the guard, which immediately caused a feeling of stupidity to engulf him. He quickly turned away as if there were something else more important on the far wall of his windowed post.

"Your relation to the prisoner?"

"I'm his brother," the stranger replied with a confidence that momentarily startled the guard because it was clear by the stranger's pale complexion and European accent that he and the African warlord were of no relation. Giving the stranger a look of disbelief, he looked down at the sign-in sheet to see what name this liar signed in under.

"John Smith? Really? That's your real name?"

"Sure is," he replied, handing the guard his identification card.

"John Smith?"

"Isn't that what the identification card says?"

"Appears so."

"Well, there you have it. John Smith it is."

"Okay, so your name *is* John Smith, but the prisoner's surname isn't Smith. Nothing close to it, and I'm supposed to believe a white 'Scot' is the brother of an African? Try me when I'm drunk, chappy."

"Shouldn't you check the prisoner's approved visitor's list before you make that assumption?"

The guard wasn't in the mood to get up and go to the large wall of file cabinets behind him, but he knew the only way he could get rid of the prankster was to prove him false. So, he pushed back on his chair, allowing the wheels and the momentum to propel him backward toward the cabinets. John watched attentively as the guard searched through several file drawers until he found what he was looking for. He quickly glanced over the sheet and exhaled deeply while lowering his head. He turned his head slightly toward Mr. Smith to see if he was watching him. John was now smiling so widely, his mouth was agape, and he was gesturing with his hand for him to return to the window with the sheet.

God, I hate that guy, the guard thought. He knew the pretty asshole would rub it in further. However, he had a job to do, and regardless of how much he loathed people like John Smith, he had no choice but to allow him entry into the facility to see Kronte. After processing the remaining paperwork, he handed John a visitor's pass and reached under his desk to buzz him in.

"Thank you, kind sir. I see this job suits you perfectly. It fills me with so much joy to see someone right where they are supposed to be," John said slyly while walking through the door.

The guard jumped out of his chair, having had enough of John's taunts and was planning on giving him some choice yet unprofessional words but then changed his mind when his superior suddenly came out to greet John Smith at the entry door.

Cheeky bastard, the guard thought while watching Mr. Smith move farther into the facility.

He led John to a small room enclosed in glass that was no more than eight feet by ten feet. The large and intimidating man known as Kronte sat at a white table in the middle of the room. He was unshackled, and from the expression on his deeply scarred and dark, coffee-colored face, he wasn't too delighted to be in the room. Kronte glared at Mr. Smith through bloodshot eyes that seemed to burn with a senseless hatred that made most uncomfortable. John was all too amused, and he smiled back at Kronte like a used car salesman on the verge of selling a lemon with a Ferrari price tag.

From the annoyed look on Kronte's face, John was no stranger to him, and he braced himself for bad . . . or insulting news.

"Father sends his greetings," John said, still smiling.

"How is Father doing?" Kronte asked, unamused with John's attitude.

"He's not doing well, brother. He's grown ill from all the bad news coming out of Juba over the past few months."

"If Father took better care of his children, he wouldn't grow ill."

"Father isn't that nurturing. You, of all his children, should know that. You should also know he doesn't take too kindly to his wishes not being fulfilled as he instructed. He specifically instructed you to stay home and not go on the farm to harvest because things were out of season, but you didn't listen, and now the crops are ruined. The family has lost a lot because of your insolence."

"The family has lost a lot? What about what *I've* lost? Over the years, I've brought a hefty harvest to Father. That should count for something, shouldn't it?"

"Was that a serious question?" John asked, staring at Kronte as if he'd lost his mind. "Listen, brother, Father instructed me to tell you that you have been disowned and cut off from the family inheritance. All your assets will be liquidated to cover the loss the family incurred from your disobedience. He can't overlook or forgive the fact that we lost a sixty-bushel annual initiative because of your actions. If, by some miracle, you beat this case, he wishes you the best on your journey in life, but Father has instructed that you refrain from continuing the family business on any level. In addition, this will be the last time you hear from Father directly or indirectly. Father's terms are final and nonnegotiable."

Kronte immediately became enraged and nearly leaped out of his chair to attack John, but then something inside gave him pause, and he changed his mind, flopping back into his chair. John seemed amused by Kronte's anger and appeared disappointed that he didn't go through with his thoughts on physically attacking him.

"Well, if I'm no longer Father's son, then you tell Father that unless he wants all the family's secrets revealed, he better find a way to grant me full forgiveness."

"Brother, you know that's impossible. Even if Father wanted to, you are in a secure position that's completely out of Father's reach and influence."

"Well, brother, *you* are his favorite son, and you've been known to make the impossible possible," Kronte responded sarcastically. "So, unless Father wants the farmer's union to come set fire to his crops, he better grant me full forgiveness and reinstate my inheritance. *This* is nonnegotiable."

John looked at Kronte, shaking his head as if he were a fool. Looking at the warlord a few seconds further, John decided the conversation was over, and he stood up to leave.

"All this trouble for a woman? She must be a rare breed. By the way, aren't you still legally married to Ms. Burundi?"

"Yes, why?"

"Just wondering," John responded, before quickly leaving Kronte sitting in the glass room alone.

Kronte's entire body felt cold as he watched John leave. He's known Mr. Smith for years, and one thing he learned quickly was John never asks questions for no reason. He didn't care if John decided to kill Ayana. He's wanted her dead for years. What Kronte didn't want was to be charged with her murder without having the pleasure of ending her life himself. That would surely seal his fate. Suddenly, he began to regret the things he'd just said to Mr. Smith.

A few minutes later, John Smith was speeding down the highway in his black Aston Martin, placing a call to "Father."

"Is this line secure?" a deep masculine voice inquired on the other end.

"Yes, sir."

"Good. Report."

"Kronte has responded with betrayal, sir. He's threatened to expose his benefactors if he isn't freed from prison, the case against him dropped by the UN, and no war crime charges are brought against him again . . . ever."

"That smug bastard! Does he understand that he cost us over sixty billion dollars annually with that fiasco he pulled? We told him to lie low and allow us to influence the outcome, but *he* decided to go it on his own. We had that entire country's oil resources within our reach. All he had to do was wait a few more weeks. Now, we're going to have to subtract that animal from the equation."

"I agree, sir. We must move quickly to get him out of UN's custody because there's no other way we can get close enough to terminate his contract."

"Do you have any ideas on how to get that done?"

"Actually, sir, yes, I do. I'll start on it now and keep you updated once the process is underway."

"Good, man."

John quickly disconnected the call and without even looking on either side of his speeding vehicle, spun his vehicle around, burning asphalt and rubber, heading back toward the UN Detention Facility to give Kronte the "good news" . . .

Chapter 28

24 Hours

Forty-eight hours later.
The University of Chicago Hospital.
Chicago, Illinois

Daniel smiled while watching Meagan play with li'l Timothy in her arms, making silly faces to amuse him. It was a beautiful day outside, and the sun enveloped the hospital room in warmth and light. Ayana's still sleeping body seemed to glow in the sun's radiance. Daniel felt that the warmth and illumination could awaken her any moment, and it was that thought that lifted his mood. He was preparing to step out to get something to eat when a foreign voice came from the doorway.

"Wow, even while in a coma, she's absolutely stunning. I get it. After seeing her in person, I really get it now."

Daniel abruptly turned toward the sound of the voice, and the man standing in the doorway immediately walked toward the doctor, extending his hand.

"John Smith," he said, while firmly shaking Daniel's hand.

"Do I know you?" Daniel asked, looking him over suspiciously.

"No, but Ms. Quinn knows me very well. How are you, by the way, Meagan?"

"That's *Ms. Quinn* to you, Mr. Smith," she snapped while slowly retreating to the far side of the hospital room, holding the baby tightly in her arms. Daniel noticed Meagan's sudden reaction toward John Smith and concluded he wasn't a friend of the family. Daniel didn't want to put anyone in danger, so he decided to remain calm and try to diffuse any confrontations.

"How can I help you, Mr. Smith?"

"John, call me John."

"Okay, John, how can I help you?"

"Well, I'm not here for you to help me. I'm here for you to help yourselves."

"How so? I don't recall needing assistance from anyone."

"Oh, I'm sure, but you see, there's been a new development concerning your dear friend Mrs. Burundi."

"That's Ms. Burundi," Daniel responded, almost jumping out of his chair and wrapping his hands around John's throat.

"Well, according to legal documents, it's *Mrs*. Burundi. She is still very much married to a mutual acquaintance of yours," John responded while handing Daniel a yellow manila folder containing several legal documents. Daniel examined them and came across a document that caused the rage he felt back in Juba to return when he saw what Satu had done to Ayana to reemerge. He immediately began to sweat and grind his teeth as he gripped either side of the document so aggressively, he almost ripped it in half. He couldn't believe his eyes as he reread the title

repeatedly—*Request for Withdrawal of Life-Sustainin*
Treatment—with Kronte's signature as Ayana's last
remaining living relative, right above Ayana's doctor's
signature of approval.

"Well, from your reaction, I can assume you fully
understand the dynamics of your situation, correct?"

Daniel closed his eyes while trying to regain control
of his anger, something he wasn't able to accomplish the
more John's Scottish accent filled his ears.

"If not, let me spell it out for you. Either drop the case
against Kronte, or he'll be forced to remove his wife
from life support. You know how these northern Africans
are. They're like pharaohs. They want to take everything
and everyone with them to the afterlife."

Having lost all self-control now, Daniel jumped up
and faced John down, breathing heavily directly in his
face. John didn't move an inch as he smiled, looking
directly in Daniel's eyes, instigating him to strike him.
Suddenly, Daniel felt Meagan tug on his arm, pulling
him away from John before things went too far. Looking
down at the floor, appearing disappointed, John smiled
while pulling on the bottom of his grey suit jacket.

"I like you, Dr. Bennett. You are a resilient man.
Almost indestructible, with a resolve very few men possess in my line of work, but you have an anger manage-
ment issue that you need to repair. When this is over, I
can send you a referral to one of the best therapists in the
world."

"I think you've made your point, Mr. Smith. Now,
please leave," demanded Meagan.

"Very well, you have twenty-four hours starting . . .
from . . . now," John responded while toying with his
expensive designer watch. "If you decide to continue

with this charade, Mrs. Burundi will be removed from
life support immediately. However, if you drop this case,
despite our mutual friend's request, I would be willing to
lose this document permanently. So decide what's more
important: justice or love. You now have twenty-three
hours and fifty-eight minutes."

"Fuck you," Daniel growled back at him.

Nodding, John turned and strolled out of the hospital
room with an arrogance that made watching him leave
hurt more than the decision they would have to make.
Once Meagan was sure John was out of Daniel's reach,
she let him go, and he fell to his knees next to Ayana's
bed, overcome with anger and defeat.

"Who is he?" Daniel asked, refusing to look away from
Ayana.

"John Smith is a male Olivia Pope with Secret Service
and counterterrorism training. Basically, the most dangerous man on earth. He represents some of the most
ruthless and powerful people in the world. Some of these
people are so powerful that their influence can make
or break economies and presidencies. If they send Mr.
Smith, they mean business, and crossing him can be a
deadly mistake. Our backs are up against the wall on this
one, Danny. Either we drop this case, or Ayana dies. And
knowing his reputation, he may not stop with her until we
give them what they want."

The more Meagan spelled out their options, the more
Daniel was overcome with grief. Tears of anger and
hopelessness poured out of his eyes. He began clenching
his fists, shaking violently, trying to contain the hurricane
of emotions bombarding his soul. After all the death and
tragedy Kronte has caused, they would have to allow
him to go free. What was the point of it all? Ayana was

in a coma that she may not ever awaken from, Victoria was dead, and many UN soldiers lost their lives—all in the name of justice. Daniel secretly wished his father was here so that he could challenge him and his beliefs that "God is in control." From his perspective, God was anything but in control, and if he were, Daniel felt he was far from concerned about justice on this godforsaken planet.

The more he looked at Ayana, the more it burned him to know she would never receive the satisfaction of knowing Kronte paid for his crimes against them both, and for taking Victoria from them.

I failed her. I failed Victoria and Timothy. But most of all, I failed myself.

"Danny, listen. I have to go and inform my superiors of this new development immediately. Trust me, I will do everything I can, but you may have to start accepting that Kronte won't see the inside of a courtroom ever again. I'm sorry," she said while handing Daniel his son. Meagan was overcome with shame, and she refused to look him in the eyes. After placing a soft kiss on Ayana's forehead, she quickly left the room, the loud clicking sounds of her heels echoing through the hall like firecrackers.

Exactly twenty-four hours after his appearance in the doorway of Ayana's hospital room, John stood in the middle of the room, wearing the same rage-inducing smile he wore the day before.

"Have we come to a decision?"

"Mr. Smith, let's not play games. You already know what our decision is, but I can tell you want to hear it. We have agreed to drop all charges against Kronte and won't file any charges in the future."

"Good choice," he replied, looking over at Dr. Bennett, who stared at him as if he wanted to do some serious damage to Smith's body. "You shouldn't look at this as a defeat but as a victory. You get to keep another man's wife, and that man gets to keep his freedom. I think that's an even trade, seeing how outlandishly attractive Sleeping Beauty is."

"You have your answer, now leave," demanded Meagan. "I can't take any more of your gloating, Mr. Smith."

"Right, good day then. Oh, one more thing, a warning really. If you decide to lose your mind and go back on our verbal agreement . . . the next time you see me . . . you *won't* see me."

There was an unpleasant look in his eyes as his smile disappeared, exposing the face of a cold-blooded killer. It was at that moment Daniel fully realized exactly who and what John Smith was, and it sent an arctic chill up his spine. John stood there, looking at Meagan and Daniel for a few seconds longer before turning and leaving the room. After he was gone, Daniel exhaled deeply and walked over to the door, closing and locking it.

Several days later, Daniel and Meagan decided to have Ayana moved from Chicago to New York so that she could get round-the-clock UN security. It was a hard decision for Daniel, but he knew she would be much safer in New York.

Months passed with very little change in Ayana's condition, and Daniel had to adjust his expectations. With his family's support in helping care for li'l Timothy, he was able to return to work. It wasn't long before the hospital promoted him to chief of medicine, and Dr. Kohlman was relieved of his position. He didn't take his firing very well. He ranted on for half an hour in the meeting with the staff about how they would regret allowing a "minority" to run the hospital. Daniel could've blown a fuse, but knowing this would be the last time he would hear Kohlman's ignorant mouth, he grinned and allowed him to make a bigger fool of himself, adding validity to his termination.

Chapter 29

A Miracle, Judgment And a Most Exhilarating Thank You

The Christmas season was back again with the city of Chicago under siege by another unforgiving string of winter storms. It was Christmas Eve, and Daniel and all his siblings gathered at their parents' home for yet another Christmas holiday. The family had gone through many changes over the year, namely trying to figure out why li'l Timothy wasn't communicating like other children his age. Daniel feared that during Satu's attack on Ayana, li'l Timothy was traumatized while in the womb, and that was affecting his mental progression. After taking him to several specialists, doctors determined that not only was li'l Timothy's brain functioning properly, it was functioning well beyond normal capacity. However, Daniel was still deeply concerned about the child's mental growth and his lack of speech during a stage in his life when he should be communicating more.

While everyone was busy playing cards in the family room, Daniel decided to sneak away and go into the office that housed the family's history. He slowly walked past each wall of pictures with a glass of eggnog in his hand. Years before, he avoided this room like the plague, but now he felt more at ease with being in this room, and he was scoping out new wall real estate to place li'l Timothy and Ayana.

He finally stopped at the last wall, staring at the picture of Victoria smiling back at him with eyes filled with life and promise. He smiled back and lifted his glass toward her. Turning to his right, he momentarily watched yet another blizzard raging outside, tossing inches upon inches of snow everywhere.

Suddenly, the office door flung open. His dad stood there with the landline phone in his hand. His eyes were bulging, and he was breathing heavily as he stretched out his hand for Daniel to take the phone. Daniel quickly moved over to his father while searching his eyes for any sign of what he was to expect on the phone. Holding his breath, he slowly placed the phone to his ear.

"Hello?"

"She's awake, Danny!" Meagan screamed hysterically through the phone. She was sniffing and crying while trying to laugh. "Oh my God, she's awake and talking! How soon can you get here? She's been asking for you all night!"

"Does she know about—?"

"No, she didn't know she was pregnant before we went to Juba, and I think you and li'l Timothy should tell her yourselves, in person."

"We'll be there tomorrow afternoon!"

"Danny, there aren't any flights leaving out of Chicago because of the weather! Wait until it clears up! You've waited almost a year for her to wake up. I think you can wait for another day. Once the weather clears, then catch the first flight out. Promise me you won't try to leave tonight with li'l Timothy with you. Promise me!"

Exhaling deeply, Daniel promised her and gave the phone back to his father, who was now staring at him with loving and endearing eyes.

"Merry Christmas, son," he said before taking him in his arms and hugging him tightly.

Forty-eight hours later, Daniel was running through LaGuardia's Airport's terminal with li'l Timothy in his arms. By the time they hopped in the UN van, he was completely out of breath but excited. Meagan greeted him inside the van with a smile he'd never seen on her face before.

"How is she?"

"She's a miracle, Danny. The doctors are saying her progress is astonishing, and she's talking and moving her limbs more than most patients who have been awake for almost a year."

Daniel smiled like a little boy anxious to get on the new ride at the biggest amusement park in town. Meagan covered her mouth, giggling at his boyish smile.

"Hey, Timothy, how are you? I missed you so much. My God, he looks so much like her."

"He does," Daniel agreed, looking down at his son with pride as he eagerly looked outside the van's window as the busy and massive city passed by.

"Did anyone tell her about Timothy yet?"

"No, not yet. I can't wait to see the look on her face when she sees him," Meagan said excitedly.

"I'm kinda worried. She may not take it well at first," Daniel said while rubbing his hand through his son's hair.

"Danny, trust me. She will be moved to tears, in a good way."

"I hope so. She's been through so much already."

Meagan nodded and began looking out the window, reflecting on the many dangers and disappointments she's faced alongside her friend.

Once they arrived at the hospital, they all hurried to Ayana's room. Outside the door, Daniel paused with Timothy in his arms. He looked his son in the face and kissed him on the cheek before saying, "Let's go meet your mommy."

And as soon as he opened the door, li'l Timothy yelled out his first complete word . . . A word he'd been saving for almost a year. A word that meant the world to him, and he practiced saying it in secret in his young mind repeatedly.

"Mommy!" he screamed at the top of his lungs, with his arms lifted above his head in celebration.

Ayana began to wail as she looked at her beautiful surprise in her love's arms. She was expecting the surprise of seeing Daniel alive, but never in a million years was she expecting to see a baby that came from her and the love that she and the doctor shared. She reached out to her son, and he leaped out of Daniel's arms on top of her, hugging her in an embrace filled with love and desperation. Daniel joined them as the three of them held each other in triumph. Although Kronte wasn't convicted, he didn't win. All the effort and hatred he spent trying to break the two destined lovers apart only brought them closer, and the miracle of their destined love filled the entire hospital wing as numerous doctors, nurses, and patients stood outside in tears watching this impossible reunion unfold . . .

Meanwhile, sixty miles from South Sudan's northern border . . .

The heat seemed to make his skin crawl as Kronte threw back another shot of the cheap liquor provided by the bartender that looked at him with disgust. Kronte was free but completely broke, and his appearance spelled just how destitute he was. Upon his release, he immediately went into hiding and attempted to withdraw his secret stash of money and gold he plundered during his days of terror, but somehow, his sponsors knew where he'd hidden everything. Now, over a year later, news of his ex-wife waking up from her coma and her speedy recovery broadcasted on every international news station only seem to depress him more. No one feared him anymore, and a few times, he was run off by an angry mob, but it seemed like the word was out that no one was to touch him. After becoming desperate for the lavish lifestyle he'd once lived, he accepted the invitation to meet John Smith at this remote location.

Fuck me! It's hot.

As if on cue, John appeared, leaning on the bar next to him, smiling brightly.

"How's it hanging, brother?" he teased while looking him over in amusement. "You look terrible, by the way. I don't think I've ever seen you so . . . What are the kids calling it these days? Oh yeah, 'rachet.'"

"Very funny. I don't have time to entertain your shit today, John. What are Father's terms for my reinstatement?"

"Oh, right down to business? Good man. Well, Father's terms are quite simple: termination without prejudice or mercy. And *these* terms are nonnegotiable."

Suddenly, the door of the bar flung open, and a ruffling of feet and metal sounded behind them. Kronte turned around to see a group of men staring at him with cold-blooded hatred in their eyes, machetes, and large wooden clubs wrapped in glued broken glass in their hands.

"Oh, and one more thing, *brother* . . . I got the results back from the DNA tests that should've tied you to the rape and murder of that little girl . . . or should I say, the rape and murder of your *daughter*."

Kronte's head jerked up violently. Violent rage, coupled with shock and horror, reflected in his eyes, and John found himself pleasantly amused by his reaction.

"That's impossible," Kronte growled back at him. "I can't have children!"

"Yeah, that's what you believed, as well as the doctors who healed that wound, but they were mistaken. The DNA tests prove that in the case of little Victoria . . . Kronte . . . You . . . Are . . . The . . . Father! So, it appears that you raped and murdered your own daughter, *and* to add insult to injury, you allowed other men to rape her too while you cheered them on. I've done some terrible things in my life, but I draw the line when it comes to children. You, on the other hand, brother, you have no shame or boundaries. All this fuss about Ayana having another man's baby . . . and come to find out, *you* were that man all along. How does it feel to be the worst dad in the history of fatherhood?"

"Fuck you, John," Kronte replied, his entire body weighed down by guilt as the revelation of his actions tore him to pieces.

"Well, time's up, old chap. It's been a blast, but I've got a plane to catch, and you have a most painful and humiliating death to attend," John said playfully, slapping Kronte on the back before walking toward the door.

Before he walked past the mob, he whispered in their leader's ear, "Make it last as long as possible. I want him to feel *everything*."

The man nodded in agreement, and John immediately walked out of the bar. Once outside, the sounds of Kronte's vicious beating blasted through the walls of the bar. His screams of pain could be heard throughout the small village, and the villagers celebrated each time they heard the agony of his suffering. He'd murdered countless numbers of his own people. No one would weep for him today. No one would feel sorrow for his passing or how he was laid to rest. To the people of South Sudan, Kronte was the Antichrist, and no amount of violent punishment would cause anyone to feel one bit of remorse or empathy for him. The world itself would rejoice when the news of his death reached all news outlets. His sponsors would rest easy, knowing that he was no longer a threat, and they would patiently wait for another chance to exploit this young African nation. For now, they will allow the country of South Sudan to mature and regroup after decades of war and death . . . until another Kronte emerges, willing to sell out his people for wealth, women, and violence.

"Gold Coast" of Chicago, Illinois

"One minute," Timothy yelled as he rushed across his condo in only a bath towel wrapped around his waist. He was slipping and sliding on the marble floor in his foyer, attempting to stop himself from falling on his ass. It was very late, at least after 2:00 a.m., and he couldn't fathom who would be at his door this time in the morning. It couldn't be a booty call, because he'd curtailed his behavior drastically once his godson was named after him. He wanted to set a much better example for his godson, so he started on the long road to recovering the gentleman that his father and mother tried to instill in him during his teenage years.

The loud banging on the door continued, and Timothy became upset and planned on cursing out whoever was at his door. He didn't even bother to look through the peephole before swinging the door open . . . to behold Ms. Meagan Quinn in a black trench coat with a mischievous grin on her face. She stepped inside the condo, wearing a pair of thigh-high, patent leather boots, and her lips were covered in a red lipstick that seemed to put Timothy in a trance. Before he could say a word, she opened her coat and let it drop to the floor, revealing an amazing body completely nude, shaven, and ready for action. Timothy's mouth flung open, and Meagan reached forward, snatching his towel from around his waist. She then bit her bottom lip as she looked him over lustfully. He was a *very* big boy, built like a tank, and she was anxious to put him to work.

It's been awhile.

She then calmly walked past him into his condo, saying, "Didn't Dr. Bennett tell you I wanted to thank you personally for what you did? Well, I'm a woman of my word, and I'm here to thank the hell out of you. Close your mouth, baby. It's rude . . . at least for now. I have a lot of things that I'll be putting in there soon enough . . ."